"As Pack creatively animates the various realms, the relationship between her two protagonists maintains the novel's bittersweet tone. Johanna and Jackson are beautifully believable, especially as they drift apart. Everything combusts in a cliffhanger finale."
—Kirkus Reviews

THIRD

CHRONICLES OF

ILLUMINATION

BOOKS IN THIS SERIES

Becoming Johanna
A Library of Illumination Prequel (novella)

The Library of Illumination
Book One (novelette)

Doubloons
The Library of Illumination: Book Two (novelette)

The Orb
The Library of Illumination: Book Three (novelette)

Casanova
The Library of Illumination: Book Four (novelette)

Portals
The Library of Illumination: Book Five (novella)

Chronicles: The Library of Illumination
Books One through Five

The Overseers
The Library of Illumination: Book Six (novelette)

Myrddin's Memoir
The Library of Illumination: Book Seven (novel)

Second Chronicles of Illumination
Books Five, Six and Seven

Third Chronicles of Illumination
Games
Book Eight (novel)

THIRD CHRONICLES OF ILLUMINATION

Library of Illumination: Book Eight

by

C. A. PACK

Artiqua Press

info@artiquapress.com

Artiqua Press

www.artiquapress.com

ARTIQUA PRESS
info@artiquapress.com
Westbury, NY 11590

TRADE PAPERBACK

February 7, 2017

THIRD CHRONICLES OF ILLUMINATION
Games
Library of Illumination—Book Eight

ISBN-13: 978-0-9979084-1-1

Library of Congress Control Number: 2016912408

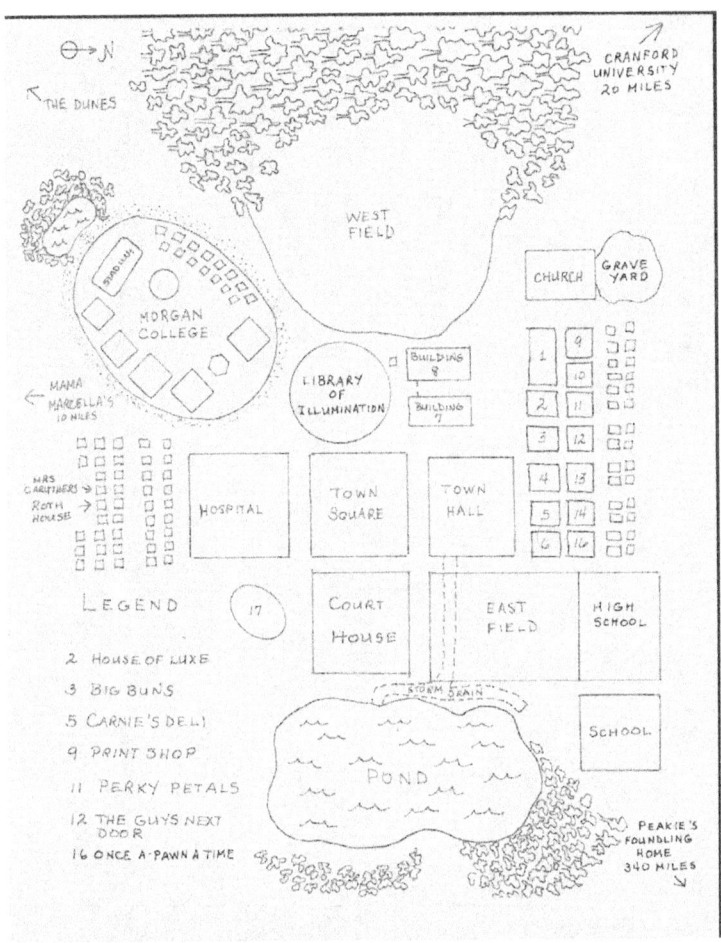

This is a map of the neighborhood surrounding the Library of Illumination on Fantasia. Considering the Ancients created the libraries on all realms, the areas surrounding them often bear similarities.

Note: You can find a list of prominent characters at the back of this book.

1

THE PERFECT BLACK cube Ryden Simmdry had given Johanna Charette started glowing. The master of the overseers had created the cube to capture Odyon, a powerful wizard trying to steal the life's work of Merlin the Magician. Library of Illumination co-curators, Johanna Charette and Jackson Roth, both knew they had to prevent the book of enchantments from falling into the wrong hands. The collection of spells and incantations—known as Myrddin's Memoir—ranged from simple remedies, like a cure for the common cold, to an obscure invocation calling for the total destruction of life as we know it.

Unfortunately, Johanna couldn't whip out the black cube in time to capture Odyon. The shapeshifter had transformed into a beam of light before he could be caught and disappeared. Instead, the tiny cube had sucked up the essence of Alianessa Anjou, the French member of the Eahta Frean fram Drycræft, a secret group of eight wizards entrusted with protecting Myrddin's legacy.

Johanna chewed on her lower lip. The eighteen-year-old had failed at what should have been a simple task, and she wanted to discuss what she could have done better with the cube's creator. "I wish Ryden Simmdry were here."

"No you don't," Jackson said. He was a year younger than Johanna, but he'd been around long enough to know where her train of thought would lead them. "Then we'd have to tell him we bungled capturing Odyon and admit the threat against the Library of Illumination is still hanging over us. He's going to give us one of those disappointed looks, like my mother gives me when I've let her down. Let him stay where he is — thinking we're saving the world."

The remaining six wizards representing the Eahta Frean fram Drycræft glared at them. One of them, Veronika Veselov, walked up to Johanna and tried to snatch the box from her hand.

Johanna twisted away from the Russian woman. "No. There's only one person who can open this now, and he's not here. I have to keep it safe until we find him."

Veronika turned to the other wizards who had sworn to protect Myrddin's memoir. "I'm leaving. Anyone who wants to further discuss this debacle, follow me." She grabbed Cathasach Caird and dragged the startled group leader from the room. The others followed, with Beck — the newest member — bringing up the rear.

Johanna grabbed Beck. Myrddin's ring and the Illumini constellation embedded in Johanna's left palm rubbed against the sigil tattooed on Beck's wrist.

Suddenly, Johanna felt lightheaded. Her knees weakened and she thought she might faint. Her lids fluttered as her eyes rolled back.

Beck grabbed her to keep her from falling. "Jackson, there's something wrong with your girlfriend."

Jackson lifted Johanna into his arms. He tried to walk away but couldn't. "Let go of her."

"I'm not holding her." Beck wriggled his fingers. "She's holding me."

"Johanna..." Jackson kissed her forehead. "Let go of Beck."

But she couldn't respond. Waves of energy and power she had never experienced before surged inside of her, and her thoughts became crystal clear yet more confused than ever.

"What did you do to her?" Jackson asked.

"Nothing. I was walking out the door. She grabbed me."

Johanna didn't know how much more of the energy surge she could take. Even as the strange new power entered her being, it zapped her own resources, and she felt herself shutting down, losing consciousness.

Her grip on Beck's wrist released when she blacked out.

He pulled his hand away. "I'm going. I don't know what you two are up to, but if it's no good, we'll be back. Otherwise, I doubt we'll be seeing much of each other."

"We've been upfront with you," Jackson said. "This is Odyon's doing, or didn't you notice how he magically disappeared when we accused him?"

Beck nodded toward the cube Johanna still

clutched in her other hand. "For all I know, he's stuck in there with Alianessa. You've taken on the wrong group if you think you can pull one over on us. We weren't selected for the Eahta Frean fram Drycræft because we're a bunch of yahoos. On the contrary, we're the most powerful wizards in the world. Pray we don't have to return, because if we do, it won't be pretty."

Jackson's voice increased in volume but lowered in pitch. "We didn't do anything."

"Two wizards are missing. If one or both of them are responsible for trying to steal Myrddin's memoir, we would have dealt with it. Internally. You did do something, and you'll have to pay for it." He stormed out of the room.

Jackson carried Johanna toward the virtual George V hotel suite they had recreated in the Periodicals Room of the library by opening a travel guide. He walked past the wizards, who argued loudly as they crowded the front door.

"How the hell do we get out of here?" Beck shouted.

"Illumination," Jackson said quietly. The door slid open, allowing the wizards to escape.

It wasn't long before Johanna's eyes flew open, her blood surging through her veins. "Where am I?"

Jackson knelt at her side with an ampoule in his hand. "The hotel suite."

She studied the re-creation of the guest room. "I've never been in one of the bedrooms before. Nice."

"Are you okay? What happened? I thought Beck did something horrible to you using one of Myrddin's spells."

"I'm fine, I think." She struggled to sit up.

"So…?"

"Something weird happened when I grabbed Beck. Like all his knowledge and power seeped into my body. He's studied Myrddin's spells quite closely, and now I feel like I know them all by heart." Her eyes glazed over as she searched her memory. "I do." She gripped Jackson's shoulders. "I know them all by heart."

"How could that happen?"

"It just did."

"I think you and I should go downstairs and have a little chat with Myrddin."

"He told me not to visit him in the vault anymore. He gave me the name of a book to use instead." She searched her pockets. "Wait a minute, I wrote it down." She finally pulled out a scrap of paper.

"It's a wonder you can fit anything in your pants pocket."

"What do you mean? Do you think they're too tight?"

He threw both hands in the air, palms facing out. "Don't change a thing," he said. "They fit you like a glove."

She made a face. "You can stop staring now."

"Just admiring your form."

Johanna set the cube down on the floor. "I hope Alianessa was telling the truth about not being able to transmogrify for any length of time."

"Why?"

"Because I'm going to set her free."

"I thought only Ryden Simmdry could do that."

"Maybe that was true, until now."

"Really? You think you're that powerful—that you can undo the protective charm the master of all the overseers placed on the cube?"

"Yes."

"Even if you could, I don't think you should."

"Why not?"

"Because she's going to be mad as hell and may try to take it out on us, and frankly, I'm tired of being defensive."

"We have to do something. We can't just leave her in there."

"Maybe you could tell Mal. He's your mentor. Write something in your diary and then say, 'Don't you agree, Mal?' He'll try to figure out what you mean and might even pay us a visit. Then we can sort this out."

"I don't know," she answered. "It doesn't sound very proactive. It makes us seem like children waiting for a parent's approval."

"Mal has never steered us wrong."

"No, he hasn't," she agreed, "and I don't want to tarnish his reputation now by dragging him into this."

"Well, that's all I'm going to say. If you want to open the box, open the box."

⌘ *You will find it is not possible.*

Jackson whirled around at the sound of Ryden Simmdry's voice. The master of the College of Overseers—which protected the libraries on twelve different realms—stared at the box in Johanna's hand.

Johanna didn't allow his arrival to distract her. She cleared her mind, envisioned a pinpoint of light, and forced it to grow larger before opening her eyes. A swirl of gray motes took form and within seconds, Alianessa

Anjou appeared. The dazed woman stood apart from them, her mouth agape.

Ryden Simmdry inhaled sharply. ⌘*Something has changed since last we met.*

"She held hands with Beck from the Eahta Frean fram Drycræft one moment," Jackson said, "and claimed she knew all of Myrddin's spells the next."

Ryden Simmdry used his mind to plumb the depths of Johanna's consciousness and found he couldn't. ⌘*Explain to me what happened with Beck.*

Johanna told him about grabbing Beck's hand and suddenly feeling both lightheaded and energized at the same time. "It's like I absorbed all his knowledge."

⌘*Did this sudden influx of information feel like it entered through the Illumini constellation on your left hand?*

Johanna thought back. "Yes."

⌘*And you were merely holding his hand… his palm?*

"No. Not his palm. His wrist." Her eyes widened with recollection. "His sigil." She opened her left palm and gazed at it. Myrddin's signet ring rested right above Fantasia.

⌘*The ring—*

A commotion coming from the main reading room interrupted their conversation. They found Alianessa pounding on the front door. "Let me out of this place."

⌘*In good time. First, I must determine why the cube chose to induct your essence. I designed this box to absorb unnatural energy that is imbued with protective powers or special charms. It chose you as the most likely source instead of Odyon.*

The Frenchwoman pouted. "I do not know of any Odyon. It's something you're making up."

Johanna held her gaze. "You were right there when I accused Robert Birk of being Odyon. You know exactly who we're talking about."

"I never knew him by that name," Alianessa said.

⌘*But you do know him. The question is, how well?*

"He's just one of the eight. I don't know him any better than the others."

⌘*That's too bad, because it would have explained why the cube worked on you. I will have to investigate your relationship more directly.* He placed his left palm against her temple.

Alianessa backed away. "Don't touch me."

⌘*I hate to involve you, Jackson, but would you please hold her?*

Jackson grabbed Alianessa from behind and wrapped his arms around her so she couldn't move. Ryden Simmdry placed his palm against her temple.

Alianessa stomped on Jackson's instep with the five-inch stiletto heel of her shoe.

"Ow," he shouted, loosening his grip on her. She squirmed away and ran for the door.

Jackson started to run after her.

⌘*It is all right, Jackson. I have what I need.* Ryden Simmdry picked up the box. Alianessa struggled but once again dissolved into a smoky haze before being reabsorbed by the cube.

"Why not let her go?" Johanna asked.

⌘*Because she is more than she claims to be.*

* * *

BACK ON LUMINA, the overseers waited patiently for Master Ryden Simmdry's return; however, they couldn't help but speculate on what their next steps should be. If Johanna and Jackson managed to stop an interloper from gaining access to Myrddin's spells, the overseers would be able to take their time while planning their next course of action. However, if the thief remained at large, they would have to re-double their vigilance, plan in haste, and second-guess every step they took.

As a group, they knew they would have to wait for the master before they could finalize their plan. They took the time they currently had to explore the avenues of action open to them.

BEFORE THE OVERSEERS sealed the portals on Juvenilia, two Terrorians escaped through the shattered back window of the library in pursuit of the children who tormented them. Most of the Juveniles quickly scattered, however, Marbol remained hidden in a tree with his sonic scrambler and soon found himself eye-to-eye with another confused Terrorian. Perspiration oozed from every pore of Marbol's fifteen-year-old body, and he shuddered uncontrollably. The Terrorian's eight oversized tentacles snaked toward the teen, but Marbol jumped out of the tree and hit the ground running. He tore around the building and bolted across the town square, racing through the neighborhood until he dove down an embankment leading to the village pond and sought refuge in a storm drain. He prayed it was too small for Terrorians to enter.

He needn't have worried. The Terrorians were not used to the bright Juvenilia sun and practically staggered by the time they hit the town square, blinded by sunlight and choking on fresh, dry air.

A quarter mile away, Marbol pushed through the storm drain, following it back into town. In some places, he stopped to hack away intruding roots with a pocket knife but eventually reached the catch basin that abutted the Juvini City Center. He waited and listened, and when he felt assured there were no Terrorians waiting nearby to tear him limb from limb, he worked to loosen the metal grid covering the drain.

FURST STARED AT his image in a looking glass. He adjusted his new Dramatican curator uniform. It was comfortable and fit well, however, the diamond-encrusted sash that contained the Illumini constellation would not fall evenly. He didn't want to disgrace himself by wearing it wrong, but he couldn't understand how to make it stay in place.

He heard an odd musical note and immediately left his quarters to see what had caused it. Overseer Pru Tellerence stood waiting at the circulation desk.

"Honored, I am, so quickly, that you returned."

The overseer looked at his new uniform with its crooked sash and smiled. ★*May I?* She stepped forward and unbuttoned Furst's epaulette. She hooked the sash on an eyelet hidden under the epaulette and then re-buttoned it.

"A trick, it is."

★*Not a trick. A simple aid to hold the sash in place.* She stepped back and looked at him in uniform, then nodded. ★*It looks very nice.*

"Too formal, it is not?"

★*This is the way the curator of a Library of Illumination should look.*

Furst nodded. "Create the same, you will, for Jackson of Fantasia?"

Pru Tellerence pursed her lips to hide her smile. ★*The people of Fantasia don't judge someone's importance by the jeweled embellishment of their clothing quite like they do here on Dramatica. The citizens of your world need to know you are in charge.*

Furst stood a little taller. "In charge, I am," he said. Then he allowed a deep breath to escape. "Disappoint you, I hope I do not."

★*I doubt that you could.* She hesitated.

★*Have there been any other problems with the Terrorians?*

"Not returned, they have. Scared them away, we have."

★*Don't let your guard down, Furst. The Terrorians are tenacious. Once they decide to invade, nothing can dissuade them. And now there's word they've invaded Romantica and Juvenilia.*

Furst's curls tightened. "Help those realms, we must."

★*For now, your place is here. You and your kinsmen must make sure the Terrorians cannot gain entrance here. However, we may take you up on your offer to help the other realms in the future. The Romanticans and the Juveniles are not as quick on their feet as you and your men.*

★*I must return to Lumina. Contact me immediately if anything out of the ordinary happens here.*

Furst looked up at the Curator's Key.

Pru Tellerence followed his gaze. ★*You won't need to climb up there*. She removed a small book from within the folds of her robe and handed it to the curator. ★*This diary is linked directly to me. Write down any questions or problems you have and I will respond as quickly as I can.*

"Yes. Do that, I can. Thank you." He rewarded Pru Tellerence with a crooked grin.

Suddenly, the air around them pixilated, then returned to normal.

Furst's eyes widened. "See that, did you?"

★*Yes. I must get back. Be on guard!*

—LOI—

2

RYDEN SIMMDRY GRABBED the black cube, said goodbye to Johanna and Jackson, and departed.

Jackson turned in time to see Johanna's eyelids flutter.

She wavered and placed her hand on his arm. "I think I need a nap."

"One minute you have all of Myrddin's knowledge racing through your brain, and the next minute you're making a date with the inside of your eyelids. You may have absorbed all of his energy but it amounts to zippo, considering he's dead."

"My head is buzzing, but the rest of me is spent. I think my brain is still trying to process all the information that passed from Beck to me. I hope it's not some short-term thing. I think I'd like to try out some of Myrddin's magic. But not right now. I'm too sleepy."

"And when you do try some of it out, you're going to teach me, right?"

"Of course, but first I'm going up to my room to

lie down."

"I guess being a great sorceress has its downside."

"I guess. Are you going to be okay alone?"

"I think I've got this down. I'll just hold things together here until the next bomb drops. It will have to be a bomb. With Ava and Chris packing heavy artillery up in the cupola, nothing less than a bomb is going to get by them."

Johanna scrunched up her face. "Do you really think the Terrorians would open a portal just to throw a bomb inside and then wait in the relative safety of their own library while an explosive here does the job for them?"

"Aarrgghh...why did you have to give me something new to worry about?"

"I never thought of it before."

"Do you have a tennis racket?"

"Non sequitur..." she said in a sing-song voice.

"It's not. Really. If you have a tennis racket, I can use it to bat back a bomb if they send one flying through."

"If you swat a bomb with a tennis racket, it will probably explode on impact, killing you instantly."

"True."

"Besides, I don't own a tennis racket."

"I guess we dodged a bullet, then."

"I guess we did." She kissed his cheek and headed toward the curator's staircase.

AFTER SLIDING THE cover aside, Marbol hoisted himself out of the storm drain. He replaced the grate and scrambled inside the Juvini City Center, bolting the door behind him. There were several entrances to the building, but he was only concerned about the one he entered through. He ran up the stairs to the "wreck-wroom" and didn't stop to catch his breath until he slammed the door behind him. Pollo and the other Juveniles were already there.

Pollo did a double take when he saw Marbol. "How'd you get away? I thought you were a goner."

"I jumped out of the tree when the beast reached for me, and then I ran as fast as I could to the pond and doubled back through the storm drain."

"Good thinking. Where are the monsters now?"

"I don't know. I haven't seen them since I took off."

A fourteen-year-old girl called Jee-Joy raced into the room. "You're never going to believe this. A couple of kids from the east side said they were in the town square and saw two big, ugly octopi wearing pants, stumbling around. I asked them what kind of sqwitch-juice they were drinking."

"They're in the town square?" Guffle cried. "We've got to ring the bell and alert everyone to the danger."

"And how are you going to do that?" Marbol asked. "The bell is in the library, and the last time I checked, it was full of monsters."

Jee-Joy cocked her head, narrowed her eyes, and placed one hand on her hip. "Very funny."

"They're real, Jee-Joy," Pollo said, "and they have to be dealt with." He turned to Marbol. "That scrambler still working?"

Marbol looked down at his hand. He hadn't realized he still had a death grip on his homemade weapon. He looked up and nodded.

Pollo grabbed his arm. "We need to get inside the library now. We need to ring the bell. And we need to free Selly and Cici and the others."

"You want to go back there?"

"Yes. We have to."

Marbol stared at the scrambler. "We're going to need more than this. We're going to need something with fire power."

"Fire! We can use the scorchers we made to stop the demon-fire from spreading past Freehollow last year," Guffle said. "The ones we used to scorch the fields so the flames would have nothing left to feed on."

Pollo started for the door. "Where are they?" he asked over his shoulder.

"Downstairs in the basement. I think we have four of them. I hope that's enough," Guffle answered.

"It will have to be," Pollo called back.

"We'll know soon enough," Marbol said, as he followed Pollo out of the room.

On Romantica, Natalia Dalura looked over Dame Erato's shoulder and noticed the message from Dean Horatio Blastoe that appeared in Dame Erato's diary. She read out loud. "The libraries will be sealed." Her brow furrowed. "What do you think that means? Sealed from invaders, or sealed so that I can't get back inside?"

Dame Erato asked the overseer to clarify his statement.

All entrances from the libraries will be sealed. Those outside cannot get in. Those inside cannot get out.

Natalia's shoulders slumped. "But it's my home."

The older woman took pity on her. "You can stay here until it's all sorted out. With the Terrorians gearing up for a fight, I'd say we'll all be facing upheavals in our lives for a while to come." The air around them blurred for a few seconds. "Something just changed. If we return to the library now, you'll probably find the door sealed."

"Maybe not. Will you come with me?" Natalia asked.

"What makes you think I want to face a bunch of war-mongering Terrorians?"

"I thought if we could get in and sneak up to my quarters, you could help me carry back some of my belongings...."

"What if we're inside with the Terrorians when the overseers seal the libraries and we're stuck there? Have you thought about that?"

"No." Natalia sighed. "You're right, of course. We'd best keep our distance."

THE TIME MACHINE would not allow additional troopers to cross the portal to Juvenilia, and instead returned them to their point of origination—Terroria. Nero 51 bristled. "We will try again!" The mechanism seemed to evaporate in thin air but again reappeared on Terroria filled with soldiers.

The curator exited the vehicle and found General Barzic 922. "What has changed?"

The general appeared confused. "Nothing has changed, what do you mean?"

"I mean we cannot deposit our troops on Juvenilia. Either the time machine is not working properly, or something else has gone wrong. Contact Plala 6 and find out if he's made any adjustments to the biometric armbands that could be disrupting travel."

"Right away," the general said, heading for the spiral staircase.

The Terrorians had removed all the stacks and obelisks from the top level of the library to make room for the time machine. It gave Nero 51 a clear view of everything happening in the library. He crossed all eight of his tentacles over his chest and glared as the general slowly made his way down the cupola stairs. The curator bellowed, "Faster, General. We need answers now." He watched as his subordinate picked up the pace.

When the general reached the main entrance, he wrapped his tentacles around the door handle and pulled the front door. It wouldn't open. He checked the lock and tried again.

"TODAY, GENERAL," Nero 51 screamed from five stories above.

"The door appears to be stuck," the general called out. He asked a few nearby troopers to help. First, they took turns trying to open the door. Then, they all tried pulling on it together as a team.

Nero 51 took a deep breath and wrapped his tentacles around the guardrail in the cupola. He jumped over the railing and used his tentacles to lower himself to the floor—five stories below. He pushed everyone out of the way as he grasped the door handle and pulled. When the door failed to budge, some of the Terrorians snickered.

The curator pointed to a stone pedestal. "Ram the window and climb out. I need Plala 6 now."

Four troopers grabbed the pedestal and propelled

themselves against the window. No matter how many times they tried to break through the glass, they failed. They asserted their efforts on various windows without success.

"Shoot out the window," Nero 51 said in a steely voice.

A soldier trained his weapon on one of the windows and fired. A micro-moment later, he and his weapon disintegrated.

"We're sealed in," one of the soldiers shouted.

Nero 51 glared at them. "I want you all to disperse immediately into the different areas of the library and look for a way out. There has to be a weakness here, somewhere, and the soldier who finds it will want for nothing for the rest of his life."

The Terrorians fanned out, looking for a chink in the library's armor that would turn into their golden key to a lifetime of riches.

THE FANTASIAN WIZARD known as Robert Birk, or Rathbarth, son of Visbur, had once been a Mysterian prophet named Odyon, who rose to the post of high priest on his native world. It was Odyon's ancestors who had negotiated with the Terrorians and Adventurans to start the Two Millennia War, and he had become a soldier—like his forebears—fighting for a better life for Mysteriose. But it wasn't enough for Odyon to win. He wanted to rule. He felt he was smarter and more powerful than the others who, to him, were merely mortal. He had experimented with alchemy and longevity and had made a number of private breakthroughs that helped him survive well past the end of the Two Millennia War.

Unfortunately, he had been separated from his realm but prospered after meeting a Fantasian sorcerer named Myrddin Emrys. They formed a friendship for a time, sharing secrets, but then they had a parting of ways after disagreeing on how far they should go to affect change with magic. Odyon already possessed the expertise that allowed him to shape-shift, but Myrddin had perfected methods of healing and time travel that Odyon would never have come to possess without having met him. And together, they fine-tuned and developed control over life forces, creating the Longevicus Blessing.

Their friendship ended when Rathbarth, who practiced déofolkræft—the black art of devilcraft—tried to use it against Myrddin to steal all his power. When he failed, Rathbarth charmed Viviane, the Lady of the Lake, into luring Myrddin to the Isle of Skokholm and using the spells he had taught her against him. Odyon told her to entomb the wizard within the sandstone cliff that rose out of the sea off the coast of Wales.

Viviane and Myrddin were long dead, yet Myrddin's spells were still out of Odyon's reach. He vowed to unlock their secrets—even if it was the last thing he'd ever do.

RYDEN SIMMDRY TOOK his place at the head of the overseers' U-shaped conference table on Lumina and placed the small black cube in front of him.

♦*Have you secured the thief?*

⌘*No. But we may have captured an accomplice.*

Ω*Who resides within?*

⌘*A witch, as powerful as she is wily. She would have us believe she is merely trying to perfect her magical skills, but on closer investigation, I discovered she possesses much stronger powers than she professes to have.*

★*Do you think it wise to have brought her here?*

⌘*There is only one way to find out.* He waved his hand over the cube, and the form of Alianessa Anjou took shape in the center of the horseshoe.

She brought herself up to her full height and scowled, before actually noticing the people surrounding her. Slowly, she looked from face to face of each overseer and visibly withdrew inside herself. "What is this place?" she asked quietly.

⌘*You like to think you have special powers. I have brought you to a place where you can put those powers to the test.*

"Is Odyon here?"

⌘*I thought you didn't know anyone named Odyon?*

Alianessa drew herself up a bit taller. "I thought we were past that."

⌘*Ahhh, yes. You know Robert Birk, but not Odyon.*

"You're the one who calls him Odyon. Is he here?"

⌘*Not yet. But I'm sure he would visit if he could figure out how. He's been here before.*

"What do you mean he's been here before? Where are we?"

⌘*This world is known as Lumina. Odyon is a high priest from Mysteriose who hasn't been seen since the end of the Two Millennia War and was presumed dead. He was curator of the Library of Illumination on that world and visited here in that capacity.*

He expanded his comments to address the group at large. ⌘*Apparently, he's been biding his time on Fantasia, honing his skills and preparing for... I don't know what. He is much more dangerous than Nero 51, in my opinion, and needs to be stopped. But for now, all we have to lure him here is Mademoiselle Alianessa Anjou from the French province on Fantasia.*

Ω*She is bait?*

⌘*Possibly. Or she can just tell us all she knows, promise to not use her powers for devilcraft, and we could return her to the location from whence she came.*

Pru Tellerence turned her full attention to Alianessa. ★*Are you the one who's trying to steal Myrddin's spell book?*

"Steal it? No. Why would I have to? As a member of the Eahta Frean fram Drycræft, I have full access to it. Besides, I know the spells by heart. I have no reason to steal it."

⌘*What she says is true. And yet, I suspect there is something she is not telling us.*

"What do you expect me to tell you? That I know this Odyon fellow? That he promised me the world if only I kept his secret? I don't know what you want from me."

⌘*You claim not to know how to transmogrify for any length of time, yet I have looked within your psyche and seen that is a lie. You successfully traveled as light and sound between your home in France and the Fantasian Library of Illumination on this very day.*

"And I would have told everyone about my break-through if the meeting hadn't deteriorated into a witch hunt. Why would I openly state I could do something, if it caused everyone to suspect and ridicule me for my hard work? At least Robert understood me. He helped me with the transmogrification spell and we experienced our success together."

⌘*So you were aware he was already proficient in shapeshifting.*

"No. We only succeeded in accomplishing sustained travel over the past few days. And to celebrate, we both traveled to the Library of Illumination using that knowledge."

⌘*That is what he wants you to believe. Robert has been an accomplished sorcerer for a very long time and has long been able to travel as light and sound.*

"That's a lie."

⌘*Not at all. The man calling himself Robert Birk and I have known each other for centuries. He is one of the most powerful sorcerers alive.*

Alianessa stiffened. "That's not true. It can't be. Why wouldn't he have confided in me? We're very close."

⌘*Finally, the truth. Please explain what you mean by "close."*

She sighed. "He told me he could help me, if I helped him. He showed me some tricks I could use to make the spells work for me. He said if I ascertained similar information from the other members of The Eight, I should tell him. And he would do the same for me, so we wouldn't be left behind when someone uncovered the key to Myrddin's magic."

⌘*And have you given him such information?*

"Only to tell him that I thought Edmund Beasom

had made a breakthrough and was holding back."

⌘*And has he shared similar information with you?*

"I already told you. He helped me perfect the transmogrification spell."

⌘*And nothing more?*

"No. We were going to start working on Totalis Pereamus next."

The group gasped as one.

⌘*Total annihilation of all living creatures?*

"That's not what it means."

⌘*That's exactly what it means—the end of life as we know it.*

—LOI—

3

JOHANNA FOUND AVA, Chris, and Jackson guarding the cupola. "Your mother would like you to go down for dinner."

"No," Ava said quickly. "We have to make sure no one breaks through our defenses."

Jackson grinned. "Listen to my little sister talking all military-like."

She butted him in the stomach with the end of the Terrorian decimator. "I was the first one put in charge here. *You* don't even *have* a weapon."

Johanna held her hand out. "You can give me the weapon. I know how to operate it. I have experience shooting Terrorians with one. You three go down and make your mother happy. Just save a little food for me, and I'll eat when you relieve me."

"No," Ava repeated. "You eat with the boys and save a little food for me."

Johanna's pupils dilated slightly, and the decimator flew from Ava's hands to her own. "Go down and eat with your family."

"How did you do that?" Ava cried.

Jackson stared at Johanna. "You're officially scaring me."

Chris nodded. "Big time."

"It's a little something I picked up from our friend, Beck."

Jackson nodded. "You're going to teach me how to do that, right?"

"After you all have dinner with your mom."

"Will you teach us, too?" Ava asked.

"Maybe. Ask me again after you get back."

The Roth siblings headed down the cupola stairs. "Your girlfriend is crazy cool," Chris said to Jackson.

"Yeah," Ava echoed.

Johanna smiled as she hitched the weapon over her shoulder. *Crazy cool. I can live with that.*

THE TWO TERRORIAN troopers could go no farther than the Juvini town square. They sat back-to-back in the center of the square trying to protect themselves, and arguing.

"My weapon was damaged by one of the explosives a kiddlet threw through the window. Where's yours?"

"I don't know. I lost it when the window shattered."

"Why didn't you look for it? No good soldier would allow himself to be separated from his firearm."

"Don't take that tone with me. Who do you think you are, Nero 51? You allowed your weapon to be damaged, which makes you no better than me."

Slowly, their tentacles snaked toward each other

as a prelude to a fight.

THE BASEMENT OF the Juvini City Center was damp and dusty, but it was organized, so it took Marbol and Pollo no time at all to find the scorchers. "We need some fat and fire-sticks to get these things going," Pollo said, handing two of them to Marbol. "And we need a couple of the other guys to help us host our barbecue."

Up on the main floor they met up with Guffle and another boy.

"Pye just got here." Guffle turned to the new boy. "Tell them what you told me."

"Two creatures have taken over the square," Pye said in a rush, "and when anyone gets too close, they snake out their long, slimy tentacles and try to snatch them. We have to do something!"

"That's what these are for," Pollo said, handing Pye one of the scorchers.

Marbol handed one to Guffle. "I guess it's us four against them."

Pye looked over his scorcher. "These need fuel."

"We can find that stuff in the kitchen," Guffle said.

"Yeah, and then let's roast us some monsters," Pollo cried, raising his scorcher into the air.

✠*LADIES*.
Natalia Dalura inhaled sharply as she spun around. "Horatio Blastoe." She placed her hand over her heart to still its wild beating. "You gave me such a fright. Thank goodness it's you."

✠*I'm sorry if I startled you,* the overseer said, ✠

but I couldn't very well arrive through the library. And since we would like to keep the situation contained for as long as possible to avoid a panic, I decided Dame Erato's cottage would be the best place to enter your world.

"It's always a pleasure to welcome you to my home, Horatio Blastoe." Dame Erato took his arm and led him to a sunny sitting area. "Perhaps you would like a brew and biscuits to sustain you?"

⌖*Although my need for food has greatly diminished since becoming an overseer, I could hardly say no to your fine biscuits, Dame Erato.* He turned. ⌖*I'm glad to see you were able to safely exit the library, Natalia. Any Terrorians who may have gained entrance are now sealed inside.*

Dame Erato set three cups on the table. "It's a shame it has come to this. What about the other libraries?"

⌖*They have all been sealed, but it wasn't that simple. Issiopia did not want to leave the Inspiracon library, nor did Dr. Infinitis on Educon. We had to stress that it was for everyone's safety and would doubly act as a preventive to keep interlopers OUT.*

Dame Erato poured the brew. "Is ours the only library that's actually occupied?"

⌖*No. Juvenilia and Dramatica have also been invaded, although there are no Terrorians remaining on Dramatica right now.*

The older woman put the brew pot down. "However did they manage to get rid of them?"

The dean smiled. ⌖*The Dramaticans proved to be too "springy" for the Terrorians. Too spry. Too quick. And they used flaming arrows, which immolated the Terrorian troopers, who apparently oil their skin. I heard the resulting odor was awful. But better a lingering stench than the threat of annihilation.*

"Is Furst okay?" Natalia asked. "He is such a kind, gentle person and has always greeted me earnestly."

✠*He is now the leader of his world. The military provost and the head of the Library Council were killed when the Terrorians first invaded Dramatica, and Furst took it upon himself to lead the Dramaticans against the infiltrators, and did so quite successfully. He's always been so unassuming, but Pru Tellerence has put an end to that by outfitting him in a uniform fit for a king. The Dramaticans look up to anyone bedecked in precious stones, and Furst's uniform has a jeweled sash bearing the Illumini constellation that no one else's attire can come close to.*

Dame Erato and Natalia Dalura laughed for a moment, before realizing that Furst's thrust to greatness was precipitated by the threat of war.

TERRORIANS—TRAPPED IN their own Library of Illumination, regardless of their brute strength and sinewy tentacles—breathed shallowly and moved erratically while they considered what might happen if the seal on the library turned out to be permanent.

"We must find a way out of here, or die trying," one stated.

"We will," Nero 51 said evenly. "However, we have everything we need to survive right here."

The general scowled at the curator. "We have no nourishment."

"Wrong again, General. You are a continuing disappointment to me. I blame myself, of course. I was too hasty in replacing General Lethro 814. I should have realized at once that you are inferior, but mourning your predecessor clouded my judgment."

"What will we do for food?" one of the troopers asked.

Nero 51 thought carefully about how much information he wanted the soldiers to know about the library. He decided revealing the contents behind one of the wondrous doors on level six would not be so terribly risky. "The library has a duplicloner, a replicator of sorts that will create whatever we need. Food, water... weapons."

"That's phenomenal," the soldier answered.

The general sneered. "Will it replenish the air we need to breathe, as well?"

"The humidifier in the front vestibule will take care of that," Nero 51 answered icily.

The general matched the curator's tone. "As long as it doesn't break down."

"We can re-create all the parts we need with the duplicloner."

"And you have the expertise to fix it if it were to break down?" the general shot back.

"This is the Library of Illumination. We can find all the expertise we need etched on the obelisks."

"And the nimble fingers to perform mechanical surgery, no doubt."

Nero 51 did not answer the general, at least not out loud. *You have outlived your usefulness,* he thought, *and I cannot allow you to continue to undermine me.*

* * *

PRU TELLERENCE HAD limited experience conjuring objects out of thin air and decided she needed to practice. She locked herself within her personal chamber and concentrated on creating a cloak that would not only hide her overseer's robe but also would contain a magic pocket that would allow her to carry her miter within the cloak without showing its bulk. She refused to be separated from it again after previously being trapped on Romantica overnight, when she had hidden her miter in Natalia Dalura's residence. She couldn't hide it there again, considering the Terrorians had invaded the Romantican library. Besides, she would feel much safer knowing she could come and go between worlds at will.

Her first attempt was a bulky, oversized garment that would be impossible to walk in without tripping over the excess fabric.

Several tries later, she had a serviceable cloak that would cover her robes but still looked bulky and did nothing to minimize her miter.

★*This has to work… eventually.* She concentrated on enchanting the fabric to remove the bulk from her robe and the hat beneath it, but the hour grew late before the cloak transformed into a cover-up that not only concealed what she wore but also appeared graceful with gentle folds of silky cloth. One more effort to change it from the color of mud to midnight blue and she felt ready to travel anywhere.

MAL'S SUDDEN APPEARANCE in the Dramatican library surprised Furst.

"To collect the taxes, have you come? Not ready, we are."

"No, Furst. I'm here to speak with you about the sealing of the libraries. Every library on every other realm, except for here and Fantasia, has been completely sealed. It's a precaution taken by the overseers to make sure no invaders get into or out of those libraries. We know they already have a presence on two other realms. We sealed all the doors and windows on most of the libraries as a precaution. Here, only your portals are sealed, so no one from another world, except for myself or an overseer, can visit. Not even a time machine should be able to break the enchantment on the current seal. You remain free to leave the library and interact with the people of your world. The same is not true on Fantasia. The overseers want Johanna and Jackson to be free to travel between realms as needed. That is the only realm without protection."

"Come to tell me, why did not Pru Tellerence?"

"Pru Tellerence is busy with another matter. I'm sure she will visit you when she has completed handling it. But I wanted you to know that since your library is only partially sealed, you could carry on normally."

"Stop training soldiers, should we?"

Mal raised his eyebrows. "Quite the contrary. Continue preparing yourselves to fight. The threat has been contained, but it has not been removed."

"Send Dramatican soldiers to Fantasia, should we?"

"I don't think that's necessary at this time," Mal answered. "But we may take you up on that in the future."

"Show them to you, I will." Furst led Mal outside to the square to watch Dramaticans take part in military drills. Farther away, near the pond, some soldiers practiced shooting rocks with their decimators while others captured mice in the weapons' force field. They allowed the creatures to go free, before capturing them again. "With moving targets, some of them practice," Furst explained.

"Yes. And they're very good at it."

"Train the eye, it does. Better able to vaporize, they are, when proficient, they become. Easier to hit Terrorians, it is. Larger, they are. But, shoot back, mice do not."

"Yes. It's infinitely more difficult to fight when you're being fired upon. Still, it looks like you have a firm grasp of the problem and have everything under control. Continue the military training. You're doing an excellent job."

PRU TELLERENCE KNEW Dean Horatio Blastoe was on Romantica, meeting with Natalia Dalura and Dame Erato, and she made a point of bypassing them when she arrived. She had not planned on returning so soon, but she worried about the safety of her child after hearing the realm had been invaded.

She materialized inside Ingur Aguri's cottage. She'd left Bel in the witch's care, knowing Ingur would take care of the toddler as if she were her own. Indeed, the old crone had already renamed the youngster Selestra and treated her like a grandchild.

"Why have you returned? I told you it would be dangerous to be seen here with the child."

★*No one saw me enter, and your window panes are hazy with age. I will make them more so.* A moment later, the panes allowed light and images to filter in but obscured anything within from being seen from outside.

"You have not explained, yet, why you are here."

★*You must not reveal what I am about to tell you. There has been a change, here. The Library of Illumination has been taken over by invaders from another realm. They are contained within the library and cannot get out, but their close proximity to someone I care deeply about has me on edge. You must be forewarned, and take precautions when you go out, in case you have to adapt quickly.*

"Selestra now wears the mark of a Maroqi priestess."

Pru Tellerence looked at the child more closely and saw the golden spiral tattooed on the front of the youngster's throat. ★*That must have been painful for her,* she exclaimed.

"Not at all. It was instantaneous and painless. I used a special ink for the mark. When people look upon the child, they perceive her as a very powerful Maroqi witch. Even someone from another realm would feel that she is not to be trifled with."

Pru Tellerence inhaled slowly, although her thoughts raced. ★*Has she shown any special powers?*

"None whatsoever, but the only people who know that are you and I."

NERO 51 ALLOWED only one trooper to accompany him to sub-level six and swore him to secrecy before opening the entrance to the Chamber of Doors. He approached the fourth door and held his left palm against the lock. The door swung inwardly and a dim light illuminated, continuing to grow brighter with each passing second.

The far wall appeared to be solid bronze and contained six large, boxy openings. An assortment of tables lined the two side walls of the room.

Nero 51 walked to a table standing in the center of the room and opened a box of small, glass files. He pulled a few out and inserted them into small ports located above each box. The duplicloner hummed gently as it started to reproduce food in one box, water in another, and merk in the third. Slowly, they filled the tables with enough food and beverages to last until the next day.

"Will that be enough?" the soldier asked.

"We will have dealt with the problem by then, I'm sure," Nero 51 answered.

"I guess we could always come back and make more if we're still stuck in here."

The curator glared at the soldier. *That is not an option.*

—LOI—

4

J OHANNA THOUGHT ABOUT Odyon as she guarded the cupola windows. *How far did he get? He might still be here, unless he exited the library with the Eahta Frean fram Drycræft.* She wondered if she would have sensed it. *Probably not.* She was too dazed from receiving an unexpected crash-course on wizarding from Beck. Her thoughts were interrupted by a pounding on the stairs.

"Okay, we're back."

Johanna turned to see the two younger Roth siblings. "Where's Jackson?"

"He didn't like what Mom ordered, so he asked room service to bring him a steak," Ava replied.

"And he's still waiting," Chris added.

"What did your mother order for him?"

Ava relieved Johanna of her weapon. "Chicken cordon bleu, and I thought it was really good."

"Did they send it back?"

"No," Ava answered. "Mom saved it in the food warmer under the room service table in case you wanted it."

"Excellent."

AFTER DINNER, JACKSON asked Johanna to take a walk around the block so he could "work off" his steak. The sun slid below the tree line and the street lights came on as they walked. He took Johanna's hand and gently rubbed his thumb over her knuckle. "I think we need a plan."

"There's really not that much we can do," she answered, "until the Terrorians strike."

"I'm not talking about the Terrorians. I mean *we* need a plan."

She pulled her hand from his. "This is not a good time to be thinking about your raging hormones. We may be fighting a war soon, and I think that takes precedence."

He let out an audible breath. "It has nothing to do with raging hormones. You talked about taking college courses. I want to take some, too. I'd like to look at a class schedule and decide what courses I want to take, but we need to make sure the library is covered. We need to coordinate when our classes will be so everything runs smoothly."

"Where's the real Jackson Roth? And who are you?"

"What?"

"You're thinking so pragmatically, you sound like me."

"Well, I was going to ask you if I could stay on living at the library after my family goes back home, but when you started in on my 'raging hormones,' I decided to switch gears."

"I knew it. But you're right."

He twirled her around. "I can move in permanently?"

"I meant about the class schedule. We really should decide on that now. Most students have already registered for the fall semester."

Jackson's shoulders slumped. "Oh."

"Let's just take a wait-and-see approach about your other 'plan.'"

He raised his eyebrows. "You mean you'll actually consider it?"

She smiled at how quickly he perked up. "It's a possibility. You turn eighteen in October, and considering you'll be old enough to get drafted or vote, I think you'll have the maturity to know you'll be living here as a curator and that we're not playing house."

"Not playing house. Right. But I could still do this sometimes, couldn't I?" He slid his arms around her and pulled her in for a kiss. She wrapped her arms around his waist, and they melted into one another in the twilight. The horn of a passing car broke through their sudden show of passion. "Get a room," someone shouted out the window.

They could hear laughing as the car drove away. Jackson shook his head. "Jokers."

"Do you hear that?"

A soft mewling sound came from nearby shrubbery.

"Yeah." Jackson walked over and bent down, pushing the branches away. A tiny white kitten with bloody fur huddled against the stem. "It's a kitten. It looks like it's injured." He reached for it. The kitten battled him with her claw, drawing blood. "And now I'm injured, too," Jackson said, pulling his hand away.

"Move over." Johanna crouched down next to him and chanted a few words from one of Myrddin's calming spells. She reached for the kitten and removed it from under the bush without a problem. "She's hurt. Let's take her back to the library, clean her up, and see what we can do for her."

"Shouldn't we take her straight to the vet?"

"Now that I have a few of Myrddin's tricks up my sleeve, I'd like to try them out."

Jackson spoke sweetly to the injured animal. "You used to be a kitten, but now you're a guinea pig."

"Don't listen to him," she said softly to the little ball of fluff. "I'm not going to let anything happen to you."

AFTER SEEING THE Terrorians in the Juvini town square, residents stayed indoors. Their reticence gave the Terrorian soldiers time to plan.

"We must find water," one of them said. "And shade from the sun."

"There has to be water nearby," the other replied. "I say we head away from the library around that building." He pointed east. "If Nero 51's maps are correct, there is a water source on the other side."

"Wait. Someone approaches."

Four Juveniles approached the square.

"This cannot be good. They're carrying weapons. We must summon all our strength and make a run for it. Now!" The Terrorians pulled their bodies into compact shapes and extended all their tentacles in a circle to propel them like wheels. They barreled across the square and around the adjoining school and didn't stop until they landed in the pond. They soaked in the moisture, and when they heard the boys approaching, they slipped under the water and waited.

It would be a while before they surfaced. Terrorians—more like whales than humans—could hold their breath for close to an hour. They planned to stay under until their bodies had a chance to hydrate, and their hunters gave up the search and left.

LENC, THE ORPHANED militia volunteer whom Furst had taken under his wing, counted the weapons three times before confirming Mudge's suspicions. "Missing, one is. Angry about it, Furst will be. But tell him, you must."

The strategist shook his head. "Under lock and key, these weapons were. Had his own key, whoever took it. Unless have it, Furst does."

"Find out soon enough, you will. Go with you, I will, to confirm."

They crossed the path known as the Steppingstones to Illumination and entered the library. Furst stood behind the circulation desk studying a book.

"Something to tell you, Mudge has. Confirmed it, I have," Lenc said before he turned to the strategist.

"Missing, a weapon is. Checked several times, I have. Too, Lenc did."

The boy took a step forward. "Three times, I counted."

"Locked in storage, it was," Mudge continued. "A break-in, it does not look like. Have it, someone with a key does." His eyes widened with hope. "Have it, do you?" he asked, almost pleading.

"No. And concerned, I am, because, the taker, I may know."

"Take it, who did?" Lenc asked.

"Just an idea, it is. Proof, I do not have. But, taken it, I believe Dungen might have."

Mudge took off his hat and scratched his head, releasing a mass of red curls. "Dungen, why accuse?"

"My reasons, I have." Furst glanced at the book he'd been studying when Lenc and Mudge first walked in. The same book had gone missing from the library before the problem with the Terrorians started. He had suspected Dungen then. Now that the overseers had replaced all the books that had been in the library, the book was back on the shelves.

"The curator, I am. Yet, missing from this library, this book was. Know how that happened, I did not," Furst said, waving the book in the air. "Out of the region, it was sent, said the card file. Yet, send it, I did not."

"Demand it, Dungen did," Furst continued, "and, threaten me, he did. But, think he removed it, I do. Make trouble, he wanted to. Curator, he wants to be."

Mudge couldn't believe the charge. "Do that, Dungen would not. A judge, his father is. A good man, Pondor is."

"A good man, Pondor is," Furst agreed, "but a good man, that does not make Dungen. Mad, he was, when the overseers gave me a new uniform. Even angrier, he was, when the overseers said 'in charge,' I am. An axe to grind, Dungen has, and, now a weapon, he has, too."

"Proof, do you have?" Mudge asked.

Furst's face lost all its animation as he shook his

head. "Have proof, I will not, until, shot, someone is. And, me, the victim will probably be."

INSIDE THE ROMANTICAN library, the Terrorians had successfully vaporized every book from the cupola down to sub-level two hundred and twenty. The top floors were easy to navigate, but they found the sub-levels, with their maze-like structure, more difficult to maneuver in. And even though the sub-levels were cooler, there were no humidifiers in this library. The soldiers wore special protective clothing to protect their skin rather than the thick oil of their predecessors, after many of those soldiers were burned to death on Dramatica. *How stupid these people must be, to have paper books that can be ruined by humidity*, one trooper thought. *Obelisks are obviously the much better choice.*

The Terrorians had brought enough food with them to last twelve hours. After that, the time machine was scheduled to return with their replacements, and take them home.

Not knowing they were locked in, the troopers continued to destroy books, all the while wishing the air held more moisture.

PRU TELLERENCE DEPARTED Mysteriose as quietly as she'd arrived. Bel was in good hands, and bearing the sign of a Maroqi priestess would protect her identity. Pru Tellerence had added another protection charm of her own for Bel's well-being, and before she departed had changed a pile of papers into gold leaves as added incentive for Ingur's continued protection.

Back on Lumina, Pru Tellerence hung her new

traveling cloak in the back of a closet and put her miter back on before climbing to the observation tower of the Library of Origination. She liked the relative peace she found gazing at the clear purple sky and allowed her mind to relax, but not too much, lest she unwittingly share thoughts she did not want the other overseers to know about.

Ingur's claim that Bel had not yet demonstrated any special powers bothered her. The youngster was only three years old, but in longevicus years, that was more than three centuries. Surely Bel had had enough time to develop some special traits by now. *Longevicus is just the starting point. Maybe it's because no one has nurtured her talents or taught her how to use them. I must speak to Ingur about working with the child to help her reach her potential.*

JOHANNA USED ONE of Myrddin's spells to heal the kitten and bathed her.

"She's such a pretty little thing," Mrs. Roth exclaimed. "Have you given her a name yet?"

"Ophelia," Johanna said as she used the low setting on a blow dryer to fluff the kitten's long white fur. "It's the name of the cat I saw in the residence when Mal first tried to convince me to take over for him as curator. He said that cat's name was Ophelia, and I commented that it was just the name I would have chosen if I'd had a cat. But then, when I moved in, there was no cat. I guess Mal didn't want to overwhelm me."

"I hope she doesn't try to sharpen her claws on the books or furniture."

Johanna looked up quickly. "Do you think she

might?"

"When the children were little, Jackson's father brought home a cat one day. He said he won it in a card game. Some prize—another mouth to feed. We hardly had any nice furniture, but I had a desk that had belonged to my grandmother that I cherished. And the cat ruined it."

"Jackson never talked about having any pets. What happened to the cat?"

"One of them must have left the door open when they went out to play, and the cat got out." Mrs. Roth's voice dropped. "I found its body lying in the road. A car had run over it."

Johanna hugged Ophelia to her breast. "That's terrible."

"We had a funeral in the backyard. Jackson made a cross out of two flat pieces of wood and wrote 'R.I.P. Cat' on it."

Johanna made a face. "Not the name? Just 'Cat'?"

"That's all we ever called it. Just…Cat."

They both turned when the entrance to the library opened. Jackson walked in carrying a five-foot high tower with several levels of carpeted shelves and a cave-like tube about halfway up.

Johanna shook her head. "What is that?"

Mrs. Roth smiled. "I was just telling Johanna how Cat ruined Maimeó Margaret's desk. And I guess you remembered, too."

"What I remember is you crying when you saw it. And I knew if that fur ball ever hurt one of the books here, Johanna would never forgive herself. So I got a…" he set down the tower, picked up the tag that was attached to it, and read, "'Multi-Level Cat Scratching Post.' She can climb up on all these different shelves and hide out in the tube when she wants to be alone. And it's got these balls on a string hanging from this thing on the top that she can bat with her paws. Hopefully, it will keep her occupied.

"And, look," he took a small package out of his pocket, "the pet store owner gave me some catnip, too." Jackson sighed. "I was going to pick up some cat food, but I wouldn't have been able to carry it. As it is, I had to leave my bike chained up in front of the pet store and walk back with this."

Johanna grinned. "You're going to make such a good daddy."

Jackson smirked at his mother. "I guess that makes you a grandmother. I think your first official duty, Granny, should be driving me to the grocery store for some food and then dropping me off to pick up my bike."

"Oh, would you please?" Johanna begged.

The cat whimpered and waved her paw at Jackson's mom.

Mrs. Roth shook her head but couldn't hold back the smile. "How could I say no to that? I just need to go get my keys."

"So, what do you think?" Jackson asked, looking around. "Should I stand the tower next to the wall by the stone stairs, or put it here next to the circulation desk, where it will get more light from the widows on the halo level?"

"I was going to leave her up in my apartment, but I guess it might get lonely up there during the day. Still, if you put it right next to the desk, it might make it too easy for her to wreak havoc with my paperwork." She walked around the main reading room. "Let's move that table from the middle of the floor and place it there. She'll get plenty of sunlight during the day and will be able to see nearly everything that's going on in the library."

Mrs. Roth walked out of the hotel suite with keys in hand. "Are you ready?"

"Yeah." Jackson turned to Johanna. "I'll move the table when I get back, okay?"

"Mmm-hmm," she said smiling.

He did his best Terminator impression. "I'll be back."

—LOI—

5

JOHANNA PLACED OPHELIA on the upper level of the scratching post when the phone rang. "Don't fall," she warned the kitten. While Johanna wrote down the particulars of a book request, Ophelia crawled inside the carpeted tube and closed her eyes.

Jackson and his mother walked in just as Johanna finished packing the book order. The Roths carried in an overstuffed princess bed for the kitten and enough food to feed her for weeks. "Mom got Ophelia the bed as a present." It looked like a small four poster bed with curtains on three sides and a puffy mattress for Ophelia to sink into. Oddly enough, it almost looked like a miniature version of Johanna's bed. "Where is she?" Jackson asked.

"The last time I saw her, she was taking a nap on the scratching post."

Jackson wandered away in search of the kitten.

Mrs. Roth gestured toward the food. "Do you want to keep half of these down here, so you can feed

Ophelia during the day?"

"I hadn't thought about it. How often does a kitten eat?"

"Three or four times a day while they're little. Twice a day when they get older."

"Okay. Let's keep a bunch of cans behind the circulation desk. I guess I should bring down a dish for her food."

"No need." Mrs. Roth removed a plate and matching bowl for the kitten.

"You didn't have to do that."

"I didn't. Jackson did. I think he's taking his parental duties very seriously."

Johanna could hear Jackson calling Ophelia's name. "My guess is he's intent on waking her up."

He returned to the circulation desk a few minutes later. "The cat's not sleeping in the tower. Where else do you think she can be?"

"Ophelia," Johanna called out as she headed toward the reading room. She continued to call the cat's name as she checked under the furniture and behind every shelf.

After a while, Jackson and his mother joined the search with no luck.

"Did you look in the closet in your office?" Jackson asked Johanna.

"No. The door is closed and I doubt Ophelia can open it."

"I guess I was thinking that's where we found… the other you."

"I can turn doorknobs that Ophelia might find troublesome."

"Ophelia," they both shouted out, going in opposite directions.

Chris bounded down the cupola steps. "What's going on down here? Who's Ophelia?"

Mrs. Roth brushed back a lock of Chris's hair as she spoke. "Johanna and Jackson found a kitten. But she seems to have wandered off. So, they're looking for her."

"How difficult could it be to find one tiny, little kitten?" he asked, yawning.

"Apparently, very difficult," his mother replied. "Why don't you try to help them?"

"Ophelia," Chris shouted. "Here, kitty, kitty, kitty."

NERO 51 COULD feel the walls of the library closing in on him. There were periods of his life when he had spent months without ever thinking of leaving the premises. But being trapped inside was entirely different, especially now that he had actually launched the invasion his grandfather had long talked about. *I'm not going to let them stop me.*

He returned to the cupola and played with the crystals used to operate the time machine. To time travel, all he had to do was touch the two crystals together and think about the time and place he wanted to go. But whenever he tried to go back to a time when the portals were open, the machine shuddered and couldn't transverse the portal. He racked his brain, trying to determine the moment when everything changed. The air had appeared to shimmer while he returned from depositing troopers on Romantica. *A temporal rift.* It had happened on Romantica, but perhaps the other realms had not been affected. He needed to exhaust all possible options by trying to travel to each realm.

"WHAT IS HE doing?" one Terrorian trooper asked another about Nero 51. "He's been fooling with the time machine for hours."

"What else is he going to do?" the soldier replied. "We're trapped in here."

They looked over at the time machine. Every so often, it appeared to waiver, but nothing more.

"He might as well give up," the first trooper said. "He's not going anywhere."

NERO 51 WORKED feverishly to locate the precise second he had traveled back to Terroria from Romantica. The time machine took up space when the rift had occurred, so it was possible that tiny hole in space might not be protected. Maybe, if he could find that precise moment when whatever now kept them locked inside was put into place, it might provide an exit path. He tried over and over again, second by second, trying to pinpoint the exact moment they returned. He berated himself for not noting the time. He had been too preoccupied with seeking intel from their previous invasion of Juvenilia.

Suddenly, he felt the machine make the leap into another portal.

"He's gone," one of the Terrorian troopers gasped as the time machine disappeared. "Nero 51 has found a way out of the structure."

"What about us?" another soldier asked. "Is he coming back for us?"

"He'll have to eventually. This is his library."

"Unless he gets himself killed," a third soldier said dryly. "Then he would never come back, and we'll likely die here."

The others felt a chill that no amount of warm, moist air could help drive away. It had never occurred to them that Nero 51 was the key to their survival. Or their demise. They had been following him blindly. Still, few of them worried. As far as they were concerned, Nero 51 would never allow himself to be killed. Period.

CHRIS MADE HIS way up the cupola stairs looking for Ophelia. He didn't believe the cat was big enough to successfully climb five flights of open spiral steps, but there was no sign of her below, and she had to be somewhere.

"What are you doing?" his sister asked when he reached the top.

He told her about the missing cat and she immediately thrust the decimator into his arms and said, "Take over."

"Where are you going?" he called, as his sister streaked down the staircase.

Her answer reverberated back to him. "I want to see the cat."

Chris could hear Johanna and his family calling out for Ophelia far below. As he looked down, he thought he saw a white streak jumping up onto a bookshelf.

Gotcha, he thought as he ran down the steps, ready to become the hero of the day.

THE TERRORIAN TROOPERS on Juvenilia strained their eyes

to see through the murky water of the pond. The soldiers could no longer hear the kiddlets' voices and hoped their pursuers had assumed they'd drowned, and had departed. Perog 2 slowly rose and allowed only his face to gently break the surface of the water. He tried to look around without making himself too much of a target. When he didn't see any movement, he signaled his colleague to rise.

Mope 98 was not as graceful as Perog 2. He allowed his entire head to rise above the surface, causing a large ripple. He quickly ducked back underwater when he saw a giant flame rushing toward him across the surface of the pond.

The orange flame lit up the air above them.

At the very least, the troopers had successfully replenished their air supply and were good for another hour. But they now knew the kiddlets had not given up and would be waiting for retribution.

HORATIO BLASTOE VISITED Natalia Dalura and Dame Erato for the better part of the afternoon, as they watched and waited for signs of a disturbance caused by the Terrorian occupation of the Romantican Library of Illumination. However, aside from the fact that Natalia could not return home, there was little indication of the destruction going on inside the great edifice.

✠*I do believe the library is adequately sealed for your protection,* Horatio Blastoe commented. He stood to take his leave. ✠*Use the diary if you need to reach me. Alert me to any changes immediately.*

"What do you think they're doing in there?" Dame Erato asked.

✠*Based on what happened on Dramatica, I would say they're probably destroying all the books.*

"That's terrible," Natalia cried.

✠*Books can be replaced. Our greatest concern is for everyone's safety. There was loss of life on Dramatica. The people of that realm bravely fought back and managed to stop the invaders from getting any farther than their library. However, a number of Dramaticans sacrificed their lives for the good of the realm.*

Dame Erato shivered. "How sad. I hope our little militia is up to the task."

Horatio Blastoe raised an eyebrow. ✠*We have never had a militia on this realm.*

Natalia lifted her chin a little. "My nature walk group has taken it upon themselves to train in self-defense. I'm sure once I've informed them about what is going on, they'll want to study more aggressive forms of offense and defense."

Horatio Blastoe grimaced. ✠*You were never given weapons with which to protect yourself.*

"Aren't weapons overdoing it a bit?" Natalia asked.

✠*The Terrorians are outfitted with weapons that can either trap you in a force field or vaporize you entirely. We have produced identical weapons for every realm to even the odds. However, I never completed delivery of your weapons because I saw Terrorians when I materialized in your library and quickly retreated. I must return here with weapons for your use.*

Dame Erato rolled her eyes. "Really, Horatio Blastoe, don't you consider that overkill?"

The overseer sighed. ✠*It depends on whom you*

want to see killed—them or you. I wish I could tell you weapons are unnecessary, but I can't. Perhaps, instead, I can find someone to help train you.

Natalia smiled. "We would be happy for your assistance."

FURST PAUSED BEFORE knocking on Dungen's door. Confronting his kinsman was not in his nature, but he believed deep within that Dungen had taken the missing firearm. Before he could knock a second time, Dungen abruptly pulled the door open.

Both Dramaticans gasped. Neither expected to see the other at that precise moment.

Dungen's face contorted in anger. "Doing here, what are you, Furst?"

"Two settings, the gun you have borrowed has, to tell you, I've come. Be careful, you must, when Terrorians, you fight. Force field, the O means, and obliteration, the X means. Hurt yourself, do not."

Furst nodded once, turned and walked away. As he retreated, he waited for Dungen to scream out a denial, but the self-proclaimed head of the library council didn't say a word.

Furst whispered the Dramatican term for *caught red-handed*. By acting like it was common knowledge that Dungen had taken the weapon and pretending to instruct him so he would not hurt himself, he had diluted the other man's ability to surprise him and possibly fire upon him. Or so he hoped.

CHRIS HAD A tough time determining which shelf the cat had jumped onto when he reached the main reading room. He knew it was close to the center of the room on the east side of the library, but that was it. The shelves all looked alike from this close up, so he had to scan each one, trying not to scare the kitten into running away.

"What are you doing down here?" his sister screamed. "You're supposed to be guarding the portals."

"Here." He handed her the weapon he had slung across his back. "You guard the portals. I need to find that cat."

"Useless," she muttered under her breath as she headed back toward the cupola stairs.

Books. Nero 51 looked around the library the time machine had come to rest in. He had broken free of the Terrorian library but wasn't sure where he had landed. He could hear several voices below saying something strange. *What is an ophelia?* he wondered.

Still, he didn't want to wait around to find out. He wanted to return to his own realm and amass his soldiers for another wave of attacks. He turned too quickly, smacking the tentacle that held one of the navigation crystals for the time machine against a shelf. He watched the crystal skitter across the floor and bounce down the cupola stairs. *Fegt!* He then realized someone was ascending the stairs at a rapid rate. He peered over the edge and saw the crystal a few steps down. He grasped it in his tentacle and rushed back to the time machine. He had no weapon, so engaging the enemy was beyond good reason. He inserted the crystal, but before he could concentrate on his destination, he saw a tiny being take aim with one of his own decimators and pull the trigger.

—LOI—

6

"MEOW," OPHELIA MEWLED when a hand closed around her.

"Come to papa," Jackson said as he nestled the kitten against his chest. "I found her," he called out.

Everyone, except Ava, followed his voice to the stacks nearest the back door.

"I think she was planning to make a break for it," he joked.

"She must have changed direction when I ran down the stairs," Chris said, banging the shelf with his hand. "I definitely saw her jump onto a shelf on the other side of the library."

The sudden move surprised the kitten, who dug her claws into Jackson's chest.

"Ow," the older Roth boy cried, thrusting the kitten away.

"Here, I'll take her," Johanna said, reaching for Ophelia and gently cuddling her.

"I'd better get back upstairs," Chris said, "before

Ava starts complaining."

A sudden boom and a flash of blue light in the cupola shook the library.

"Ava," they all screamed in unison.

MAL ENTERED THE overseer's chamber to request permission to begin visiting realms, ostensibly as the Chancellor of the Exchequer.

⌘ *Avoid the libraries, Malcolm. As you know, they are sealed. But you carry with you the ability to transport anywhere. Much as our miters help us travel among realms, your chaperon, or hat, contains the same power.*

"I was thinking of starting with Terroria."

⌘ *I would wait before visiting that realm. I'm sure the Terrorians are livid about the library being sealed. I think it might make more sense to start elsewhere, perhaps one of Terroria's former allies.*

"Mysteriose and Adventura?"

⌘ *Yes. It might be interesting to hear their opinion of what is happening with the libraries.*

"Do you have a preference?"

⌘ *They are equal. Choose whichever one you'd like to start with, and tread carefully.*

DAME ERATO COULD understand Natalia Dalura starting a militia, but didn't know how effective it might be if Romantica were ever invaded. "Just what is your little group capable of doing?"

"We are very effective at archery. Only Cecilia has failed to ever hit a target, but the rest of us have fairly decent aim. We can start a fire using a metal file and a rock. And Alicia is very good at spear-fishing and is teaching the rest of us." Natalia smiled. "Madam Beech is putting together packets for each of us, survival kits you might call them, with fishing line and hooks and seeds for plants if we're ever forced out of our homes and have to live in the woods."

"That's good," Dame Erato replied, "if you're forced from your homes by fire or storm, but how will any of that help protect us against Terrorians?"

✠*Perhaps these will help.*

The two women, startled, turned to find Horatio Blastoe and one other person standing behind them, their arms filled with oddly shaped tubes.

"What are you holding?" Dame Erato asked.

✠*These are Terrorian weapons. The Dramaticans captured a number of them and we've had them dupli-cated for all the realms. If the Terrorians are going to inflict this kind of firepower on others, it's only fair they be prepared to face it themselves. And I've brought someone with me who can teach you how to use them to best effect.*

The person standing behind Horatio Blastoe laid the weapons he was holding on the floor.

"Furst!" Natalia Dalura cried, running over to give the Dramatican curator a hug. "I'm so glad you're well."

"My services, I volunteered. To fight off invaders, there are many Dramaticans trained. So, to teach you how to fight Terrorians, I've come."

"That's wonderful, but it will have to wait until morning. Everyone is home, asleep."

"For no one, war waits," Furst said pragmatically.

✠*Furst is right. But there's no need to wake everyone yet. Show us where your militia has been practicing, and we'll take the weapons there.*

MYSTERIOSE LOOKED EXACTLY like Mal expected. The skies were gray with an odd silver glow escaping between layers of...*What? Clouds, perhaps?* The structures beyond those lining the town square were more like mounds—inset with rocks—than buildings. And there were masses of dark, dreary trees, their trunks covered with lichen and their branches draped with silvery-gray threads. A proliferation of webs connected many of the trees, the remnants of insects and small creatures entangled in their hold. The air was damp and Mal shivered, glad of the heavy robes he wore as Chancellor of the Exchequer.

Dean Proteus Bligh noticed Mal's discomfort. Ψ*It's not the cheeriest looking place, especially when compared to Lumi, but many of the people are pleasant enough if you respect their culture. Come. Let us go to Town Hall.*

The exterior of the Mysterian Town Hall looked similar, in architecture at least, to the town halls on other realms. However, the interior had wide open stone seating pits rather than rooms filled with traditional furniture; hand-woven Mysterian tapestries hung from the rafters, dividing the space.

Proteus Bligh led Mal to the largest of the seating pits, where a wizened old man led a discussion about the need to protect the trees from thieves trafficking in firewood.

The old man nodded to the overseer and continued

his discussion.

Proteus Bligh led Mal to seats on the outer ring of the circle. Ψ*This is as good a point of observation as any*, he whispered.

Mal nodded once in agreement. He studied the Mysterians attending the discussion. Many of them were older and their eyes seemed to be as black as coal. They dressed in drab fabrics with the only color coming from their wildly-hued scarves. All of the younger attendees were males with long locks, varying degrees of facial hair, and multiple tattoos and piercings. Their most arresting feature, however, was their silvery eyes. Unlike their elders, Mysterian youths' eyes glowed with an unearthly light. He leaned his head toward Proteus Bligh. "I notice there are no young women in attendance."

The overseer nodded. Ψ*On Mysteriose, the males are the politicians, the laborers, the warriors. They keep day-to-day life operating on an even keel. The females are the priestesses, the spiritual leaders, the healers. They are more powerful than the men in many ways but wouldn't be able to function without them.*

"Has it always been this way?"

Ψ*It has been this way since the Two Millennia War. Before that, the males were powerful priests, as well as politicians, warriors, and laborers. But many of them were killed in the war, and the women adapted to the change—growing incredibly powerful. Eventually, the men seemingly lost their ability to perform as priests while the women reached a pinnacle by which they all cultivate their power as priestesses. However, many of the older women have the knowledge and experience to realize it's beneficial to keep an eye on what the men are* *doing. So, they attend these discussions. The younger women don't yet have the knowledge that comes with experience and are too busy honing their craft to attend.*

The people around them began to disperse, however, the speaker and a few of the other men sitting closest to the center of the circle approached the overseer and Mal.

As NERO 51 FUMBLED with the crystal, Ava's finger tensed on the trigger of the decimator. But, before she could pull it, a flash of light blinded her and a percussive explosion knocked her to the ground.

The shock made Nero 51 freeze in place, until a bit of fog seeped into the time machine and took shape as Odyon.

"I suggest you get us out of here," the wizard said, using a translation charm to converse with the Terrorian.

Nero 51 closed his tentacles around the crystals, and a moment later they were back in the Terrorian library.

Terrorian soldiers picked up their weapons and targeted Nero 51's companion.

"No need for that," Odyon said, and with a wave of his hand, the weapons seemed so heavy the troopers could no longer hold them in the air. "That's better," he continued. He pulled off his left glove and showed Nero 51 his palm. "Who's in charge here?"

"I am," answered the curator, displaying the Illumini constellation on his seventh tentacle.

"Then I suggest we find someplace private to talk."

* * *

THE ROTH BOYS kept pace with each other as they raced up the cupola stairs. They arrived on the top level to find Ava lying on the floor, unconscious, with her finger still on the trigger of her weapon.

Jackson pushed his younger brother out of the way and eased the weapon out of his sister's hands, before lifting Ava.

"Jackson?" His mother's unasked question hung in the air.

"She's breathing. Let's get her downstairs."

Chris started toward the stairwell, but Jackson stopped him. "No. Check the weapon and make sure it works, even if you have to destroy a book. If it does, you've got to stay here and guard the portals."

"No," Johanna said as she reached the top of the steps. "I'll do that. All of you need to be there for Ava. I'll protect the portals."

The Roths trudged down the five flights of stairs, silently praying Ava would be all right.

Back in the comfort of the hotel suite, Mrs. Roth used an ampoule to revive her youngest child. "I'll need one of you boys to go to a pharmacy and buy some more of these. We seem to go through them like water."

Ava's head moved from side to side as she tried to escape the aroma of spirits of ammonia. Finally, her eyes sprang open and she pushed it away. "That stuff stinks."

Mrs. Roth kissed her daughter's forehead.

"What happened up there?" Jackson asked.

"Maybe we shouldn't force her to remember," Chris said.

"If this were just about us, I'd agree. But so

many other worlds are involved, I need Ava to remember whatever she can."

"There was a bubble. And an octopus. And a ghost. And a flash of light."

"Is she hallucinating?" Chris asked.

"No," his mother said. "I've seen the octopus before in the cupola, but only for a moment before he disappeared. I thought the light was playing tricks on me."

"Okay. The bubble sounds like the time machine, and the octopus is probably Nero 51 or some other Terrorian," Jackson said. "I need to know more about the ghost. What makes you say it's a ghost?"

Ava took a deep breath and closed her eyes. She took her time. "It appeared out of nowhere."

"What did it look like when you could finally see it?" he continued to prod.

She scrunched up her face. "Like a rich business man."

Chris's shoulders relaxed. "That's your idea of a ghost?"

"Shhh…" Jackson concentrated on reading his sister's face. "I want you to think very hard about this next question. It will sound silly, but it's very important. Was he wearing gloves?"

Ava's mouth opened and she pushed herself up on her elbows. "Yes. I saw him take one off, and he had one of those," she pointed to Jackson's Illumini constellation, "on his hand. I don't remember anything after that."

Jackson gave his sister a huge, sloppy kiss on the lips.

"Ewww!" she shrieked. "You kissed me on the mouth. That's disgusting."

"Yeah, bro," Chris said. "What were you thinking?"

JACKSON RACED UP the cupola stairs. "Nero 51 was here."

"How do you know?" Johanna asked.

"Ava saw an octopus in a bubble. Then she saw a ghost. One who materialized into a 'rich business man' who removed his glove and has one of these." He flashed her his left palm.

"Odyon."

"He was here, but not anymore. The last Ava saw of him, he was in the bubble. So if that's gone, so is Odyon."

"Where are they going to go if all the portals are sealed?"

"Didn't they say only the windows and doors were sealed on Terroria, but not the portals? I'll bet dollars to donuts Odyon went back there with Mr. Personality. Umm…donuts. I could use a couple of those right about now."

"No one thinks about eating more than you do."

"Chris. He eats more than me. Maybe I can talk him into going out to get some donuts."

"It's late. All the donut places are closed. We need to think about—"

"Room service! I'll bet we can order some."

"You're more likely to get French pastry than donuts."

"Yeah, but—"

"Stop. We need to contact the overseers and tell

them what's happened."

"So write to Mal in your diary."

"Exactly." She thrust the gun in his arms. "Guard the portals."

UNDER COVER OF darkness, the Terrorians slowly made their way through the water to the far end of the Juvini pond. Perog 2 signaled Mope 98 to stay behind, before he slowly slithered up onto the embankment beneath the bulk of a heavily boughed tree. He saw his tormentors sitting on the opposite end of the pond, toasting something over a fire. They were totally immersed in their conversation and didn't notice the Terrorian had emerged from the water. He snaked a tentacle into the pond and wrapped it around Mope 98, pulling him slowly to the shore. The two Terrorians stealthily crept into the woods beyond in an attempt to evade the flamethrowers.

"We must circle back to the library and look for our weapons."

"What if there are kiddlets there?"

"They may be too scared to go back there. Besides, there's nothing there for them anymore."

"Except our weapons. What if they found them?"

"Even if they got them to work, being decimated is a better end than burning to death. Nero 51 says it's painless."

"I wonder how he knows? It's not like he's ever been decimated."

"Follow me, and be quiet. We can't afford to make noise or speak." Slowly, they circled around darkened buildings, through the quiet alleys protected by the darkness of nightfall. If anyone had been about, they would have heard the squishing of the Terrorians' feet before they actually saw the invaders who blended exceptionally well into the shadows of night.

—LOI—

7

THE POLITICIANS OF Mysteriose were curious about the man in the vivid green robes and oversized green hat that flopped over to one side of his head. "Who accompanies you, Proteus Bligh?"

Ψ*Malcolm Trees has been appointed by the College of Overseers as its Chancellor of the Exchequer.*

"We are unfamiliar with his title. Is he an overseer?"

Ψ*In a manner of speaking. Malcolm Trees is the receiver of taxes—*

One man raised his voice. "Of tithes, you mean?"

Ψ*Call it what you may, we are here to discuss your need to tax your people in preparation for war.*

"What war is this?" asked the speaker, who had addressed the group earlier.

A voice came from behind them. "Gentlemen, I did not know you were here," Mysterian curator, Hue the Elder, cried as he rapidly approached Proteus Bligh and Mal. "What have I missed?"

"War taxes!" one of the politicians bellowed. "Yet, we are not at war."

Hue the Elder sighed. "I was planning to discuss what has occurred, but I have been busy relocating."

"Why would you relocate?" Sean of Oster asked. "Have you been expelled from the library?"

Hue the Elder slumped onto the nearest bench. "The library is off-limits. Sealed against intruders. I have had to find space to stay elsewhere while the threat of war lingers in the air."

"Who would fight us?" another person called out.

Ψ*Let us all be seated and I will explain. Or maybe it would be better if you told them what you know, Malcolm.*

"Gentlemen, and ladies," Malcolm began, taking note of the two women who stood at the fringe of the group, "one of the realms has decided to destroy the contents of the Libraries of Illumination, to gain control of all knowledge."

"It matters not," one of the women said. "We carry our knowledge within."

"Of course," Malcolm noted, "and no one can take that away from you. But, sometimes we need to refer to older texts of what has come before, and if that were suddenly to go missing, it could affect your daily lives."

Ψ*I'm sure there are some chants and spells that are much too complicated to be committed to memory. Imagine if one day you consulted the writings passed down to you from learned ancestors and found the pages blank.*

One of the women gasped.

Ψ*That is the threat of this war.*

"Who is carrying out this atrocity?" Sean of Oster asked.

Ψ*The Terrorians.*

The atmosphere immediately changed. The Mysterians let Proteus Bligh and Malcolm Trees know in no uncertain terms that their meeting was over and they would discuss nothing further with them. It didn't matter how long ago they had chosen the wrong side in war. Some taints failed to fade.

HORATIO BLASTOE AND Furst carried the decimators to a small glade west of the Library of Illumination. Dame Erato and Natalia Dalura followed, the curator strapping on her bow and quiver. Romantica's twin moons illuminated the clearing, and Natalia explained how her group of seven naturalists enjoyed walking the surrounding forest trails where they could study the various plants and herbs growing there.

Furst pulled an arrow out of a tree. "The plumage you use is substantial. Does it not weigh the arrow down?"

"No," Natalia answered. "It is light enough to allow the arrow to fly true, yet heavy enough to propel its trajectory. It is beautiful, no?"

⚓*It is light and lovely like everything on Romantica.*

Natalia inserted the arrow, drew back her bow string, and aimed it at a low-lying branch. The arrow hit its mark and severed the branch. She retrieved the branch and showed it to Furst. "This is what we use to make our arrows. Notice how it snapped cleanly? We used to use arrows made from live branches, thinking the moisture in them would make the arrows flexible, but as they dried, the arrows no longer stayed true. Now we make them from dry wood, like this. The arrows break more easily, but they hit the target more often."

"I, may?" Furst asked.

Natalia handed him her bow and he aimed an arrow at a narrow sapling. The arrow split the wood just below the joint where it branched out. A bird sitting on one of the branches took flight, seeking solace in a bigger tree with higher branches.

"Very nicely, it works."

Natalia examined the shot as she pulled the arrow from the tree. "You're an excellent shot, Furst."

"A lot of practice lately, I have had."

"Do the weapons you brought shoot arrows?"

Furst looked at Horatio Blastoe before answering. "A projectile, they do not shoot."

"Then what are they good for?" Dame Erato asked.

Furst picked up a weapon and set it on stun. He saw a rabbit feeding at the edge of the clearing and nodded toward it. Before Natalia Dalura could say, "Furst, no!" he had caught the rabbit in a force field.

"Is it dead?" she asked.

"No. Move, it cannot. Away, step." He shot it again and it scampered away.

"Oh. I like this weapon." She reached for it.

"No," Furst said, stepping back. "This first, you must see." He showed her how he switched the lever and then took aim at a rock. "The rock, watch."

Natalia and Dame Erato turned to watch the rock,

and a moment later, it was nothing more than dust.

"Where did it go?" Natalia asked.

"Gone forever, it is."

"You cannot shoot it a second time so it comes back?"

"No. Kind, this weapon can be. Or fatal."

"Oh!" Dame Erato exclaimed, realizing the potency of the weapon.

"I could never use such a weapon," Natalia whispered.

✠*You will have to,* Horatio Blastoe advised, ✠*because Terrorians won't hesitate using the same weapon on you. You must fight them with their own weapons if you wish to save yourselves.*

"But I won't have to, will I?" Natalia asked. "After all, isn't that why you sealed off the library?"

✠*I do not know how long it will take for someone to figure out a way to undermine the seals. I hope no one ever does. But at the very least, we have given you some time to prepare.*

A GLIMMER OF sunlight dappled the glade. Dawn had broken. ✠*It is time to summon your militia. Advise them about the threat of war and ask them whom else they know who could join your ranks. It will take more than a handful of you, and you need to start training.*

"It will take some time," the curator replied.

✠*Go as quickly as possible.* He turned to Dame Erato. ✠*Perhaps, while we wait you could prepare a small meal for Furst?*

"Of course," Dame Erato replied. "Go, Natalia. Rouse your friends and tell them to meet us here in two hours' time. I think that should be enough to alert everyone."

Natalia walked toward the village with them but left before they reached the library. She had a number of stops to make, including visiting some people who had expressed a desire to join the group but had not yet done so. She planned to tell them enough to fire up their imaginations and draw them to the glade but would leave the more frightening details for Horatio Blastoe and Furst to impart.

Three sisters lived at the first home she came to. Only Felicia, the middle sister, belonged to her nature group, but after listening to the curator speak, the other two asked if they could join in.

"All are welcomed," Natalia said. "All are needed."

"I think being part of a war is very exciting," the youngest sister, Milencia, said.

"You are ridiculous," the oldest sister, Arraba, replied.

Natalia smiled at the young girl, who looked taken aback by her sister's rebuke. "We are all unfamiliar with war except for what we have read, however, I've been told it's very dangerous, and our lives could be at stake. It is not romantic or comfortable. War is tolerating the intolerable to gain or maintain the freedoms we hold dear. You will learn through experience, as we all will. You are most welcomed to join us, but you need to understand sacrifices may have to be made. Painful sacrifices."

Milencia lifted her chin. "Even if it is not easy, I am ready to fight." She thought about it for a moment. "Can I ask my friends, too?"

Natalia nodded. "Meet us at the glade before the sun has risen above the tree line."

They agreed to split up and recruit as many volunteers as possible to the cause.

Natalia realized she must move more quickly. She still had five members to visit in the agreed upon time frame.

MAL, SENSING THE question Johanna wrote in her diary, turned suddenly toward Proteus Bligh. "Nero 51 has been sighted on Fantasia. It's believed he has now returned to Terroria, and he's brought Odyon with him."

"Odyon," one of the politicians repeated. "That is the name of the most powerful wizard in the history of Mysteriose. We have many wizards, but none have reached Odyon's level of greatness. He is long dead, however, having died in the Two Millennia War."

"Apparently, Odyon did not perish, and is now on Terroria."

One of the politicians drew himself up. "Odyon may be a Mysterian, but that does not mean we will necessarily side with him in the event of war. He chose to hide himself from us for many millennia and no longer commands the people of this realm."

✠*Then you are willing to rise up against Odyon if he sides with Terroria in battle?*

Murmuring grew loud among the people in the crowd. Some of them agreed to defy Odyon, but others hurried away, knowing if he still possessed the power he once held, they could not make such promises.

✠*We must take our leave, but we will soon return to continue this meeting. I'm sure there will be a lot to discuss among yourselves, for this latest development is, indeed, a most serious one.*

As they returned to Lumi, Mal asked Horatio Blastoe, "Do you believe the Mysterians who say they will take up arms against Odyon?"

✠*I do. Unfortunately, it bodes badly for the people of that realm because it means it will be a world divided.*

"DID YOU GET in touch with Mal?" Jackson asked Johanna when she returned.

"Yes. He sent me a one-word answer."

"Which was…?"

"'Understood.'"

"Doesn't say much, does it?"

"No."

Chris came up the stairs carrying a plate of pastries. "Room service told Mom the kitchen does not serve donuts, but if she was willing to wait for them, they would search the city for an American bakery that specializes in them. She told them 'pastries are just fine.' So, here."

"What is this?"

"Paris-Brest."

"I guess it's round like a breast, but shouldn't there be two of them?"

"Not boobs, you idiot. Brest is a city. François says it's named after a bicycle race between Paris and Brest."

"François?"

"The guy from room service."

"The way I see it," Jackson said, "bicycles have two wheels, so there should still be two of them."

"If you don't want it, I'll eat it."

Jackson snatched the rich pastry off the plate before Chris could grab it. "Hey," he said, his mouth filled with pastry and cream, "this is pretty good."

"I'm glad you like it. I ate two downstairs."

"Why didn't you bring us two? Now Johanna doesn't have one."

"You could have shared yours," Chris said.

"Am I interrupting?"

The three teens turned to find Mal standing at the top of the stairs. He still wore his Chancellor of the Exchequer robes.

Jackson wiped his hands off on his jeans. "Nice hat! Where'd you get those threads?"

"Weren't you aware that the College of Overseers appointed me Chancellor of the Exchequer for all realms?"

"The title sounds familiar, but that's it. I guess it's been kind of busy around here lately. So, you write checks?"

"No. I receive the checks. Or the taxes, to be more precise."

"We have to pay you taxes?"

"It's more to allow me to travel to all the realms and listen in on their rumors and innuendoes."

Jackson smiled. "You're the gossip guy? You could have fooled me. I think you look more like a college professor from some fancy-schmancy school."

Mal grew serious. "Who saw Nero 51?"

"Ava did. There was some kind of explosion that knocked her out, so she's sleeping now. But Mom made sure she came to first, and that's when she said she saw

Nero 51 take Odyon away in the time machine."

Mal nodded. "I'd like to talk to your sister."

"Mom probably won't let you until morning," Jackson said. "But considering it's almost morning already, you probably won't have long to wait." He handed the decimator to Chris. "You have the watch." He grabbed Mal's arm and turned him toward the cupola stairs. "While we wait, we can have some really good pastries from room service, unless," he raised his voice, "Chris ate them all."

THE TERRORIAN SOLDIERS stared into the back window of the Juvenile library. A beam of moonlight glinted off something on the floor and Perog 2 said, "I see one of the weapons." He tried to hoist himself up through the window but couldn't.

"What's the matter?" Mope 98 asked.

"There seems to be some kind of force field where the window used to be. It's preventing me from entering."

"Here, let me give it a try." Mope 98 snaked his tentacles up along the building to grab hold of a higher window sill and pulled himself up but was not able to enter the library. "Now what?"

"Wait here. I'm going to see if I can enter through the front door. Don't do anything. Don't make any noise. You don't want to call attention to yourself. Wait for me here."

Perog 2 crept around the building, even though he knew he was in danger of being discovered because the sky was growing lighter. He pushed the front door and gained entry to the front vestibule. But he could not gain further access into the library.

Through the glass, he saw the light from a torch across the way and saw two boys walking together. They didn't appear to have a flame-thrower, or any other weapon, but he still plastered himself against the wall, hoping they wouldn't notice him. He could clearly hear their voices and they seemed to be getting louder.

Out back, Mope 98 felt shivers run along his tentacles when he heard a twig crack. It sounded like someone was sneaking up behind him. Slowly, he snaked his tentacles up the tree behind the library and hoped the branches were strong enough to support his weight. He felt for two sturdy boughs and grasped them, shortening his tentacles to pull himself up into the tree. It was hard to find a comfortable position, but he couldn't afford to make any noise, so he held himself uncomfortably still, praying Perog 2 would soon return—with a weapon.

As Mope 98 hung on for several long moments, he felt his body cramping and shifted his position. A branch cracked. He hoped there was no one around to hear it, but then he heard another twig snap and he knew someone was in the woods behind the library.

—LOI—

8

Jackson led Mal to the George V room.

"It's very important that I speak to Ava as soon as possible," Mal stressed, "before she starts to forget details."

"You've got to convince Mom," Jackson replied.

When they arrived at the suite, they found the lights dimmed. "I don't hear anyone," Johanna whispered. "Your mother probably went back to sleep after jumping through hoops trying to find donuts."

"Thanks for reminding me." Jackson picked up the phone and dialed room service. "Bonjour, this is Mr. Oswald-Fitzpatrick of New York. I'd like three orders of your Paris-Brest pastries with coffee for three, please. ... Very good. Thank you."

Mal narrowed his eyes. "Mr. Oswald-Fitzpatrick of New York?"

Johanna shook her head. "Don't ask."

"What's going on?" A very sleepy Ava in an oversized T-shirt walked into the living room.

"Just the young lady I want to speak with," Mal said, smiling.

Ava stared at his hat.

Jackson followed her line of sight. "I told you that hat is a show-stopper," he said, picking up the phone. "You want coffee?" he asked his sister.

"Tea. And French toast with strawberries."

"Got it." Jackson added her choices to their order and pulled out a chair for her at the table.

She looked at Mal. "You want to know about the octopus, don't you." It was more of a statement than a question.

"Every little detail. Don't leave anything out, no matter how minor it seems."

Ava rubbed her eyes. "I was running up the stairs when I saw a crystal fall onto one of the top steps. I reached out to pick it up, but a tentacle snaked down from the cupola and snatched it. I had the gun slung around my back, so I grabbed it and pulled it forward. That's when I saw a huge bubble sitting in the cupola. I aimed the decimator, but then a man appeared inside the bubble with the octopus. I didn't know who he was, or if I should shoot, and before I could figure it out they were gone."

Mal leaned forward. "Describe the man who appeared in the bubble."

"He looked like he owned a company or something. He looked like he had money. I thought I saw him pull his hand off, but then Jackson said it was a glove."

Mal looked up. "You told her it was a glove?"

"No," Jackson corrected them. "I asked her if he

was wearing gloves, and she said yes."

"It made more sense that way," Ava continued, "because he showed the octopus his hand, and he has that same design Jackson has on his palm."

"Like this?" Mal asked, showing her his left hand.

"Am I the only one who doesn't have one of those?" Ava whined. "Although, maybe I don't want one considering the octopus had one on his tentacle."

"Are you sure?" Mal asked quietly.

"Yes, I'm sure. And then everything went bright white and...I woke up when Mom held one of those smelly things under my nose. One of those ampoules." She exaggerated her pronunciation of the word, making it sound ridiculous.

"Do you remember anything else?"

Before she could answer, they were interrupted by a knock at the door. Room service wheeled in breakfast. After they were settled, Mal continued his questions. "Did you hear anything?"

"No." She stopped. "Except the octopus sounded like he was having an asthma attack."

Jackson sucked out some of the cream from the center of his pastry. "I think Mal means the explosion."

"I didn't hear any explosion. There was just a bright light. That was it."

"Did you hear the man and the octopus speak to each other?" Mal asked.

Ava stopped chewing. "I think they spoke. I saw the man's lips moving. But I couldn't hear anything they were saying."

"I thought I heard people out here." Mrs. Roth

took a seat at the table. Before she could say another word, Jackson was on the phone ordering toast and tea for her breakfast.

"We get to feast on rich pastries," Mal said, laughing, "and all your mother gets is toast and tea?"

"That's all she ever eats," Jackson replied.

"It's true," Ava added.

Mrs. Roth smiled. "My children know me well."

Jackson turned back to Ava. "I'm surprised you didn't hear the explosion. There was a loud boom."

"No," Ava said. "I just saw a flash of light, and that was it."

Mal still had questions for Ava. "Are you sure you saw an Illumini constellation on the creature's tentacle? Maybe you dreamt it when you fell asleep after the explosion."

Ava popped the last piece of French toast in her mouth and chewed thoughtfully. "No. It was real. I would bet my life on it."

THE FOLLOWING MORNING, a council of elders met on Mysteriose. Both males and females had been encouraged to attend. Their discussion centered on Terroria's new attempt to invade its neighbors, as well as the "tax" to pay for war preparations. The Mysterians knew they would have to have a unified front before they spoke to Proteus Bligh, or anyone else the College of Overseers chose to send their way.

Val Dvir, a priest from the village of Mecox asked, "How do we know the Terrorians initiated an attack? Maybe the overseers only made the claim as an excuse to assess taxes."

"I trust Proteus Bligh," Sean of Oster replied. "He wished to provide us with weapons to ward off the attack."

"So that we'd feel compelled to pay for them," Val Dvir said. "It makes the transition to taxes that much easier for them."

"We have our own weapons," a high priestess replied. "Why would we use theirs?"

Ψ*Because the weapons we are prepared to give you were designed by the Terrorians. You would be fighting them with their own technology.*

Sean of Oster bowed his head in reverence to the overseer. "We welcome you, Proteus Bligh. We are not convinced the need to wage war against the Terrorians is warranted."

Ψ*Some might feel you prefer to fight with them.*

Anger flashed in Val Dvir's eyes. "You lie to incite us," he shouted.

Ψ*No,* Proteus Bligh answered. Ψ*Every realm is being given the same weapons. We know there are brave citizens on each realm who will do what they must to protect their homes and liberty. We offer you weapons because we've offered everyone else weapons. Whether you use them against the Terrorians or residents of other realms, the College of Overseers feels satisfied knowing all aggressors are evenly matched.*

"What is this tax you want to collect from us?"

Ψ*It is a small amount we believe all your residents should pay to help you keep up with the necessary expenses of war. Homes may be damaged and need to be rebuilt. Supplies may be destroyed and may need to be replaced. Your taxes will not leave this realm.*

Malcolm Trees, the Chancellor of the Exchequer will see to that. He will make sure it is not squandered by your politicians. Your taxes will only be used to make quick reparations for whatever items you lose during battle.

Usterice, a high priestess, rose to her feet, and everyone around her quieted. "How much is this tax and when is it due?"

Ψ*You must decide on the amount as a group. You know what your homes and possessions are worth. You must decide on an amount that will cover their replacement and fairly apportion an amount for each to pay.*

"What if we choose to have no taxes?" Usterice asked. "What if each of us wants to be responsible for our own losses?"

Ψ*That would be very generous of you, especially if you alone lost everything and had to pay to replace it all, while your neighbors lost nothing. Think how you would feel, after putting your life on the line to protect them and their possessions. Wouldn't you consider it an unfair burden upon yourself? Taxes help even out that inequity regardless of who bears the loss.*

"I'm surprised your tax collector isn't with you today."

Ψ*Our Chancellor of the Exchequer is busy on another realm. But I will ask him to return, if you wish to discuss ways in which to make the payment of taxes easier.*

A FEW HOURS later, the glade behind the Romantican library filled with dozens of women of varying ages.

"Many, you have recruited," Furst said. "What

you are already doing, perhaps you could show us."

The original members of Natalia Dalura's nature walkers demonstrated their abilities with bow and arrow, stick fighting, and bodily maneuvers to evade physical punches and blows. When they were done, Furst gave the group a demonstration of how the Terrorian decimator worked.

✠*I believe the best way to approach this is to divide by strengths. Everyone who believes they are strongest in archery, line up behind Natalia. Those who believe they excel at stick fighting, move to the other edge of the glade with Felicia, and those who would like to learn weaponry, move here behind Furst. Those remaining will be guided in hand-to-hand combat.*

Most of the women gathered behind Natalia and Felicia. Few assembled behind Furst, and only one woman remained who was interested in physical grappling.

"Even out, we must," Furst said. "Learn everything, everyone will. But, too lopsided, the groups are."

Dame Erato and Horatio Blastoe divided the women into four platoons, and Natalia was reassigned to physical fighting while Arraba took over archery training. Each group anchored a corner of the glade, with the two more dangerous groups aiming their weapons away from the town proper and out toward the forest that divided the western edge of the capital city of Roma from the Wellendra Region.

PEROG 2 WAS soon awash in sweat, caused by the fear of being spotted by the Juveniles walking in front of the Library of Illumination. Apparently, the teens were so wrapped up in their conversation, they didn't notice the Terrorian hiding in the vestibule. The Terrorian waited for the Juveniles to disappear from sight and then waited some more. When he finally felt safe, he exited the vestibule and crept around the building but soon found himself again hiding from a Juvenile confab in the rear of the library.

He stood in the shadows of the building, working up the courage to peek around the corner in search of Mope 98. A quick scan did not reveal his countryman, and he wondered what hiding spot his fellow soldier might have found. He stayed hidden. *How long can these kiddlets talk?* He soon learned they could talk for a very long time about games, and weapons, and killing monsters. *Why don't they go home to their beds?*

A few of the boys walked away, and the Terrorian relaxed, thinking they soon would be gone. But instead, the wanderers returned with twigs and branches and began to build a fire.

I cannot stay here, Perog 2 thought. *I was better off hiding by the pond. Maybe that's where Mope 98 has gone.*

A drop of wetness dripped onto his forehead from above. He looked up into a tree to see Mope 98 hiding among its branches.

They had outrun the kiddlets once before and they could probably outrun them again. But there was always the possibility that the group with the flame-throwers would be waiting at the pond. They needed to get away from the library and secure a hiding place, but that wasn't going to be possible as long as Mope 98 was stuck up a tree.

* * *

MAL, JOHANNA, AND Jackson stood in the cupola talking about what Ava had seen.

"There's not much you can do about it right now," Mal said. "I'll return to Lumi to tell Ryden Simmdry what happened and confirm Ava saw Nero 51 on Fantasia in possession of the time machine. I'm sure he'll be interested to learn that Odyon and Nero 51 are traveling together."

Jackson nodded once. "What should we do in the meantime?"

Mal rubbed his beard. "Aren't you still in school?"

"Ye-ah," Jackson said tentatively.

"Shouldn't you show up for some classes?" Mal continued.

Jackson closed his eyes and grimaced. "Aww, Mal, why'd you have to say that? Besides, Johanna needs me here."

"No I don't," she replied. "You graduate soon. Aren't you supposed to be getting ready for finals or something?"

Jackson's shoulders slumped. "I don't even know what's going on in school anymore."

Johanna pushed him toward the cupola stairs. "Go call Logan. Tell him you need a refresher before you can take your finals. And while you're at school, see Old Man Benson and tell him you're sorry you haven't been to all your classes, but you have family obligations that have prevented you from attending."

Jackson perked right up. "I can't believe you just called him 'Old Man Benson.'"

Johanna's jaw dropped. She thought back to what she had just said. There was no denying it. She punched Jackson in the arm. "Your bad habits are starting to rub off on me. We're spending way too much time together. Go to school. And do not, I repeat, do not call him Old Man Benson, regardless of what I said. I was wrong."

"I can't wait to tell Logan you did that. He's going to love it." Jackson happily bounded down the cupola stairs, ready to catch up with his best friend.

"The two of you are usually so mature," Mal said, "I sometimes forget Jackson is still a kid in many ways."

"I don't think I was ever that young, Mal. I don't remember ever acting like a kid."

"Running away from Peakie's Foundling Home was something a kid would do."

"I told you about that?"

Mal paused before answering. "I learned a lot about your background before we ever met. I had to know if you were the right choice for the Library of Illumination. So, I may know some things about you that you haven't personally revealed. But I don't know anything about you that I don't accept wholeheartedly and that doesn't make me proud to know you."

Johanna fought tears as her nose prickled. "I'm surprised you were able to link me to Peakie's."

Mal smiled. "There was no Johanna Charette at Peakie's. Just a bright, young girl named Josefina Charo who had completed her education and couldn't wait to make her mark on the world."

She sniffed. "Yeah."

He put his arm around her shoulders. "I wonder if there are any more of those French pastries left in the

Roth's suite? I think we could use a little pick-me-up right about now."

"Uh!" Johanna gasped.

"What is it?"

"I just saw Nero 51 and the time machine make a flash appearance. Just for a split second."

"Was Odyon with him?"

"I don't know. It was way too fast."

No sooner had she spoken than Ryden Simmdry appeared.

Mal nodded in acknowledgement of the overseer. "You just missed a momentary visit by Nero 51."

⌘*Not at all. He's trapped in the portals. I detected him transporting and realized he'd found a way to continue his travels. But now that I've sealed off this library and his own, he's trapped in the portals between the layers of time and space. I stopped here to warn you. I must go tell the others.*

JACKSON AND CHRIS fell into step with Logan outside the high school.

"Where's Cassie?" Jackson asked.

Logan shrugged. "She has the mumps."

Jackson stopped walking. "Didn't she just get over them?"

Logan turned and made a face. "What have you been smoking?"

"Today's April 6ᵗʰ, right?" Chris said a little too loud.

Jackson felt a chill wash over his body. "Yeah. April 6ᵗʰ." He had forgotten about the time warp that occurred while he and Johanna were in Wales. He'd have to be very careful about what he said or did."

The three boys split up as they made their ways to separate classrooms. Jackson stopped by the boy's room and heard the bell signal the start of homeroom. Late again.

The classroom door was closed and he looked inside through its small glass window and stopped in his tracks. He could clearly see himself already sitting at a desk. He started to sweat. *Okay, okay, okay. This happened to Johanna. Go home. Now. So you don't meet yourself.*

—LOI—

9

THE PLATOONS ON Romantica worked diligently to perfect their skills. As the day wore on, several people moved between sections so each platoon contained females who were strongest in that particular ability. There were some small sacrifices—friends separated from each other, women hurt by the critiques of their abilities—but the platoons grew stronger.

Grappling was an especially uncomfortable pursuit, and the Romanticans voluminous skirts did nothing to aid the process. Instead, flying fabric added spectacle when the diaphanous material ballooned around the wearers as they rolled in the grass.

Furst stood with his hands on his hips as he observed hand-to-hand combat. "Uniforms, they need," he said aloud.

Horatio Blastoe nodded. ✠*A splendid observation.*

"To Dramatica, it is what Pru Tellerence and Master Ryden Simmdry contributed."

✠*I will speak of it to the overseers.*

"Know what women need, Pru Tellerence will."

✠*Of course. Can I leave these women in your capable hands?*

"Do my best, I will, to train them."

Dame Erato walked over to Furst and the overseer. "Pru Tellerence could visit to see the women in action. She will understand the problems they face."

✠*You listened in on our conversation?*

"I may have been eavesdropping. It is a necessary evil in times of war."

Furst jerked his head back. "But, the enemy, we are not."

"Listening-in is a common practice on Romantica. A hobby of sorts. We are known for sharing in the triumphs and agonies of our friends and neighbors. When it comes to uniforms, I think Pru Tellerence would be especially insightful."

Horatio Blastoe smiled. ✠*I will make your request. If I'm unable to return before day's end, please find lodging for my friend Furst.*

Dame Erato smiled. "That will be no problem at all."

DUNGEN STOMPED UP the Dramatican library steps, the hem of his long blue velvet cloak sending up swirls of dust in his wake. He howled when he could get no farther than the outer vestibule and yelled for Furst to unlock the door. He continued screaming for several minutes, even though he got no answer.

Lenc observed the head of the Library Council's tirade from across the square. Finally, when he couldn't take the racket any longer, he approached Dungen.

"Here, Furst is not. Off-world, he has traveled."

"Mean, what do you? Gone, where has he?"

"Not sure, I am," the boy replied. "To help others fight the war, he has gone. To train them, he is helping."

Dungen scrunched up his chin, causing his lower lip to jut out. "Here, he should be. Running this library, he should be." He stomped off in the direction of Town Hall.

Lenc watched as the wind lifted the edge of Dungen's cloak, revealing the weapon hidden beneath its folds.

PEROG 2 MOVED closer to the tree where Mope 98 hid to see if it was visible to the Juveniles who had settled around a small fire. The trunk was out of sight, hidden by the corner of the building; however, some of the branches remained in full view. Any movement could draw unwanted attention.

Perog 2 closed his eyes as he thought. *We were sent here to destroy books and capture kiddlets in a force field. We are not prepared to be set upon by mercenaries.* His imagination churned as he tried to think up a plan of escape. He motioned to Mope 98 to stretch his tentacles and grasp a ledge on the roof. He mimicked stretching and pulling himself onto the roof. *He will need a diversion.* Again, he closed his eyes and inhaled deeply. A plan formed in his mind. He opened his eyes, startled to find a young girl standing in front of him clutching a rag doll. The kiddlet was tiny with a round face and very large eyes. Her eyelashes reminded him of *drit*—spiders—that infested parts of Terroria.

He stretched his tentacles toward the roof. "Mope

98, now!" he commanded as he hauled himself up. The two soldiers nearly collided on top of the library.

Down below, the youngster emitted an ear-piercing scream.

Perog 2 surveyed the area around them. There were no adjacent roofs to aid their escape. They attempted to flatten themselves against the roof to avoid detection.

The Juveniles abandoned the fire and ran to the side of the library. "What's wrong, Dee-Dee?"

The little girl pointed up at the sky. "Bugga-boos go up, up, up."

"Where's Marbol and the scorchers?" another boy asked.

"I'm pretty sure they're patrolling the pond," a girl named Rika said. "Rascal, Looper, take your BB guns and tell a couple of them to bring their scorchers. The rest of you, ready your weapons."

The Terrorians found no solace on the Juvenile library roof. It was clad in metal and shaped like a dome. A small foothold existed but proved inadequate for the fat, flat feet of the Terrorians who desperately clung to the top of the dome, afraid of losing their perch. Unfortunately, their sweat glands worked against them.

Mope 98 felt his tentacle slipping. "My grasp is weakening. I don't think I can last much longer. What should I do?"

"Land on the kiddlets. They'll soften your fall, and you in turn will soften mine," Perog 2 answered.

"Couldn't you fall on some kiddlets of your own?"

"I will do my...eeeeeeeeeeeeeeeeeeeeeeeee!" A hail of BBs bounced off Perog 2, but one injured his eye.

He thrashed out with his free tentacles smacking Mope 98, who lashed out with one of his own, and the two of them lost their grips and plummeted downward.

THE MYSTERIANS SPOKE among themselves about taxes long after Proteus Bligh left. They had reluctantly agreed to create a pool of reserves by turning raw mineral ore into coinage. But they were unsure how to disburse the coin and collect it as taxes. They had always traded in raw minerals and herbs, which could be used for poultices, charms, and favors. Dealing in coins created a new set of problems. The mineral ore was communally owned by all the residents, so they each had a right to coinage. But if they just gave everyone coins, there would be no mineral reserves for lean times.

They were reluctant to ask the Chancellor of the Exchequer for recommendations. He might ask too much in return. It would be better to control their tax system themselves, but they hardly knew how to do that.

RYDEN SIMMDRY DEPARTED Fantasia, only to return an hour later.

"To what do we owe the honor of your return?" Mal asked.

⌘*I've come to inform you, you're needed on Mysteriose. Apparently, Proteus Bligh has suggested the Mysterians speak to you about taxes. They were reluctant to pay them until asked how they would feel if they alone suffered losses and had to bear the entire cost while their neighbors did not. That concept did a lot to motivate them. Proteus Bligh addressed their discomfort by saying you could make objective recommendations without requiring any compensation whatsoever in return. Ever. They are now ready for your visit.*

"I'll go at once." Mal turned toward Johanna. "Stay alert."

"I will," she replied. "If there's one thing I've learned, it's not to underestimate Odyon, or Nero 51."

After they left, Johanna realized she was quite alone. The Roth siblings were all in school, and Mrs. Roth had gone to work. She checked the day's mail and phone messages and started putting orders together. It felt so normal. *I should enjoy the peace and quiet while I can.*

But in reality, she was bored. Being busy had made time pass faster, but now that she had finished her chores, time stood still while she waited for something to happen.

THE LIBRARY DOOR swung open just as the grandfather clock chimed three o'clock.

"Did you miss me?" Jackson leaned across the circulation desk and planted a quick kiss on Johanna's lips.

"I did." She answered. "I had to personally deliver several orders of books. It was like old times. It reminded me of when I first started working at the library. But all I could think about was leaving the cupola unprotected. If you had been with me, at least one of us would have been here to protect everything."

His jaw dropped. "No one guarded the portals while you were gone?"

"No. We've had a couple of flash sightings of Nero 51. However, Ryden Simmdry says he's trapped in the portals between the layers of space and time."

Jackson hoisted himself into sitting position on the circulation desk. "Is that even possible?"

"It is according to Ryden Simmdry. He says space-time is curved, so even though space and time are intrinsically linked, they're located on different planes of existence."

"I don't get it."

"Don't look at me. I'm not Stephen Hawking."

"You are the smartest, most beautiful, most wonderful girlfriend ever." He leaned over and gave her another kiss, this one lasting a little longer than the first. "Where can I find books by Stephen Hawking?"

"Look in the science section. There should be several."

Jackson disappeared into the stacks while Johanna thought about their trapped enemies. Her co-curator quickly returned carrying two copies of *A Brief History of Time*.

"You brought one for each of us?" she asked.

"No. This one," he laid a book on the desk, "is a first edition. This book," he placed the second one on top of the first, "was printed just a few years ago and contains updated material. I guess we should use the second one."

"Probably."

"Here goes." Jackson looked at the table of contents and opened the book to the appropriate chapter. Stephen Hawking appeared. He stared at the two teens in front of him.

"You gotta help us out," Jackson said. "There are a couple of guys in a time machine stuck between the layers of space and time, and we want to make sure they can't get out."

The theoretical physicist's synthesized voice caught Jackson by surprise. "Time travel used to be thought of as just science fiction, but Einstein's general theory of relativity allows for the possibility that we could warp space-time so much that you could go off in a rocket and return before you set out."

Jackson nodded. "Oh, we know there's time travel. We've done it. And let me tell you, it's not pleasant on a full stomach, if you get my drift."

Johanna stepped forward. "The people—if you could call them that—who are trapped are not very nice. We need to know how easy it would be for them to escape?"

Hawking answered, "Before 1915, space and time were thought of as a fixed arena in which events took place, but which was not affected by what happened in it. Space and time are now dynamic quantities.... they not only affect but also are affected by everything that happens in the universe."

"So what can we do in this universe to prevent them from getting out?" Jackson asked.

"I cannot answer that without more information." The physicist paused. "If I had a time machine, I'd visit Marilyn Monroe in her prime or drop in on Galileo as he turned his telescope to the heavens."

Jackson closed the cover on the book. "I don't think he's going to be able to help us."

"Neither do I," Johanna said. "As a scientist, he relies on proven data, statistics he's seen and comprehends.

"We're talking about a Terrorian and a

shapeshifter," she continued. "While he might believe there is other life in the universe, I don't know if Nero 51 and Odyon are what he has in mind."

Jackson's face lit up. "Do you think H. G. Wells can help? He wrote *The Time Machine* and thought up the Morlocks and all, so he might understand what we need." He hit his forehead with the palm of his hand. "Doh! *The War of the Worlds*. If he wrote that, he believes there are beings totally unlike us who live in other parts of the universe."

"He's primarily a writer. A fiction writer. He may know a lot about science, but I don't think he could help us." She tilted her head. "I wonder if Myrddin could help us?"

"A magician? Really. You think a guy who's been long dead is going to know more about this than Stephen Hawking?"

"You wanted to ask H. G. Wells just a moment ago, and he's not exactly alive."

"I'm brainstorming, here!"

"So am I," she replied.

MOPE 98 SLOWLY opened his eyes. His head ached, as did his body. He tried to rub a painful muscle and found himself immobilized. He was tied up in such an intricate way, he could not move. He could see a small fire burning next to him and remembered being on the roof of the library. Now, he found himself sitting on the ground with his back up against something lumpy. He heard a groan. "Perog 2, is that you?" he asked softly.

"We're tied up!" Perog 2 answered.

"Yes. They've done an admirable job. They've

braided our tentacles and bound them together at intervals with some type of cord. It's a very effective way to subdue an enemy."

"Instead of praising them, think of a way to get us out of here. Where are they, anyway?"

"I don't know," Mope 98 replied. "We appear to be alone."

"Then we must act quickly to get out of these binds and away from here." Perog 2 began working his strongest tentacle against a knot, hoping to loosen it or break it altogether.

It took all his strength to loosen the cord just a little. He could feel the play of extra space but not much else. The knots had been cast so tightly, his tentacles were numb. It took him a while, but he finally pulled the tip of a tentacle out of its binding, and in doing so, had more dexterity to work on the next knot.

"Ayyiiieee!"

The scream startled the Terrorians. They looked up to find dozens of kiddlets—each making the same sound—forming a circle around them. The kiddlets' appearances had been altered. Each wore a different color face paint, and they had twigs and feathers stuck in their hair. Around their waists, they wore rope belts from which strings dangled, and attached to the end of each string was a rock, gemstone, shell, or polished bit of wood. Once the circle was complete, the kiddlets began to chant in an eerie sing-song manner and dance around the Terrorians. Every so often, one of them would punctuate the song with a scream, and the others would hop in place in a full circle, before moving forward and continuing their chant.

Mope 98 began shaking. *Nothing good can come of this.*

—LOI—

10

D<small>EAN</small> A<small>RTEMUS</small> R<small>EXANA</small> materialized in the Adventuran town square in search of curator Prophet IAN c. As usual, the square was deserted except for detritus blowing in the wind.

All of Adventura had a decayed and abandoned look—like a ghost town—although that hadn't always been the case. Before the Two Millennia War, Adventura had grown into a world of burgeoning metropolises that other realms could scarcely dream of emulating. Then, Adventuran forefathers sided with the Terrorian and Mysterian realms to launch what they called *The Great Battle,* but would later become known as the Two Millennia War. Their descendants, unfortunately, found themselves on the losing side of that war and became intent on preventing their military adversaries from enriching themselves on Adventuran assets. In retaliation, the Adventurans detonated a series of nuclear devices aimed at depriving the victors of the spoils of war. However, that arrogant decision had a devastating effect on their world, leaving much of it derelict. Citizens had taken cover in underground caves, with sufficient supplies and food to last a solar year. When they emerged, they found their cities in ruins, their fertile farms and factories obliterated, and wild packs of mutated animals—vicious and difficult to kill—in control of the land.

The bulk of the population, who might have known how to surmount these problems, had been killed in battle. The survivors—the thinkers—were less suited to foraging for food and necessities, and rebuilding. Radioactive fallout soon took its toll on them, causing massive health problems that couldn't be treated because the bombs they'd planted had destroyed their hospitals and pharmaceutical laboratories.

As radioactivity lessened on Adventura, those who had adapted to the changes on the realm were able to carve out a new life using their knowledge of cyborg technology. They repaired mechanically what they could not repair surgically. Over time, the inhabitants mutated and no longer needed some of the organs they once possessed—eventually evolving into hu*bots. They had human hearts and brains but seventy-five percent of their bodies were robotic. They no longer needed to maintain excess muscle tissue or worry about organ damage. The brain served as the control center, and the heart generated the pulse that kept the brain functioning and the hu*bots running. Scientists developed a polymer that mimicked the appearance and feel of skin but not the color. Adventurans looked like humans, but their skin was an almost artistic pattern of blues, purples, and greens. And while their brains denoted a difference between the thinking of males and females, the body design for both was identical. Ironically, what appears to be a belly button on humans became a real button on hu*bots and was used to shut down the body for sleep mode. Adventurans had no need to eat, because they were sustained by a nightly intracranial drip of nutritional fluids — distributed from the brain to the heart — and an infusion of oils and lubricants for their mechanical sections.

Being mostly robotic helped wipe out petty differences among the sexes. Adventura and Romantica had been the first two realms created, and in the beginning, residents had often used the portal system to travel between worlds. Unfortunately, a schism occurred between the males and females of both planets because of a miscommunication before the start of the Two Millennia War. As a result, Romantica evolved into a female dominant realm, while Adventura became a world populated primarily by males. Members of the opposite sex continued to live on both worlds, but they were subservient and treated as nothing more than breeding stock and laborers. Those early inhabitants had been human. After the nuclear devastation, breeding was no longer important on Adventura, however survival was, so those who lived eventually evolved into hu*bots.

Regrettably, the Adventuran Library of Illumination fell into disrepair because hu*bots preferred to download information rather than learn it from books. All the information, previously stored in paper tomes, was uploaded to chips housed within the library walls. And since there were no longer any patrons to speak of, the library — for the most part — appeared neglected. It was maintained only as a shrine to knowledge, and the few books that remained were seen as archaic relics.

Oddly enough, the curator remained a powerful figure, if only for his connection to the College of Overseers and his influence with his peers on other realms.

ADVENTURAN OVERSEER ARTEMUS Rexana found the realm's curator in one of the engineering labs.

"We are honored by your presence." Prophet IAN c.'s voice lacked pitch and intensity because of his robotic voice box, yet his human brain guided the flow of his words, so his speech, while flat, sounded more natural than manufactured.

∑ *I'm not sure if you've realized yet that we have sealed off your Library of Illumination. I would have told you sooner but had to return to Lumi on an urgent matter. I hope the change did not affect your people too much.*

Prophet IAN c. nodded. "You're right. I've had no need to visit the library, so I'm not aware of the change. Are the Terrorians responsible?"

∑ *It would seem so.*

"If they choose to make the same mistakes over again, must we, too, be punished?"

∑ *Not if you're not involved, and I feel your society has evolved to the point where you would not chase the Terrorians into this particular wormhole.*

"What can we do for you?"

∑ *I have weapons of Terrorian design that I would like to leave here, in case they pay you an unwanted visit. Right now, Nero 51 is trapped in the portals, but he may eventually escape, and if he does, I'd like you to have adequate means to protect yourselves.*

"What can the Terrorian weapon do?"

Artemus Rexana removed it from the folds of his

robe and demonstrated its two abilities.

"We are not in need of their weaponry." Prophet IAN c. pointed his forefinger at a chair sitting alone in a corner. A moment later, it disintegrated. "Like the Terrorians, we too can eliminate our enemies, however, we don't need a separate weapon to do so. We developed this technology several years ago, and all Adventurans can now request this modification, if they can show need for it. Because competition among our technology laboratories is so heated, we have established a security force with this capability. I, and a number of town leaders, have already had the ability installed. It is expensive, preventing many citizens from requesting it. However, those of us who have already adopted this technology can protect ourselves adequately against interlopers.

ΣI don't suppose your technology comes with the more humane capability of capturing your enemy in a force field?

"No. But Adventurans have a highly developed ability to determine when someone is prevaricating—or trying to mislead. If someone chooses to lie to us, they deserve no better than the full force of this technology. However, if someone proves fair and truthful, no weapon is needed."

ΣAnd you're saying a small number of your population already have this built-in weapon?

"I would say one-in-five Adventurans have this ability."

ΣThat's twenty-percent of the population. Not a small amount by any means.

"Perhaps not, but still a minority."

* * *

THE CHANCELLOR OF the Exchequer entered the Mysterian Town Hall and took a seat on the outermost circle of the main discussion pit. Sean of Oster wrapped up his lecture and immediately announced Mal's presence, which was met with much more cordiality than his first visit.

The Mysterians explained their limitations in issuing coinage for payment of taxes.

Mal nodded. "Using up your most important natural resources to adopt an unnatural taxation system would place an undue burden on your society. However, you have no shortage of trees. Are your library books printed on paper?"

Sean retrieved a book laying on the innermost circle. "They are printed on a medium made from the ground root of the briars that are overly abundant here. It provides a fine material that is rolled into thin sheets and is impervious to moisture or decay." He opened the pages to show Mal what he meant. The pages were smoother than paper, almost glossy, yet had a subdued tint that enhanced the contrast between the words and the page. "Is this expensive to manufacture?" Mal asked.

Sean laughed. "No. We have an overabundance of briars. Producing books," he waved the one in his hand, "is our way of keeping invasive briars from encroaching on our cities."

"Then might I suggest a paper currency? Each note could designate a specific amount of the natural resource it represents, without actually using up that resource. People could pledge the currency as taxes, or relinquish it in exchange for the resource it represents."

Sean stroked his chin. "What would keep people from making their own currency?"

"Ah," Mal sighed. "That is the trick. You would need a special ink or mark that is not easily duplicated to decorate your currency. I will speak to the overseers. They may have some ideas about resources not easily obtainable on this realm, but which could be imported from another world to make your currency unique. We do not wish to deprive you of what you need," Mal continued. "However, we should have something in place to buffer the losses of future victims who may be deprived by war."

"And if no war comes to pass?" Sean asked.

"Then nothing would be spent, and citizens would be reimbursed with currency they can trade-in to replenish the natural resources they need."

"But the cost of creating such a currency is a loss of resources unto itself."

Mal sighed. "Let me speak to the overseers. Perhaps they can shed illumination on another way of dealing with this matter."

Surprised Dramaticans watched as Lenc ran up the Steppingstones of Illumination, chasing after Dungen. He finally got close enough to grab Dungen's shoulder. "Right there, stop. Authorized, you are not, to carry beneath your cloak, the weapon you have hidden."

Most of the witnesses scurried away, not wanting to be party to the confrontation.

Dungen sputtered as his face turned red. "Talk to me like that, how dare you? To protect myself, I am allowed."

Ozzro emerged from a nearby shop, but ducked back into the shadows when he heard his countrymen arguing. He would enjoy watching Dungen get cut down to size. Dungen had treated Ozzro badly on several occasions. But he knew there would be repercussions if the head of the library council saw him standing there, so he remained out of sight but not out of earshot.

"Authorized to carry that weapon," Lenc repeated firmly, "you are not. Confiscate it, I must." He held up the palms of his hands to receive the weapon.

"Merely a boy, you are," Dungen shouted. "Talk to me like that, you cannot."

"A soldier, I am. A citizen, you are. The weapon, give me." The boy was much smaller than Dungen, but his voice was firm and confident. "Now."

Dungen unstrapped the weapon from beneath his cloak, but rather than handing it to Lenc, he fired it at the boy, vaporizing him.

Ozzro gasped, and flattened himself against the wall, praying Dungen had not seen or heard him. He had witnessed something unheard of on his realm—one Dramatican killing another. *Get away with this, Dungen cannot. Protect myself, I must. But, tell others, I must, as well.*

The question was, how? In what way could he let others know what Dungen had done, without it leading directly back to him?

JOHANNA OPENED THE book Myrddin had instructed her to use to contact him. He spoke before she had a chance to say a word. "Have you caught the perpetrator who would steal my life's work?" The wizard apparently didn't believe in reacting to intrusions with subtleties like, *how nice to see you again,* or, *what do you think about this weather?*

"Right now, he's trapped between the layers of space and time," she answered. "But we're afraid he might get out, and then we'll lose track of him."

"The layers of space and time..." Myrddin echoed. "That reminds me of being impressionably young. I amazed myself when I first discovered how to perform that spell."

Jackson stepped forward so Myrddin could see him. "You know how to trap someone between the layers?"

"I do believe that is what I have said."

"So then," Jackson continued, "you must know how to release them."

"Of course."

"Which is what we want to do." Johanna completed Jackson's thought. "However, once they're released, we want to be able to control where they reappear."

"They will enter where they exited," Myrddin said matter-of-factly.

Jackson grabbed Johanna's arm with such force, she almost dropped the book she held. "That puts them back in our ball-park," he said. "Because if Odyon is with him, they entered from this library. That's what Ava saw. So we just have to wait for them and capture Nero 51 in a force field and Odyon in the black cube."

"What makes you think I can capture Odyon now, when I wasn't fast enough to capture him before?"

"Tell me about this black cube you speak of?" Myrddin demanded.

"It's small but heavy, and the master of the overseers created it. It sucks in imperfect energy." Johanna sighed. "But Odyon was too quick for it."

"You speak of a very small, extremely dense object like this?" Myrddin extracted a cube from his pocket and held it out.

Jackson reached for it, but his hand sliced through Myrddin's image. "He's not real."

"Of course he's not real," Johanna whispered. "You're looking at a holographic image of the spirit of a dead man. He instructed me to use this book so no intruders could gain access to his memoir."

"Right."

"I designed this, of course," Myrddin said, staring at the cube in his hand. "I would very much like to speak to the man who claims he created it for you."

"You want to talk shop with Ryden Simmdry?" Jackson asked.

"Ryden Simmdry," Myrddin repeated the name. The expression on his face clouded. "I must speak to this man at once."

"Of course," Johanna answered. "We've just got to get him here, first."

Jackson looked at her. "Diary?"

"Diary," Johanna answered.

"WE ARE DOOMED," Mope 98 cried, as the circle of kiddlets danced around him and Perog 2.

"Speak for yourself," the other trooper said, as he freed the tip of a second tentacle.

"What do you think they are going to do to us?"

"I don't know. At least they haven't built a fire under us."

Mope 98 moaned. "I don't want to die!"

"Be quiet. You're not acting in a way befitting a Terrorian, and I will have no choice but to report you to General Barzic 922."

"I think there's a rodent gnawing on my tentacle."

"That's me. I'm trying to find a way to undo these ropes and set us free."

"How did you do that? I can't move."

"Neither could I, but I found a way to loosen the rope. I should just leave you here. Anyone who can't help himself as a soldier does not deserve to live."

Mope 98 tensed. "You would leave me here to die?" He felt himself getting angry and tried to turn to face Perog 2. One of the ropes that bound him snapped. He snaked his one loose tentacle around Perog 2 and shook him violently. "Why would you do that to me?" Another rope snapped, releasing one of Perog 2's tentacles. He used it to push Mope 98 away. The two Terrorians wrestled with each other, and in doing so, more of their bonds gave way.

"The monsters are getting loose," a young boy cried. "Where are the flamethrowers?"

"We left them in Town Hall," a second boy answered.

Another rope snapped and Mope 98 found he was nearly free.

"Untie me," Perog 2 demanded.

"Untie yourself," Mope 98 said.

"They're gonna eat us!" a little girl cried and started running away. The other Juveniles followed suit, screaming as they fled.

—LOI—

11

PRU TELLERENCE AGREED with Furst and Dame Erato that the militia on Romantica should have uniforms to facilitate combat. Romantican women's love of voluminous, soft fabrics in multiple diaphanous layers would not serve them well on a battlefield. Yet, Pru Tellerence knew their highly developed sense of self would make them turn their noses up at anything less than beautiful. The overseer watched their movements and noted the limitations of the garments they wore. A design started to form, almost subconsciously, and she hurried back to Lumina to discuss her ideas with the same tailor who had created the uniforms for Dramatica.

★*It is important,* she explained, ★*for the pieces to flow, yet not impede.* Her design appeared Grecian in drape and feel. Light, silken fabric would drape from the right shoulder, across the bodice, and fasten at the left ankle. It would also drape from the left shoulder, crossing to the right side to fasten at the right ankle. It would give the appearance of a gown with a deep center slit. Beneath the gown, each militairre, as they asked to be called, would wear narrow pants that would fasten to the gown at the ankle. For their feet, she requested ankle-high animal hide boots that had to be both durable, yet flexible and comfortable, and she asked for them in shades of navy blue, light blue, or silver to complement the ombré shades of the uniform. The militairres would also be given a second dress uniform, completely white with gold dress boots. Over either uniform they would wear a crisscross harness fastened to a belt, designed to carry the decimator in a backpack, a quiver over the left shoulder, and a sheath for a dagger at the waist.

★*It's imperative that we have them immediately.*

"I don't know if that is possible," the designer answered. "We are still making uniforms for the Dramaticans."

★*Can you make me prototypes? One of everything would do.*

"I will work non-stop on it, if I must. I will have it for you before first light."

Ozzro signed in for duty at the Dramatican military barracks. His platoon practiced shooting for a while and then went on to march in formation. During both activities, he asked various people, "Seen Lenc today, have you?" Each person he asked proceeded to ask others the same question. Most Dramaticans had an innate desire to help each other, and they wanted to let Lenc know Ozzro was looking for him. But it soon became apparent no one had seen Lenc. And the question continued to multiply as people realized the boy might be missing.

One of the military strategists approached Ozzro.

"Invaders have Lenc, do you think?"

"Of knowing, I have no way. However, protected, Furst says the library is."

"Looking for Lenc, why are you?"

"Homeless, the boy is. Share a meal with him, I want to. Now, worried, I am."

"Here, Furst isn't." The strategist sighed. "Know what to do, he would."

"In his place, in charge, who is?"

"Designated, no one has been. Told to carry on, we have been. Perhaps, Dungen, you should see."

Ozzro's ringlets tightened. "Talk to Dungen, I prefer not to."

The strategist nodded knowingly. Ozzro had not been Dungen's only recent target. "Speak to Pondor, I will," the strategist said. "Know what to do, he will."

"A good man, Pondor is. Wise," Ozzro said. "Take after him, his son Dungen did not."

ODYON LEANED AWAY from Nero 51. "I'd quite forgotten how vile Terrorian body odor is."

Nero 51 did not respond. He considered Odyon nothing more than a curiosity. He cared little that the shapeshifter didn't like the way he smelled. What he wanted to know was how Odyon had appeared in the time machine out of thin air. Nero 51 believed his unwanted passenger was the reason why he was stuck in the portals, and he thought if he could get rid of Odyon, everything would be put right again.

He considered ways to evict the shapeshifter. Most Terrorians were not known for their subtlety, especially Nero 51. In a flash, he wrapped a tentacle around the shapeshifter's neck to fling him out of the vehicle. Before he could complete the action, Odyon dissolved into a beam of light and reappeared on the Terrorian's other side.

"That was uncalled for," Odyon said icily. "Don't consider doing it again, or I will be forced to focus your deadly intent back upon yourself. However, if you do as you are told, we may be able to form an alliance."

Nero 51 felt his jaw clamp tightly. "Alliance?" the Terrorian repeated incredulously. "Why would I want to partner with you?"

"Because, together we could rule the world."

"I do not need you to rule the world," Nero 51 claimed. "I'm already close to doing that myself."

Odyon sneered. "Really? Stuck in an endless loop while the overseers discuss the best way to punish you after they allow you to escape into their trap. I could teach you how to disappear and reappear at will. Of course, that's not to say it's easy to learn. You would have to work hard at it. But it's a good skill to have. And I'm sure I don't have to tell you how useful it could be."

TRUE TO HIS word, the Luminan designer tasked with creating uniforms for the Romantican militairres delivered the prototypes to Pru Tellerence not long after she asked for them. A Luminan model accompanied him, to show off the outfits.

The fabric was deeply ruched and draped beautifully. The boots were as soft as kidskin, yet protective. And the crossover harnesses looked like works of art, done in silvery mesh for the everyday uniform and golden links for the dress version.

"You said these were for Romantican women. I know how exacting they are in their dress. I have taken the liberty of having quivers made that match the boots. The knife sheaths are a complementary color, and a metalsmith has designed daggers that should be easy to access. He has provided me with both gold and silver daggers, as well as gold and silver arrows for the quivers."

★*You have done remarkably well.* Pru Tellerence picked up one of the uniforms. ★*They're lighter than air.*

The designer smiled. "What you don't see," he said, taking a uniform, "is the lining. It is lightweight and silky, yet it's made with auroriumide, which has been woven into a protective material that is as strong as any diamond or metal. An arrow or projectile will not pierce this material, although the flesh beneath it will bruise from the impact."

★*It's that strong?*

"Yes. But the overall design is not foolproof. Your militairres' heads, necks, and shoulders will be exposed.

"With that in mind, I took the liberty," he continued, "of having one of my finest apprentices put together short jackets with a hood and long sleeves. It will protect the wearers against weather changes that often plague the others realms. They will be made of the same hides as the boots and be lined with the same protective material. I will have them delivered to you by tomorrow."

★*You have more than risen to the task. Thank you.*

* * *

MAL AND RYDEN Simmdry arrived on Fantasia together.

"Rather than answer your diary entry, the master and I thought it would be better to stop by instead."

Johanna turned to Ryden Simmdry. "Myrddin wants to talk to you, personally."

⌘*I'm sure he does. Did you say you were keeping him in the vault?*

"Yes, but he has asked us not to enter the vault until the person trying to steal his memoir is found. We have a book that he answers us through. Would you like to speak to him here, or would you prefer the privacy of my office?"

⌘*This is as good a place as any. Is the book here?*

"Just a moment. I'll get it for you." Johanna walked to the circulation desk and removed the book from one of the lower shelves.

Ryden Simmdry had followed her and now stood across the counter.

She handed him the book. He paused before opening it, his face oddly emotional. She felt a chill. She'd never seen Ryden Simmdry's countenance so unguarded.

The overseer looked at her. ⌘*What you witness here must remain among us. It is, what you might call, classified information.* He lifted the cover. Myrddin popped into view. At first, neither one said anything.

"It is true, then. We have gone on to become master of the College of Overseers."

⌘*Yes.*

"I suspected as much after she said *you* had created the black cube, when I knew full well that I had devised it. In retrospect, there could be but one answer. How is it I am dead and you are not?"

The overseer smiled. ⌘ *Your depth of experience ended in the caves of Skokholm. But one of our associates from Lumina had summoned us through a diary. I appeared to him in Lumi. Suddenly, I felt free, and I chose to stay. I tinkered with the Longevicus Blessing, which we had worked on with Rathbarth, and was able to reform it completely. My only limitation is here on Fantasia. I cannot leave the confines of this library, because it is on this realm that we were cursed. If I were to walk out the door, I would be transported back to the cave where I would once again be trapped.*

"So you guys are brothers?" Jackson asked.

"No," Johanna answered. "They're two parts of the same psyche. Ryden Simmdry *is* Myrddin Emrys."

"Of course," Myrddin said. "You should have known that at once. His name—Ryden Simmdry—is merely an anagram of my own—Myrddin Emrys."

Jackson gaped.

Johanna gently slipped her fingertips under Jackson's chin and closed his mouth. She turned back to Ryden Simmdry. "It's your life's work that someone is trying to steal."

⌘ *Yes. And, at this point, I am very sure it is Odyon. There was a time when we were friends and worked on our magic together. As I've mentioned previously, he is a very powerful wizard. But there were some levels of power he could not attain. And it is better that way, because they could change life as we know it, forever.*

While he spoke, Jackson worked out the anagram

with paper and pen. "You're talking about Totalis Pereamus, right?"

"Total annihilation," Johanna added.

⌘ *Your depth of perception never ceases to amaze me.*

"Both names have the same letters." Jackson slapped the pen back on the counter. "So just to confirm— Odyon can't do that, right? Totalis Pereamus?"

⌘*Not right now, but that's not to say he won't perfect that curse in the future. His specialty, after all, is déofolcræft.*

They all fell silent. Jackson paced the length of the circulation desk, before turning and retracing his steps several times. After a minute, he stopped and looked at Johanna. "I've got nothing. I can't even think up something ridiculous that we could do to solve this. How do you fight a guy like that?"

"If only there was a way to transport the black cube directly into the time machine," she said, "then it would suck up Odyon, and we'd only have to deal with Nero 51."

"Who now seems cuddly in comparison," Jackson said, smirking.

Johanna laughed but stopped abruptly when her eyes met Mal's. "Oh my goodness, I didn't even ask you how you are."

"That's perfectly all right," he said, giving her a hug. "You've had a lot on your mind."

"Where have you been in all your greenness?" Jackson asked.

"Trying to work out a tax system for Mysteriose," Mal replied.

"Mysteriose," Johanna repeated. "Isn't that where Odyon is from? Won't he try to go back there?"

⌘ *Right now, I don't think Odyon cares where he ends up, as long as it's not here. Although I'm sure he would want to take a crack at your vault if he knew my memoir was inside.*

"Do you want to take it with you?" Johanna asked.

⌘ *No. I think your vault is the safest place for it. Leave it be and forget it's there.*

"That's kind of hard to do, isn't it?" Jackson said. "It's like carrying a bag of peanut M&M's in your pocket. Sure, you can ignore them. But there's so much temptation to just pop them in your mouth."

"Bag and all," Johanna said under her breath.

Jackson nudged her with his elbow.

⌘ *There is something we could do, but it would mean opening the vault.*

"It's safe to do that, isn't it," Mal asked, "considering Ava reported seeing Odyon in the time machine before it became trapped in the portals?"

⌘ *It would seem so. We should hurry, though.* Ryden Simmdry led the way to the lower level with Johanna, Jackson, and Mal trailing behind him. Once they entered the Chamber of Doors, he approached the one in the middle.

Jackson tried opening each door in turn, without success. "What's behind all these doors?"

⌘ *Right now, we're only concerned with what's behind this door. Johanna…*

She walked over to the door and held her left palm to the lock. The door sprang open and a light automatically came on.

⌘*This is the Duplication Room. Please, give me a moment of silence. I need to concentrate.*

As they watched, Ryden Simmdry approached a compartment in the wall, closed his eyes, and started to hum. His lips moved ever so slightly as he called upon a spell. He held his hands parallel to the surface for about a minute, then quickly clapped. In front of him appeared a copy of Myrddin's memoir. He waved his palm in front of a button on the wall and identical books started piling up on top of the first one. He levitated several of them to a table as even more of them appeared. Within minutes, there were hundreds of books.

"What are we going to do with all those?" Jackson asked.

"Camouflage the real one," Johanna answered.

⌘*Precisely.* The overseer spent several more minutes touching various books and chanting. ⌘*As an added precaution, a few booby traps are in order.*

"That's hilarious," Jackson said. "Exactly what did you do to them?"

⌘*That's not important. What is important is that you don't touch them. Only I can approach them.* He turned to Johanna. ⌘*It's time to open the vault door.* He dug into the pocket of his robe and pulled out a black cube.

Jackson pointed to it. "Is Alianessa Anjou still in there?"

⌘*No. This is a duplicate cube. Johanna, please hold this in your right hand and open the vault with your left.*

"I can hold the cube," Jackson volunteered.

⌘*No. Johanna generates much more magical power than you do. I don't think Odyon is nearby, but if he is, this will be a deterrent. Johanna...*

She followed his instructions and opened the vault door. Within an instant, all the books he had duplicated started flying into the vault, swirling around the original, which eventually lifted into the stream and swirled with the others until it was impossible to tell which one it had been. Just as quickly, the books settled down into haphazard piles along one side of the room and Ryden Simmdry pulled the vault door closed. He looked at the cube in Johanna's hand. It emitted a soft pink glow.

—LOI—

12

JACKSON LOOKED FROM the cube in Johanna's hand to Ryden Simmdry. "Does that pinkish light mean she caught someone?"

⌘*No. It means the status quo is unchanged.* Ryden Simmdry waved his hand over the cube, and the light disappeared. ⌘*We should return upstairs and forget all about Myrddin's... my... memoir.*

"We're still not any closer to capturing Odyon," Jackson pointed out.

⌘*Oh, but we are.*

"How?" Johanna asked.

⌘*You pointed out the solution yourself. We just have to transport a black cube into the time machine. It should be possible, but I'd like to give it some thought, first.*

Ryden Simmdry's stomach grumbled. ⌘*How odd. It seems far too soon for my annual meal. It must be because I've expended much more energy than usual lately.*

"Do you like French food?" Jackson asked. "There happens to be a great place really close by where we can get some tasty tidbits."

Johanna looked at him quizzically. "You want to go to Le Chat for lunch?"

Jackson spoke with a phony French accent. "No. I want George V to bring zee lunch to us."

"Lead the way," Mal said.

Ryden Simmdry broke into an odd smile when he walked into a luxury suite in a space previously designated for periodicals.

Jackson handed him a copy of the room service menu. "Order whatever you like."

After much discussion with Mal on the differences between nouveau cuisine and classic Gallic cooking, the two men ordered a veritable seafood feast. Johanna and Jackson stuck to their usual order of burgers.

⌘*I wonder if the original overseers had this in mind when they made Fantasia a class L realm? They meant for the books to come to life and be enjoyed, but I don't think this is exactly what they planned.*

"Probably because travel guides hadn't been invented yet," Jackson replied. He watched Johanna smear béarnaise sauce on her burger. "Why must you insist on ruining a perfectly good hamburger?"

"I'm not ruining it, I'm enhancing it. And I'm doing it because I can," she said, before taking a bite out of her burger. "Umm umm!"

They didn't mention Nero 51 or Odyon during the course of the meal, but once they finished and room service waiters had removed every last utensil, they picked up their earlier conversation.

⌘*One issue clouds the clarity of our intended action. The time machine is not static. Even though it's trapped outside the portals, it does not rest at a singular point. Instead, it travels along a string of time that lies between the closed portals. That makes teleporting the cube inside of it very difficult, because at any moment, it may be anywhere along the string.*

Jackson leaned forward. "Couldn't you send one of us—me, for example—out into the same trapped space, where I could throw the cube into the time machine when it appears? I've got a pretty good throwing arm."

⌘*A string of time is not a straight line. It's long and tangled,* Ryden Simmdry waved his hand, ⌘*... like spaghetti. I need to give this serious thought.* He stood. ⌘*I must travel back to Lumi. I'm sure I will find the answers I need in the Library of Origination.*

"Is the Library of Origination different than a Library of Illumination?" Johanna asked.

⌘*It is very similar. You would find all the same books that you have here in our library. However, there are two major disparities. The first is that our library is not part of a closed circuit. While every new piece of literature that is introduced into being anywhere automatically appears in every realm's library, including ours, information only flows into the Library of Origination. It does not flow out. So there is knowledge housed within our walls that the twelve realms do not have access to.*

"Why?" Jackson asked.

⌘*We are privy to information that the realms may not be ready to handle. It is disbursed when the time is right.*

"What's the second difference?" Johanna asked.

⌘ *Our oracle.*

PEROG 2 STRUGGLED to remove the rest of his bindings. He meant what he said about leaving Mope 98 behind, but had to admit the other trooper's temper had allowed them to break free. "We have to find a way back into this library."

"They're getting the flamethrowers. I'm going back to the pond where I can at least escape them." With that, Mope 98 revved up his tentacles and propelled himself away from the library, looking for a way to double back to the pond without being seen.

Perog 2 reluctantly followed. *We're stronger together than apart.*

The pond appeared deserted when they arrived. Mope 98 dove into the water; however, Perog 2 took a moment to look around. He found the storm drain and drew in all his tentacles to make himself compact. He moved inside the drain and found it would easily accommodate him. As he pushed forward, he found the storm drain remained a uniform size. Watery runoff collected at the bottom of the drain, and Perog 2 found the humidity it caused helped ease some of his discomfort. They could last indefinitely in the drain, if they had food. *I'd better get Mope 98 in here so we won't have to hold our breath like we do in the pond.*

He retraced his steps but stopped short of exiting the drain when he heard voices. He stood back and watched as several kiddlets walked around the pond, poking the surface with long sticks.

"Hey, I found something," Pollo called out, and the others rushed to gather around him. He kept poking at something and then waded into the pond. He ducked down and reached for something in the water. "I need help here," he screamed.

Marbol waded out to meet him. He reached under the water, and together they tugged.

"Heave-ho. Heave-ho. Heave-ho," the others chanted.

Finally, they dragged a large kayak-like object onto the shore.

"Hey," Pye called out. "That's my floaty that sank last year. Do you think it still works?"

"Sure," Marbol answered. "But you'll have to clean all this stink-mud out of it. It's really slimy." He stuck his finger in a hole. "And you'll have to plug this. There must have been a knot in the wood that popped out."

"Nope. No knot," Pye answered. "I was taking on water and drilled a hole in the bottom so it would drain out."

"You knucklehead. Everybody knows you should only drill a hole on dry land," Pollo said.

Pye defended his honor. "It was an emergency."

"Let's take it to the cottage. We can fix it there."

The group picked up the foul-smelling boat entangled with decomposing weeds and carried it away en masse.

After their voices faded, Perog 2 crept out of the storm drain to search the pond for Mope 98. He swam across the pond using his tentacles as feelers. He grasped onto Mope 98 and pulled him above the surface of the water.

"Oh. It's you," Mope 98 said. "I thought, for a

moment, the kiddlets had found me."

Perog 2 let go of the other soldier. "I've found another place to hide where we can actually breathe."

"Where?"

"Follow me." He crawled out of the pond and led Mope 98 into the storm drain. They traveled inside for a hundred feet or so, until they came to a junction.

"Which way?" Mope 98 asked.

"I don't know."

"Well, I say we go right."

Perog 2 started down the other tunnel. "And I say we go left."

Mope 98 sighed in exasperation but followed the other Terrorian.

MAL RETURNED TO Mysteriose after discussing its taxation problems with the College of Overseers.

Sean of Oster, who sat at an outer tier observing a discussion, rose to greet him. "Do you have insight into our dilemma?"

"I do," Mal answered. He pulled out a bundle of printed notes from his robes. He removed one and handed it to Sean. "It is made from your own briars using the same manufacturing process you use to make paper; however, these notes have been embedded with a special microscopic chip that cannot be reproduced in your realm. The notes are numbered sequentially, so they can be recorded as representing a specific resource in your reserve. Do you have a central vault?"

"The rare herbs, minerals, and chemicals are kept in a series of protected caves west of the city. An accounting of what is in the caves is stored in a vault somewhere in the Library of Illumination. It is time we visit Hue the Elder."

"Your curator?"

"Yes."

The two men left Town Hall and made their way to a small bookshop nearby. Behind a very long, narrow counter, a man sat hunched over an old book.

"Hue, we have a visitor from the College of the Overseers. This is the Chancellor of the Exchequer."

"Since when does the College of Overseers have a Chancellor of the Exchequer?" Hue the Elder, who had looked diminutive hunched over a book, slowly stood up until he towered over Sean and Mal.

"I know I shrunk in height as I grew older," Mal noted, "but you seem taller, if anything."

"Malcolm Trees. How absolutely wonderful to see you. What's all this talk about Chancellor of the Exchequer? If curators were allowed to apply for such a position, why don't I know anything about it?"

"I'm no longer a curator. I'm working for the deans, now that the threat of war has forced them into asking realms to prepare for the inevitable. We're creating systems that equally divide the burden of reparations, if property is lost due to an attack. I'm here to help with that. We have been calling it a tax, but in essence, your citizens would just be putting away a portion of your communal resources to make restitution to victims who might suffer unfairly."

"Taxes? Restitution?" Hue leaned back in his chair. "How do you plan to accomplish that?"

"With a system of notes." He showed Hue the same note he had shown Sean. "Sean says you keep a record of Mysterian resources in the library vault. These notes are numbered sequentially and also have a numeric value assigned to them. So, the lowest numeric value could represent a low number of shares of your most common resource— for example, a sheaf of grain—while the highest numeric value could represent shares of your most scarce and valuable resource, like rare minerals or gems. Each note should be backed by a specific reserve, that is put aside, and will only be surrendered when the corresponding note is presented. Instead of the allotments of resources put aside for each citizen every year, the elders could hand out one of these notes, and citizens could choose which denomination they want to remit as taxes. Of course, diamond would be much more valuable than wheat on a general scale. But a baker may prefer not to pay in wheat, because he needs it to make his wares, while a blacksmith would be reluctant to give up the metals or coal he uses in his work. You could set up an exchange where citizens could barter notes among themselves so they could amass the resources they consider most necessary. But all should be asked, in some way, to contribute their share of "taxes," which are to be held until they are needed. Is my explanation clear?"

"It is, Malcolm," Hugh said. "Abundantly clear. And it sounds like it would not be too difficult to set up."

Mal sighed as if the weight of the world had been lifted from his shoulders. "As Chancellor of the Exchequer, I will help you in any way I can and act as liaison with the College of Overseers, if any difficulties arise. I am here only to advise you and keep a record of your tax system. I require nothing in return."

"That's a shame," Hugh said with the hint of a smile, "because I was going to ask you to share supper with me. But since you require nothing in return...."

Mal's eyes brightened. "A bit of, what is it you call it, essential water, would certainly help relax me after making this trip."

"And maybe a little red bread stew would help soften the impact of the essential water," Hue added.

"That would certainly be kind of you."

"Come." Hugh led Mal and Sean out of the bookshop and pulled the door closed. He threw an arm around Mal's shoulder as he led him away. "Maybe a little essential water will go a long way in persuading you to enlighten me about why I've been thrown out of my library."

JACKSON'S FACE LIT up with surprise. "You have an oracle? That is so cool!" Then he whispered to Johanna. "What is an oracle, exactly?"

She laughed. "How can you say it's cool if you don't know what it is?"

"Isn't it Greek or something? Doesn't it tell you the future?"

⌘*There were oracles in ancient times on Fantasia, but they differed depending on the era and region. Essentially, oracles make predictions. Greek oracles were women—believed to be the mouthpieces of the gods—however our oracle is different. It is an object rather than a person. It is located deep within the Library of Origination and we meditate in the Oracular Chamber when we have a particularly difficult problem to solve. Our oracle is a gemstone that looks like a massive Fantasian opal, and it has the power to align our thoughts and remove distractions. The way to resolve a particular problem soon becomes clear.*

"So it doesn't actually speak or anything." Disappointment tinged Jackson's voice.

⌘*Not out loud in words or sentences, but the outcome is the same. It helps us clearly see the path that must be taken.*

"Then we shouldn't keep you," Johanna said. "We'll await your return with advice on how to proceed."

After Ryden Simmdry left, Jackson slumped onto the sofa. "I don't mind telling you, I'm a little disappointed. No, wait. That's a lie. I'm a lot disappointed. I was expecting an oracle to be some big deal, not just some stupid little stone they make jewelry out of."

Johanna sat down next to him. "I'm sure it *is* a big deal. Ryden Simmdry didn't make a fuss over it, because he's used to it. But he did call it a major difference between our library and theirs. And it's something they turn to when they need help. They're overseers. They know everything. So if an oracle—regardless of what it looks like—helps them see an answer, then it's a very big deal."

"Yeah. You're probably right. I guess I was expecting the Hollywood treatment. If a famous director ever put an oracle in his film, it would command center stage with a light show and lots of sound effects."

"I think the overseers have a pretty firm grasp of creating special effects. Just think back to Plato Indelicat's memorial and the Overseer's Competition. Or were you too busy flirting with Natalia Dalura to notice what went on there?"

Jackson smiled. "Are you jealous?"

"Do I have anything to be jealous about?"

"I'm not saying," he teased.

She pulled away to emphasize the space between them. "Then the next time you want to know why our relationship isn't progressing as quickly as you'd like, think back to this conversation."

"Ouch!"

PRU TELLERENCE PUT the duplicloners in the Library of Origination to good use. Before long, she had a large collection of uniforms and weapons ready for the Romantican militairres. All she needed was the delivery of the jacket prototype, and once she had replicas made, she could deliver everything to Romantica.

She telekinetically moved the uniforms to her quarters, and they floated behind her like a parade of laundry on washday. During the journey, Ryden Simmdry crossed her path.

⌘ *What have we here, Pru Tellerence?*

★*Uniforms for the Romanticans. Their gowns impede their fighting efficiency, however, I believe these will suit their aesthetic tastes while making movement easier.*

⌘*It appears we have mutated from a strictly advisory capacity to that of manufacturer of uniforms, equipment, and currency.*

★*Currency?*

⌘*Yes. Our Chancellor of the Exchequer has found that some realms don't use currency, nor are they knowledgeable about the process of taxation. They need assistance. The Dramaticans have found a way to make their barter system work for them, but we had no such luck on Mysteriose. So Malcolm introduced them to the idea of paper notes that would represent the standard resources each Mysterian receives annually, and they will decide which notes they are willing to pay in taxes, yet still be able to continue their day-to-day productivity.*

★*Couldn't they print their own notes?*

⌘*Mysterians are naturally resourceful, and the elders felt some citizens might take it upon themselves to manufacture their own currency. So I had a printer in the Besta outcrop create notes out of Mysterian briar. Each contains a mineral chip that is only available here on Lumina. Before a Mysterian can trade their notes for natural resources, it will have to successfully pass through a scanner.*

★ *Calling them "resourceful" is very diplomatic. I would have said "greedy."*

⌘*Diplomacy is a required attribute that serves me well. Will you be making a grand presentation of uniforms on Romantica, like the one on Dramatica?*

★*Yes. Proteus Bligh and I will be doing that tomorrow. Would you like to join us?*

⌘*I'm not sure I can. I'm on my way to consult the oracle. It may take a minute. It may take a month. I am hoping for expediency, but nothing is certain.*

★*What's the problem?*

⌘*We believe Odyon—the Mysterian shape-shifter—is stuck in the time machine with Nero 51, and I am looking for a way to transport a black cube of my own creation into the time machine to absorb the essence of Odyon, so when we recapture the vehicle, we'll only have one nefarious criminal to deal with instead of two.*

I seek clarification of the best way to proceed.
    ★*Then I hope the oracle swiftly illuminates you.*

JOHANNA'S REMARK ABOUT their relationship cut deeply, and Jackson slipped away to shoot hoops behind his house.

Logan rounded the corner. "What's going on?"

Jackson tossed the ball cleanly into the hoop. "Need you ask?"

"Johanna, huh?"

"Yeah."

Logan's face lit up. "You know what you need?"

Jackson stopped dribbling the ball. "You're not going to drag me to a tattoo parlor, are you?"

"That's just plain freaky. How did you know I wanted to do that?"

Jackson shook his head. He'd never explained to Logan how almost everyone had lost three weeks in a temporal shift, and he didn't want to start now. Instead, he thought about the tattoo. "Okay. Let's do it." He already knew which one he would get, but this time he would let the artist go to town embellishing it.

Jackson handled the process of getting tattooed like it wasn't out of the ordinary, and Logan commented about how easily he had submitted to the pain.

"So why don't you get one, too?" Jackson asked.

"I think I will." Logan looked through a book of art and chose a freestyle black and white arabesque for his shoulder. He grimaced when the needle started puncturing his arm. "How long do you think this will take?" he asked through clenched teeth.

"Depends," the artist said. "If you want a very

simple-looking tattoo, a half hour. If you want the one pictured in the book, we'll do it in a couple of hourly sessions."

Logan grimaced. "An hour of this?"

"It would be worse if I wasn't using the machine," the artist answered. "This thing punches the needle in about a hundred times a second." It would take much longer if it wasn't for the machine."

Logan winced as he looked at Jackson. "Did I ever tell you how much I hate needles?"

"Yes." Jackson smiled.

"Why did I let you talk me into this?"

"I didn't," Jackson answered. "It was your idea. But, you know, you were right. I am feeling better already." And he continued to smile as Logan scowled through clenched teeth.

—LOI—

13

JOHANNA SAW THE bandage on Jackson's neck. "You didn't."

"It's my neck and I will do with it as I please."

"Wait till your mother sees it."

"I'm not some seven-year-old whose only wish is to please his mother. I've traveled off-world. I've fought Terrorians. I'm graduating high school in a couple of weeks, and I'll be eighteen in just a few months."

"You won't be eighteen for ten years," she answered. "Longevicus Blessing. Suck it up, sonny, you're going to be a minor for a long, long time."

He glared at her. "I used to think I liked you."

"I used to think I liked you, too."

What is going on here? Jackson wanted to know. Someone had stolen the girl he loved and replaced her with Kate from *The Taming of the Shrew*.

He wandered over to the literature section and pulled a copy of Shakespeare's play from the shelf, opening it to the middle. Petruchio and Katharina came to life. "Asses are made to bear, and so are you," Katharina said to Petruchio, her words dripping acid.

Jackson shut the book. *Yep. That's Johanna.*

He headed toward the hotel suite, hoping Chris was out. His neck bothered him and he wanted to take aspirin and a nap.

His luck held. *At least I can rest for a while before I have to explain the bandage on my neck. Maybe I can figure out why Johanna is acting so cranky.*

> *Jackson stood in the middle of a dance floor with strings of twinkling lights decorating the ceiling above. The air was misty, making the walls recede. He saw Johanna walking toward him. She looked beautiful. She wore a beaded crop top that twinkled liked the stars in the sky and a long flowing skirt. He reached out for her, but another male tapped her on the shoulder. She began dancing with the other guy. When the music ended, Jackson approached her. She smiled, but turned to yet another male and began dancing with him. Jackson started to worry. He felt like he had to dance with her immediately or lose her forever. The music ended again and she walked toward him. This time his gym teacher swept her off her feet, literally, and waltzed around the room carrying her in his arms. He didn't even know his teacher knew how*

to waltz. The edges of the room began to swirl. Something's wrong here, he thought. Maybe it's a temporal rift. He chased after the waltzing teacher. The music ended and Jackson sighed with relief, but before he fully exhaled, dozens of guys crowded around her, blocking him. He elbowed people out of the way to break through to Johanna, but when he got there, he found her in a wedding gown kissing a groom who was definitely not him.

A MESSENGER DELIVERED the Romantican uniform jackets to Pru Tellerence earlier than expected, and she used a duplicloner to make jackets for all the militairres.

Afterward, she met with Horatio Blastoe, and they strolled through the gardens at the College of Overseers as they planned their visit to Romantica.

★*We had what amounted to a ceremony on Dramatica, but that was only because its citizens were already having a meeting. It will be less formal with the Romanticans.*

✠*The militairres will be together, but not the general townspeople. Still—Romantica being what it is—word will spread quickly. Everyone will know about the militairres and their new uniforms before the day is out.*

★*If they like them enough, we may even find the outfits attract a few new recruits.*

Horatio Blastoe stopped walking. ✠*We will have to broach the subject of taxes.*

Pru Tellerence waved him off. ★*We don't have to concern ourselves with that, now. It is a task best left to our new Chancellor of the Exchequer. He has successfully introduced individualized tax systems on both Dramatica and Mysteriose and appears to be at ease doing so. If he's available, I'll ask him to join us.*

✠*Good. We would have to propose the subject sooner or later. Best to do it now, if possible.*

"Did you see these tracks?" Duddu asked Marbol when they returned to the pond. "They lead right into here." He pointed inside the storm drain.

"How'd they fit? They're really big."

"I don't know. Maybe they'll get stuck." The two boys laughed, imagining what a couple of stuck monsters would look like.

"Should we follow them in?"

"I don't know. Do you have a flamethrower?"

"Wait, I'll get one." He ran to the old hollow tree. The Juveniles had stuck the flamethrower inside so they'd have their hands free to carry the floaty they'd found back to the owner's cottage. He returned with it and motioned Duddu inside.

Duddu shook his head. "I'm not going first. You have the weapon. You go first."

"Some leader you are."

"Then give me the weapon."

Marbol had to think about this. He didn't want to go first, but he knew the one with the weapon would automatically get the bragging rights. "I'll do it." He pushed ahead of Duddu and proceeded cautiously.

The storm drain didn't smell great. It never did.

But now that it had two Terrorians crammed inside of it, it smelled even worse. They proceeded until they reached the junction and sniffed.

"I think they went left," Marbol said.

"Why would they do that? The left side leads to a dead end."

"Yeah. But they don't know that."

"If we follow them, we're going to get stuck in there with them," Duddu said.

"How far does it go before it ends?"

"I don't know. Maybe two hundred sticks."

"Do you think the flamethrower will reach that far?"

"Probably not."

"Then we have to go in there. But we have to be careful, because they could have turned around when they reached the end and may be coming right at us."

JOHANNA CHECKED ON Ava, who had been guarding the portals since she got home from school. "Don't you have homework to do?"

"Yeah. I did my math homework during lunch, but I still have to write a poem. I'm thinking about it while I guard the portals. Who knows? Maybe I'll get inspired."

Johanna laughed. "I hope you do. If you need me, I'll be in my residence."

"Okay."

Johanna retreated to her apartment. Before the Roths moved into the library, she had often felt lonely. Now, she sometimes looked forward to being alone so she could process everything that had happened. The first image to pop into her head was Jackson's tattoo. She remembered how the first one had gotten infected. She feared it might happen again. The idea that he'd done it without asking her first irritated her. And the fact that she felt irritated about it annoyed her even more. She had no more right to give Jackson grief about his tattoo than he would have telling her how to cut her hair.

Would I care if he were my brother? No. She would probably have a live-and-let-live attitude if he were her brother. *Would I care if I didn't like him?* No. If she didn't like him, what he did wouldn't matter to her. *Would I care if he were my husband?* She felt herself blush, heat building in her face. Just thinking of herself married to Jackson made her nerves tingle. As much as she fought facing her feelings about him, she knew it was time to do so. They were almost always together. They saw each other every day and she had practically adopted his family as her own. They worked well together as co-curators of the library. And they had fun together when their lives weren't being threatened by enemies from other realms or dimensions. She sat back on the sofa and closed her eyes. She allowed Jackson to enter her daydream. He pushed her down on the couch and kissed her. She wrapped herself around him. They had kissed like this a few times and she had felt like she was part of him but then had pushed him away. *Why?* She allowed the scene to play out in her mind. Jackson took a small silver band off his pinky and slipped it on her finger. *"I want you to know I'll be there for you, always,"* he said, *"no matter what."* *"Me, too,"* she answered.

Johanna opened her eyes and sat up. The room

had darkened as the hour grew late. Her fingers found the switch on the lamp next to the couch. She didn't want to think she had been dreaming. She had just allowed herself to commit to Jackson, at least in her imagination. *I love him.* After thinking it, she said it out loud. "I love Jackson." She realized she'd been pushing him away because she didn't think she should allow herself to fall in love with him. However, her subconscious just permitted what her conscious mind would not allow her to admit—and it was time for her superego and her id to get their act together. *I'm in love,* she thought again and smiled. Then she imagined Jackson being decimated by a Terrorian weapon and felt tears sting her eyes. There was a lot to be said about keeping someone at arm's length— you could protect yourself from being hurt if anything happened to them. But she was going to hurt whether she admitted she loved him or not, so she might as well admit it. She felt a wave of happiness surge through her body. It was time to let Jackson in.

SOON AFTER ARTEMUS Rexana departed Adventura, Prophet IAN c. called together a meeting of the realm's ruler*bots. They looked like every other hu*bot, except their right arms were solid metal instead of covered in polymer. The most prestigious Adventurans had gold arms, followed by platinum, silver, and copper. Non-ruling hu*bots had titanium arms covered with multihued artificial skin.

The rulers stood in a circle around Prophet IAN c. "Fellows," the curator began, "there have been changes in the outer worlds that may affect us. Allow me to explain." He spent the next half hour recounting the

Terrorians' latest incursions into other realms.

"We will not side with the Terrorians again, will we?" asked Prophet DAVID 1.

"No," the curator replied. "We will not allow ourselves to repeat the past, knowing it does not work out in our favor. And while I do not consider the Terrorians our enemies, I certainly do not consider them friends. I would freely eliminate them if I felt they threatened our world."

The others were fully in accord with the curator. "Say! Say!" they chanted in response.

One of the ruler*bots took a step forward. "Before the meeting, you mentioned the overseers are planning to tax us. Isn't that punishment for our ancient alignment with the Terrorians?"

"They are sending their Chancellor of the Exchequer to discuss a tax with us. Since we engage in communal living, there is no need for a tax. Those who sustain war losses will merely be brought back to their state of being before the loss occurred."

"Do you think this Chancellor of the Exchequer will allow that?"

"We'll soon find out."

WHEN JACKSON WOKE up, he decided it was time to have a serious chat with Johanna about their relationship. He found her packing book orders at the circulation desk.

"Johanna."

She turned to him and smiled.

He rushed his words, knowing if he took his time, he might change his mind. "I've been doing a lot of thinking lately," he said, "and I'm finally beginning to see the light."

"Um-hmm," she answered.

"We're good together. We're friends. We're co-curators. I know you always have my back when there's a problem, and I want you to know I'll always have yours."

"I do know that," she said. "Hiring you was one of the best moves ever."

Her answer unnerved him a little, but he pushed on. "I can see now how being together so much can drive us apart in some ways. So I want you to know, I'm backing off. You can date whomever you want. I'll go out with some of the girls I've met in high school or will meet in college. And that will give us the ability to work together without our emotions getting in the way. I've got to say, sometimes you really get into my head, and I feel awful about something I've done—when I shouldn't have to—like getting this tattoo. I think it's because we're in this weird pseudo-relationship. But how much of a relationship can we have with my family living here and us being thrown together all the time?"

She felt like the bottom dropped out of her stomach. "It sounds like we're already married," she said, her voice flat.

"Right. But without the perks. Romance should be a little mysterious. A little sexy. And very pleasing," he continued. "I'm finally realizing what we have together is not romance. It's friendship, for sure. And, at times, it's exciting. But there's no mystery. And I'm craving that. So I just want to say I'm going to start dating, and I want you to feel comfortable about doing the same."

"Okay." She continued packing books without

looking at him.

He didn't notice the blood draining from her face. "Right," he said again, before walking away thinking, *She doesn't even care.*

PEROG 2 AND Mope 98 inched their way through the cramped storm drain until they reached a large obstruction—metal louvres spanning the height and width of the opening—that completely blocked their path.

"What is it?" Mope 98 asked.

"I don't know."

"Knock it out of the way."

Perog 2 slammed his right side against it. It didn't budge.

"Maybe if we pull it," Mope 98 suggested.

Both Terrorians snaked their tentacles into the louvres and took hold, pulling. The top opened toward them, but the bottom swung away. The large, round louvre rotated on a central pivot.

"Grab the center," Perog 2 instructed, "and pull on my command." He took a deep breath. "Now!"

The two Terrorians pulled with all their might, but the pivot refused to budge.

"I told you we should have gone the other way," Mope 98 said.

"Fine. Follow me."

Mope 98 turned around but stopped in his tracks when he heard muffled voice. "Someone's coming," he whispered.

"Maybe they'll go down the other tunnel," Perog

2 said.

"Maybe."

Rather than follow Perog 2, Mope 98 wrapped his tentacles around the louvres in a last-ditch effort and began tugging with all his might.

—LOI—

14

MARBOL COCKED HIS head to one side. "Did you hear that?"

"What?" Pye whispered. "I didn't hear anything." The squeak of a metal hinge startled them. "Oh. That."

"They can't be that far away," Marbol reasoned. "The dead end is right around the bend." He snuck up to the bend in the storm drain and held his breath as he listened. He could definitely hear heavy breathing. He hoisted the flamethrower over his shoulder and jumped out into the middle of the storm drain after he turned the bend, switching the flamethrower on full.

"THEY'RE HERE!" MOPE 98 whispered. "They're going to kill us."

"They're just kiddlets," Perog 2 answered.

Suddenly, there was a loud whoosh directly in front of them. Perog 2 opened his eyes as wide as possible to see what caused it. He wished he hadn't. A giant fireball hurtled toward him and he knew he was going to fry. He shielded his face with the tentacle that contained the biometric armband. There was a small case attached to it with a dose of poison. Perog 2 sucked out the poison and hoped it would act quickly. It did not stop him from screaming in pain.

Mope 98 had the same armband and poison device but could not maneuver it to his mouth because Perog 2 was pressed too tightly against him. He could feel the intense heat and smell burning flesh.

Perog 2 stopped screaming as the poison did its job. Mope 98 prayed he would be protected by Perog 2 and that the kiddlets would run out of firepower before they could kill him, too.

CHRIS ROTH HAD stayed after school watching his girlfriend, Brittany's, cheerleading practice. Afterward, he greeted her with a kiss. "You must be hungry. I thought we could go back to my house for a nice, quiet dinner."

"What's your mom making?"

"Nothing. She's not at home. No one is. I thought we'd pick something up along the way."

A honking horn diverted her attention. "My mom's here. I told her I'd go shopping with her. I don't suppose we could do it tomorrow?"

"Sure," Chris answered. "Tomorrow would be great."

She winked at him. "I'll see you then."

Chris thought about his date all the way home. *I'll get something good from Piccolo Italia.* He wondered if his mother had a bottle of wine in the house? Probably not. *Cassie's older brother works in a liquor store. I'll ask him.*

Candles. He'd seen a movie where there were dozens of flickering candles in a seduction scene. *Girls like that stuff. I'll stop at the florist and get a single red rose, too. That should seal the deal.*

JACKSON SLID INTO his seat at the dinner table.

"Where's Johanna?" Ava asked.

"She's guarding the portals."

"Oh."

Mrs. Roth sat down. "What's wrong, Ava?"

"Nothing. I just wanted to read her my poem."

Mrs. Roth spread her dinner napkin across her knees. "I'm sure we'd all like to hear it."

"Yeah," Ava said, "but I want to read it to Johanna first."

Jackson grabbed a dinner roll. "Johanna and I are no longer...dating." He said it casually but felt funny saying it, like it was wrong.

Ava gasped. "What happened?"

"It was by mutual agreement. We've been spending a lot of time together, which is fine. And we enjoy working together and all. But there's no magic. We're still really good friends. Just nothing more."

"That's a shame," his mother said, laying her knife down. "I had the feeling you two were made for each other."

"Yeah. Well, now we're unmade."

Chris snickered. "Like a rumpled bed."

"Except our bed never got to the rumpled stage," Jackson muttered.

Mrs. Roth put her fork down. "I want you boys to stop talking like that in front of your younger sister."

Jackson popped a French fry in his mouth. "It's not like Ava doesn't know anything about the birds and the bees."

"Why are you dragging me into this?" Ava complained.

"Why not?" Chris answered.

"Jackson Ryan Roth, I have half a mind to send you to bed with no dinner. And you too, Christopher Daniel."

"Really, Mom," Jackson said, "aren't you being a little melodramatic?"

Mrs. Roth stood up and threw her napkin down on the table. "Ava, why don't you run upstairs and read Johanna your poem. As for these two, don't listen to a word they say."

"Good idea," Ava said, escaping the tension in the room.

Naimh Roth turned to her sons. "I thought I raised you better than this." She walked out the door.

"Awkward," Jackson muttered.

"Hilarious," his brother answered.

AVA FOUND JOHANNA at the top of the cupola stairs. "Hey, Johanna. Can I read you my poem?"

"Sure. Let's hear it."

The fourteen-year-old stood straight and read from the paper in her hand.

"Abandoned...

"I sit alone in silence.

"No birds sing.

"No dogs bark.

"There is no sound of the rustling of

leaves.

"I look around.

"No flowers bloom.

"No children play.

"There is no one around to give a friendly greeting.

"Is this the result of man's knowledge and accomplishments?

"Why?

"Am I to wither away like the former life known to me?

"Through others' hatred, ignorance, and greed, I have been...

"Abandoned."

Johanna stared at Ava. "That's pretty deep, Ava. And a little morbid."

"I know." The younger girl sighed, "But sometimes when I'm here by myself guarding the portals, I think about what might happen if the octopus succeeds."

"We're going to do our best to protect you from that."

"How can you, now that you and Jackson aren't a couple anymore?"

Johanna couldn't hide the grief on her face or the tear that escaped quickly and involuntarily. "I guess Jackson told you..."

Ava dropped to the floor and sat crossed-legged. "He announced it at dinner. He said it was by mutual consent." Ava looked at the tear Johanna had failed to wipe away. "It wasn't, was it? It was my brother's idea.

Chris said it's because you're not sleeping together."

Johanna's face turned a deep shade of red. "Nice dinner table conversation."

"Mom was mad about it. She got up and walked out after yelling at the boys."

"It's not like we're not friends anymore," Johanna said. "And I consider you the little sister I never had."

"Me, too. Not that you're my little sister, but like you're my older one."

Johanna crouched down next to her and gave her a hug. "I'm pretty sure if they don't pack you off to the school psychiatrist for fear that you're suicidal, you'll get an A on that poem. But you can't tell them what prompted you to write it."

"I know. I'll just tell them I watched a doomsday movie and it made me think of it."

"That'll work." Johanna stood and lifted the decimator. She aimed it at the portal. "I'll be here, guarding the fort."

The time machine flashed into view with Nero 51 and Odyon inside. Startled, Johanna pulled the trigger without thinking. It caused a flash.

The time machine disappeared, but exactly what happened to it was anybody's guess.

MARBOL KEPT THE flamethrower turned on high until it ran out of fuel. When the fire died out, he turned and ran, gagging on the smell. He didn't see Pye until he got out of the storm drain. The other boy stood at the edge of the pond vomiting in the water.

Marbol dropped the flamethrower. "What's the matter, Pye? Can't take—" He felt his stomach heave, and a moment later, his stomach contents defied gravity as well.

"Did you ever smell anything that gross?" Pye asked. "My clothes smell like that, and my hair, and I'm going to smell that stink forever."

Marbol wiped off his mouth on the hem of his shirt. "It had to be done."

"Whose gonna remove what's left?"

"Why do we have to remove anything?"

"Because it's going to block the storm drain. And if it blocks the drain, it's going to back up into the pond when it rains. And the pond is going to overflow. And the homes on the low side are going to get flooded. And those people won't have anyplace to live. Do you want them to come live with you?"

Marbol leaned over and propped both his hands on his knees. Another wave of nausea rippled through his stomach. "No. We killed them. We did our job. Some of the others should have to clean them out of the storm drain."

Pye stood a little straighter. "That's a good plan."

"Okay. Let's go back to Town Hall and tell them the deed is done, and it's their job to clean up the remains."

Pye pulled the front of his T-shirt away from his chest and looked down at it. "I'm kind of dirty. I need a swim first." They both looked at the pond and saw bits of vomit floating on the surface. "Or maybe I'll just go home and wash up, instead."

Marbol nodded. "Yeah."

* * *

CHRIS WATCHED JACKSON climb the stairs to the cupola when it came time for his older brother to guard the portals. As Jackson disappeared, Chris entered the bedroom they shared and rummaged through their dresser drawers. *C'mon, bro, you have to have some protection in here.* His hand closed around something unusual, but it wasn't the kind of protection he was looking for. *Whoa! What are you doing with a gun?* He turned the firearm gently in his hands, making sure he didn't press the trigger by accident. He would never be able to explain that to his mother, or his brother. And he didn't want to hurt himself before his big date with Brittany.

He smiled. He hadn't found what he was looking for, but this was ammunition he could hold over Jackson's head. Besides, he could stop at the drug store near school and buy the protection he needed.

"YOU DECIMATED THE time machine," Ava said to Johanna.

"I doubt it. It may have just disappeared on its own. But I'll check with Mal, just to play it safe."

They turned when they heard Jackson thumping up the stairs. "What's going on?" he asked.

Ava narrowed her eyes. "What do you care?"

"I came to guard the portals. I thought Johanna would like to go down for dinner."

"And eat alone?" Ava's comment dripped with sarcasm.

Jackson's shoulders slumped. "This isn't about you, squirt."

Ava bristled. She hated when he called her squirt. "Do you want me to guard the portals while you go find your diary?" she asked Johanna.

Johanna smiled. "It will be more fun if you keep me company." She handed the decimator to Jackson. "Here. It's time for you to earn your paycheck."

"Hey. You're the one who told me to go back to school."

The girls disappeared down the stairs.

Jackson sighed. His face clouded over and his lower lip trembled, but no one was there to see it.

MYSTERIAN ESSENTIAL WATER turned out to be stronger than Mal remembered, and he woke in his Lumi apartment the following day with a blazing headache. It was early in the morning, but Pru Tellerence had left him a message asking him to go to Romantica with her for the presentation of uniforms.

He'd certainly enjoyed Hugh the Elder's red bread stew, but it did nothing to ease the impact of the essential water. Mysterian fermentation techniques went a long way in ensuring their favorite beverage packed a punch, yet its taste rivaled only the sweetness of pure fruit nectar. It was the wallop that followed a few hours later that caused Mal's suffering, and everyone else's who drank it. But no one really cared, because essential water went down smoothly and made a body feel like a god in a world of mortals.

He took the Luminan equivalent of aspirin, put on his Chancellor of the Exchequer robe and chaperon, and headed out.

PRU TELLERENCE AND Horatio Blastoe traveled with Mal to Romantica and led him to the clearing that had become the unofficial headquarters for the militairres.

They found that Furst had instructed some of the Romanticans to dig out and level a large area of land at the edge of the glade and pave it with uniformly-sized stones. Now, four large wooden tables flanked by benches sat in the space, and a large tent, usually used for village fetes, shielded them from the sun. The tent's side panels had been fastened at the corners, giving it an open appearance. The women had erected poles in the middle of each table and fastened a handmade flag to the top of each one. A rust colored flag contained an arrow pointing straight up—bisected by a bow turned on its side. A yin-yang design on a green flag represented two people grappling. A red flag looked like it had a gold sunburst in its center, however, as Dame Erato pointed out, it was the blast of a decimator—representing the women in the weaponry division. The final flag was a beautiful shade of azure and contained a slender X representing crossed fighting sticks.

⚐*I see there have been some developments here since I left.*

Furst nodded. "A sense of solidarity, they needed. A small start, this is."

★*We have something that may help with that*, Pru Tellerence said with a smile. ★*Please have the militairres gather around us.*

"If I might interrupt?" Mal asked the overseers.

★*Yes, Malcolm?*

"I'm sure the Romanticans will be pleased with their uniforms. It will unite them as a team and give them an instant identity as a group. They may not be as pleased to learn about a war tax. So I'm wondering if it would be better if I preceded you in today's presentation, so we can end on a positive note, rather than something that will not be as well-received. From there, I'm hoping Horatio Blastoe will accompany me into Roma, where we can speak with residents who chose not to enlist and further explain how necessary it is that they support the militairres."

⚜*I would be happy to do that with you, and I think softening the sting of a tax with the gift of uniforms is an excellent idea.*

★*Yes. Let's begin.*

Horatio Blastoe asked Natalia Dalura and Dame Erato to introduce the overseers and say they had two important announcements to make.

Once the militairres had seated themselves in a large circle on the grassy glade, Natalia Dalura introduced Horatio Blastoe.

⚜*I am pleased to see the progress you have made. It shows our faith in you is not ill-advised. Now that you are in place as this realm's militia, there are steps that must be taken to assist you. I would like to introduce the Chancellor of the Exchequer for the first of our announcements today.*

Mal talked about the history of how Johanna and Jackson unwittingly breached the portals, the "punishment" that followed, and how Johanna's imprisonment on Terroria revealed a mounting invasion threat. He then segued into the need for a tax and explained how it would go a long way toward making reparations, as well as paying for supplies like tents and banners. As he predicted, the crowd was not very happy to hear what he had to say, but he remained upbeat about his topic and said he would be available for questions. He then introduced Pru Tellerence.

★*Good morning. As I'm sure some of you have realized by now, hand-to-hand combat in skirts is less than desirable.* Many of the women in the group laughed. ★*Several people have already pointed out how a uniform might be more beneficial.*

One of the militairres groaned. "You seek to take away our individuality."

★*No. I seek to streamline your ability to fight as militairres, without losing the wonderful grace and style you all possess. Allow me to show you what we've come up with.*

★*Natalia, would you help model the new uniforms?*

"Of course. Where are they?"

★*Just stand here in the center of the circle. I will handle the rest.*

As the militairres looked on, Pru Tellerence asked Natalia to twirl in a circle.

"As you wish," the curator said, laughing.

By the time the rotation was completed, Natalia was dressed in the blue ombré uniform, complete with boots and cross-brace. Pru Tellerence described the features of the uniform as Natalia walked around so the militairres could get a closer look. As the overseer spoke of each specialty, the appropriate weapons appeared. Pru Tellerence asked Natalia to twirl again, and the militairres applauded when her uniform turned white and her boots gold. The overseer continued to describe the dress uniforms and the officer's metal mesh cross-braces, and ended the presentation with the matching jackets that everyone would receive. Pru Tellerence clapped her hands twice, and enough uniforms for every militairre appeared on the tables under the tent. The women went in search of their uniforms and soon closed the sides of the tent so they could change into them.

Afterward, Pru Tellerence visited with each militairre and used a special enchantment to make the uniform fit each woman perfectly. She asked them to sit at their respective tables and stopped at each one, where she stared at the emblem on the pole for a few seconds while whispering another chant. When she finished, she nodded, and the emblem of that unit appeared, embossed on the side of the militairres' boots and the backs of their jackets.

The uniforms were a big hit, and as Mal had predicted, did a lot to remove the sting of his talk about taxes.

—LOI—

15

NERO 51 FELT himself thrown against the interior of the time machine with so much g-force, his body flattened like a pancake. Suddenly, the velocity stopped, and he crashed to the floor.

Odyon resumed his human form. "This is no time to nap, Terrorian. We seem to have arrived someplace new." He exited the time machine. "Ugh. And it's filled with more of your kind."

The decimator blast aimed at them by Johanna Charette had released them from their entrapment in between the layers of time and space.

Terrorian troopers crowded around the duo, all speaking at once.

"Nero 51, did you find a way out?"

"Yes, Nero 51, where did you go?"

"Have you found a way for us to exit the library?"

"What are you doing on the floor?"

They were all brimming with questions that Nero 51 chose not to answer. "I am going to my chamber.

Under no condition am I to be disturbed."

"Not even if we find a way out of here?" Odyon asked.

"I've had enough of you." He turned to the troopers. "Seize him." But before they could wrap their tentacles around Odyon, he disappeared into a pinpoint of light.

MAL LEFT ROMANTICA after explaining, ad nauseam, how a tax system would work. It was up to the citizens to decide who should pay and how much. He could do no more than guide them in their decision. He collected his thoughts and concentrated on his next stop of the day. A moment later, he appeared in Adventura's town square, where Artemus Rexana stood waiting.

Σ *Have you ever visited Adventura before?*

"No. But I read up on its history. Is everyone a hu*bot, or are there some humans mixed in?"

Σ *All humans per se have perished, but their minds and hearts live on.*

"What about children?"

Σ *There are no children here.*

"How do they perpetuate? Surely all the beings here can't be several millennia old."

Σ *The Adventurans are quite adept at cloning. When the human parts of an Adventuran start to fail, the hu*bot goes in for maintenance. Bits of brain tissue and heart muscle are removed and cloned. When total failure is imminent, the flawed parts are replaced with the cloned parts, and the hu*bot continues to thrive.*

"That's incredible. Are there as many hu*bots now as there were, say, a thousand years ago?"

Σ*It depends on your interpretation. The population of hu*bots is constant. However, the diversity of personalities is limited. Sometimes the cloning process fails completely and that personality is lost forever. However, there are multiple clones of several of the hu*bots' more important predecessors, and if one personality dies out, the hu*bot continues to function with the clone of another noted ancestor.*

"Are you telling me there may be more than one Prophet IAN c.?"

Σ*He wouldn't be called Prophet IAN c. He would go by the name of the hu*bot who died. That is to say, if Prophet PATRICK c. died and a clone of Prophet IAN c.'s heart and brain is inserted into the dead hu*bot's shell, he'd still be called Prophet PATRICK c.*

"I can see how that could start to limit the Adventurans as a civilization."

Σ*Possibly, but they won't grow extinct any time soon. I dare say they'll outlive you and I, even with our Longevicus Blessings.*

They walked into the lab where the curator conducted his experiments. Prophet IAN c. nodded in acknowledgement but did not break away from what he was doing until he had completed his task. "Horatio Blastoe, is this the Chancellor of the Exchequer?"

Σ*Yes. Have you arranged a meeting with your peers?*

"It is not necessary. We have discussed the need for tax and find there is none. Adventurans are each part of a communal society. We only exist to help the whole of our civilization continue to advance in science, mathematics, and engineering. We are not individually competitive, although, we must acknowledge that teams of Adventurans, especially those working in the pharmaceutical fields, have become somewhat zealous, if only for the honor of making greater advancements and discoveries."

"Pardon me for my ignorance," Mal interjected, "but if Adventurans are seventy-five percent robotic, why is it you need pharmaceuticals?"

Prophet IAN c. did not appear to be phased by the question. "We hope to discover ways to strengthen our hearts and brains and improve our ability to function. We do not wish to become a race of artificially intelligent robots. We embrace our humanity. And in order to prolong our existence, we are always looking for remedies to the problems that threaten our lives. Every so often, a congenital weakness hidden in an originator's cells must be dealt with. Cancers, dementia, naturally occurring structural changes in cellular proteins. One lab discovered a way to strengthen heart valves. Another found a way to improve sinus rhythms. We are always working toward the perfection of being.

"The competition stems from the developer's ability to produce stronger progeny. We are not paid in money but are rewarded by prestige. Our bodies are equal in strength and structure and are all equally provided for in their repair and ability to function. Our brains, however, even after years of evolving into a homogeneous civilization, are prideful and require praise. The greatest praise is in the continuance of our line. And the hu*bot with the greatest number of descendants is looked at with great reverence."

* * *

Juveniles did not have patience for boring meetings, and it always took a long time to gather enough of them together in one place for what could be called a productive gathering. However, they adored the game Bullaroot, and wouldn't miss a match for the world. Duddu, Pollo, Guffle and Marbol agreed to captain competing teams and would address the problem of disposing of monster carcasses during the pre-game build-up and the post-game toast.

A group of fourteen-year-olds formed a human perimeter around the field adjacent to the school to keep the overflow of Juveniles from spilling over onto the playing field. The field was surrounded by seatless bleachers, where everyone seemed smashed together — for row upon row — as they all clamored for a good place to stand and view the game. Those who didn't arrive in time for a spot in the bleachers gathered on the grass directly in front of the square playing field, and the massive number of latecomers threatened to encroach on the field of play.

The game of Bullaroot was simple: four teams containing thirteen players each had an assigned color with a ball, a corresponding net on the field, and a color-coded target eight feet above the ground on the opposite side of the field. In a free-for-all competition, it was up to each team to score as many net and target shots as they could while facing interference from the three other teams. Net scores could be kicked in while on the move. Target scores had to be thrown from a stationary position. If a player threw a ball while on the move, he was immediately disqualified. The targets were fitted with pressure points so that balls that struck the outer rings did not score as many points as balls that hit the target dead center. The game was refereed by two dozen twelve-year-olds, six along each outside perimeter. Every referee swore to uphold the principles of the game and took his or her job very seriously.

The crowd cheered as Duddu took the field with a megaphone in his hands. He started by announcing the teams and the players and their respective colors. In a ceremony complete with horns playing, drums banging, and flags waving, each team ran out from a corner of the field, joining with the other teams to jog in a large circular pattern at its center, before splitting up again to form a cross—with the captain closest to the center of the field and his teammates extending outward toward their net.

The referees passed around cards and asked spectators to write their names and the colors of their favorite team. This was well-subscribed to because those who supported the winners knew they would receive extra leisure time and prizes for making the right choice.

After the cards were collected, Duddu motioned for the spectators to quiet down. "As many of you know, monsters have invaded the library." Feet stomped the ground to indicate they were aware of the invaders. "Marbol and Pye trapped the monsters in the drainage tunnels and fried them."

The crowd roared their approval.

Marbol took the megaphone. "It was scary and disgusting, but we did what we had to do. However, we can't leave them in the storm drain 'cause they'll clog it, so the losing team and its backers have to clean out the drains."

This was met with some "boos," some applause, and a lot of shouts and whistles.

Duddu took back the megaphone. "Everyone who voted for the top three teams will be able to celebrate this afternoon. Those who chose the losing team must carry out the penalty for losing. It is the way it must be. But once they are done, they can also join in the celebration because we will have beaten the monsters!" Everyone began stomping their feet, and the stadium shook with energy. "Play on!"

THE MYSTERIAN DISCUSSION rings were crowded the following day with people who wanted to learn more about the rumors they heard concerning a new currency and taxes.

"We promise you," Hue the Elder spoke over the crowd, "that you will have a say in what you donate in taxes." He explained everything Mal had told him about the currency system, including how they could barter notes.

"But we'll still end up with less than we get now," one herbalist called out. "So even though we can 'barter,' we end up with less to barter away."

Hue the Elder took a deep, calming breath. "Every year, we all receive a portion of antimony. How much antimony do you use?"

"I use none!" the herbalist answered. "So, you see, I would end up with even less than everyone else."

"What happens to your share of antimony?"

"I don't know." She shrugged. "I imagine it reverts back to the ruling council and is handed out again the following year."

Hue nodded. "So you lose it."

"Yes."

"Under this new system, you would be given currency denoting your annual allotment of antimony, along with currency for everything else you're entitled to. But now, instead of losing it, you could just hand it over as your share of taxes. You wouldn't even notice the loss, yet you would satisfy your tax contribution."

The herbalist's head jerked back slightly. "Oh!"

"There are others here who have allotments they don't use. The coal monger may have no need for herbs. The innkeeper may not use his ore allotment. We all have something we don't use that could be contributed to the common good during wartime."

"And yet," Drace the Elder replied, "we have seen no signs of war. I believe this new currency system being rammed down our throats by the overseers is an unnecessary tactic to control us."

"I do not believe the overseers would take such an action," Hue replied.

"Really?" Drace countered. "You believe them because they are known to you. I do not know them, nor do most of the people here." Loud murmuring replaced what had been total silence.

"Considering no one person will be forced to give up anything other than what they don't currently use," Hue replied, "I do not see the need for agitating the crowd."

"I bring it up," Drace said, "because they are trying to rob us blind without our realizing it." The noise level continued to grow. "And this currency with a special chip—whatever that is—could be some kind of device that slowly robs us of our strength, or poisons our air, or tracks us where we would prefer privacy. Has anyone here ever heard of such a thing?"

The crowd became unruly. Clearly, selling the Mysterians on taxes and currency would be no easy task.

OZZRO DID NOT sleep well, even though the Dramatican season had reached its most comfortable level. And when he did sleep, he dreamed of Dungen vaporizing his enemies one-by-one. He awakened haggard and grumpy.

"Tired, Ozzro, you seem. The problem, what is?" one of the Dramatican soldiers asked.

"Something horrendous, I may have witnessed. After me, the person may be, if he knows I saw him."

The other soldier moved closer and lowered his voice. "See, what did you?"

Ozzro shook his head. "Tell you, I cannot. Too dangerous, it is."

"Yet, tell Lenc, you would."

"Lenc!" Ozzro said, not able to hide his surprise. He thought better of giving away too much information. "Seen him, have you?"

"No. But, looking for him, I know you are."

"Yes. See me, tell him to, if see him, you do," he said, even though he knew no one would ever see Lenc again.

JOHANNA CHECKED HER diary hourly but didn't hear from Mal until much later. *I am busy on Adventura, but have relayed your question to Ryden Simmdry. He will meet with you later.*

No sooner did she read the message than the

overseer appeared. She explained how the time machine had suddenly appeared and how she had shot at it without thinking.

Ryden Simmdry took a few moments before he answered. ⌘*I don't know if a blast from the decimator could change the dynamics of the time machine. The decimator is a Terrorian weapon, and I regret to say I have not paid much attention to it, other than noting the devastating effect it has on the life force. I imagine a blast could reverse the polarity of the time machine and, like a slingshot, send it back to its point of origin, but I can't say that with any certainty. It is merely speculation of a possibility.*

"What about the oracle. Have you determined a way to propel the cube into the time machine?"

⌘*There is a way, but it would require a very dire maneuver that would put one or more lives at stake. It is a solution only of last resort.*

—LOI—

16

EACH BULLAROOT TEAM captain simultaneously hurled a ball in his team's color toward their target to signal the beginning of the game. The Juveniles cheered, stamping their feet in approval, and the mayhem that typified any Bullaroot game ensued.

Before Bullaroot, Juvenile sports usually pitted two teams against each other, but in many of those games, there were long scoreless stretches of time that bored the spectators. Then, someone got the idea that double the teams would mean double the excitement, and Bullaroot was born. Having each team defend itself against three others kept everyone on their toes and entertained the crowd. Today's game was no different, and there wasn't one Juvenile who wanted to be associated with the losing team, so they all cheered their teams to score and booed their missed chances.

Marbol played especially hard. He had been in the tunnels and didn't want to return. Duddu, Pollo, and Guffle wanted to win but didn't have that extra impetus to avoid losing at all costs.

Marbol's red team scored first with a double-rebound play. The captain himself rocketed the ball toward his team's red bullseye, where it hit dead-center for the highest number of points and bounced back toward the field with the maximum force provided by the spring action loaded behind each target. Pye was ready for the rebound and forcefully kicked the ball in an arc that missed scores of other players on the field and descended gracefully into the red team's net to double their point score.

The other teams scrambled, but three of Marbol's defensemen had been instructed to thwart scoring by the competition at all costs. So instead of trying to gain control of their own ball and score, those three players roamed the other teams' quarter fields, and they did whatever they could to disrupt the flow of competing games.

The red team scored a second time, hitting the target. Moments later, Duddu's blue team scored when they successfully kicked their ball into the net. This caused frenzied action by Guffle's green team and Pollo's yellow team, who didn't want to lose the day. But their nervous energy caused them to make mistakes, while the red and blue teams each scored additional points.

Marbol focused all his energy on scoring. He threw hard, intercepted with agility, and kicked ferociously. By the end of the first tri-match, the red team was firmly in first place, while the yellow and green teams had failed to score.

* * *

"So, are you going to ask Emily out or not?"

Jackson looked at Logan like he was a thorn in his side. "I'll ask her when I'm ready."

"No, you won't. You may have broken up with Johanna, but she still possesses your heart."

"You sound like a freakin' poet."

"That's why I have a girlfriend who loves me." He pushed Jackson toward Emily Brent. "Make your move. She just broke up with Zach Maybrecht. She's running for prom queen. She needs a king. You can be her king."

Jackson sighed but didn't move.

"What if it's a double date? Dinner and a movie. Cassie and I will go, too."

"Yeah? You'd do that for me?"

"Yes." Logan gave Jackson a push. "Just go ask her."

Emily gasped when she shut her locker door and found Jackson standing on the other side, waiting for her.

"Hi, Emily." *That sounded so lame.*

"Jackson. You startled me." She smiled.

Jackson could feel Logan's stare boring into the back of his head. "I was wondering if you're doing anything Wednesday night? We don't have classes on Thursday, and I thought if you're not busy, maybe we could go out? On a double date? Dinner and a movie?"

She paused before answering.

Jackson could feel himself deflating.

"I'd love to."

"You would?" He was totally surprised by this turn of events.

"Yes, I would." She linked her arm in his. "Walk

me to class?"

"Sure." He felt someone bump into him. *What the....* It was Logan. It would be a long time before Jackson forgot the smirk on Logan's face.

That afternoon, Jackson stopped at Logan's house after he walked Emily home. "I need to go to a cell phone store."

Logan's eyebrows shot up. "I thought you didn't have space in your life for 'frivolities' because you're saving for a car?"

"Emily asked for my phone number. I can't have her calling me on the library phone. Besides, I've been meaning to get one for months."

"Little Jackson Roth is finally growing up."

Jackson punched Logan's arm.

"Watch it, bud. If you're not nice to me, I'll let out all your secrets when we double date tomorrow night."

Jackson groaned.

Logan smiled as he unlocked the car. "That's what I like to hear. Total capitulation."

THE ROMANTICAN MILITAIRRES moved with ease in their new uniforms as they practiced their specialties. The militairres were neither strong nor stealthy, but they developed great precision and could think quickly in the face of adversity.

Still, no one could be sure how they would react when battling a real enemy.

Natalia approached the dean. "I would like to take a small contingent of militairres inside the library."

✠*Absolutely not.*

"I need to take my library back, Horatio Blastoe."

⚕*And very well sacrifice your group's lives in the process?* He gently placed his hand on her shoulder. ⚕*You're not ready. Continue to practice fighting. Hone your skills. When the time comes, you'll need to be razor-sharp, not only in your specified skill, but also in the other military disciplines.* Natalia walked away, shoulders sagging, and joined her platoon.

"Why so glum?" one of the militairres asked.

"I think we're ready to fight the Terrorians in the library. The dean doesn't agree with me."

Felicia overheard Natalia's comment and spun around. "The dean is right. My team is doing well playing nice with each other. But I don't know if they're ready to handle deadly force. They still need to toughen up."

Arraba joined the discussion. "The militairres don't want to hurt each other, but if there's one thing I know, it's that they're all extremely competitive.

"What if we initiate a series of games?" the eldest Jolen sister continued. "Maybe if our militairres are fighting to win, there will be more fire in them."

Milencia, the youngest sister, shook her head. "What kind of competition could we have with decimators? They're already pulverizing rocks. I don't want them pulverizing each other."

Natalia's eyes lit up. "The decimators have a force field setting. As the leader of your platoon, it would be your duty to make sure each militairre's weapon is locked on the lower setting. But then they could shoot at each other. They'll be moving targets. And the spirit of competition will sharpen their wits."

"We can't do that with archers," Arraba pointed out. "It's a shame we don't have access to the library. We could travel inside one of the books and shoot at fictional animals to improve our aim on moving targets."

"We could bake clay and feather mud balls and catapult them into the air as targets," Felicia said. "That would work."

"Okay." Natalia nodded slowly. "That takes care of archery and weaponry. What about stick fighting and grappling?"

⚔*May I join this conversation?*

Natalia turned to the dean. "Horatio Blastoe. Of course."

⚔*Since I've been told that listening in on others' conversations is commonplace on Romantica, I couldn't help but exercise that option after I saw how defeated you looked when I said I wouldn't let you inside the library. I believe the idea for a series of competitions is a good one. But it needs a motivator. I think there has to be something in it for the winner, like co-command.*

Felicia folded her arms. "What do you mean?"

⚔*Each platoon has a leader—the four of you—and your responsibilities will continue to grow. The competition could be to assign troop leaders. Start with two in each division. The top two grapplers would each take over half the platoon. They would then report directly to Natalia. The four of you would retain command of your unit, but you would each gain two assistants to work with. Perhaps while the top assistants work on your group's specialty, the second assistants could work on a different form of fighting with her troop of militairres.*

"Two co-captains to boss around," Milencia said. "I like it."

⚔*They would allow for more mixed practices.*

And, you, as platoon leaders, would have more time to either practice yourselves, strategize like you're doing right now, or view your militairres' practice in other specialties.

"That could work," Natalia said. "And we have nothing to lose trying it."

Felicia frowned. "If they're going to be co-captains, what are we? The word 'leader' doesn't sound as impressive as 'co-captain.'"

✠*How about "commander?"*

"Ooh. I like the sound of that." Arraba saluted. "Commander Arabba Jolen at your service."

The others laughed.

"I'll make up signs," Felicia volunteered, "to announce the competition. When do we want to have it?"

✠*I would suggest you give yourselves two days' time. One day to make sure everyone knows about the competition in advance; a second day to give people time to get fired up about it and practice.*

"This sounds exciting." Milencia grabbed her sister Felicia's arm. "I'll help you make the signs."

✠*What about your platoons?*

"I'll take care of that." Milencia walked over to the militairres who were waiting for their team leaders to return. "Let's all break for lunch. Afterward, we have something exciting to tell you."

"What?" one of the militairres called out.

"You'll find out soon enough."

DURING THE BULLAROOT game on Juvenilia, Duddu noticed Fibber, one of Marbol's players, trying to anticipate the path of his team's ball. The infiltrator constantly interfered with it. Duddu refused to play second fiddle. He called aside two of his people. "Boxer. The red team's messing with us. Patrol their quarter field and knock their ball out of play." He turned to the other player. "Elmie. Shadow the filcher who's boogering our plays and prevent him from interfering."

The next tri-match was more heated than the first. While the red and blue teams concentrated on getting in each other's way, the yellow team managed to score a target shot, and the green team scored a net shot. The red team remained in the lead, but only by a point.

The teams broke for a small intermission. The captains strategized with their players while the crowd traded trinkets for cotton candy and sweet water.

The last match of the game would prove to be intense. Now that all four teams were on the board, the crowd anticipated bloodlust.

JOHANNA PUSHED HER food around her plate, not really eating. Ryden Simmdry had not been very specific about the meaning of "dire maneuver." He'd left her alone in the library, saying only that he needed to give the problem more thought.

Worse, he said there was a possibility that the blast from her decimator may have reversed the polarization of the time machine, allowing it to escape the portals.

What am I doing, eating, when I should be guarding the cupola?

She pushed herself away from the table and dumped what was left of her salad in the trash. She grabbed a bottle of water and a protein bar to hold her until one of the Roths came to take over for her. *I used to be curator of one of the most exciting places in the world. Now, I've been demoted to guard duty.*

She hoped something exciting would happen just to break the tension she felt.

NERO 51 DID not notice the barely perceptible swish of air that followed him down to level 333 — his private lair. He saluted his grandfather's picture when he entered. "Garpa, we have encountered a small problem, but it is nothing we cannot overcome in time. The overseers will do everything in their power to thwart us, but I will not let them. I will unite the libraries under the Terrorian flag once and for all. For you, Garpa." He settled down in a corner to meditate. While he did, he felt so attuned with life, he could hear the walls hum.

Two hours later, when Nero 51 opened his eyes, Odyon was standing in front of Garpa's picture, studying it.

"How did you get in here?" the curator roared.

"I came in with you, of course. I was just studying, what did you call him, Garpa? He resembles you, but then again, all you Terrorians look alike."

Nero 51 huffed. "How is it you even speak Terrorian?"

"I don't. I created a translation charm many millennia ago that is still in use by the College of Overseers. I am speaking English — a language I learned after centuries of living on Fantasia. I'm originally from Mysteriose and can speak several of those dialects, as well. You are speaking Terrorian. With the translation charm, it doesn't matter what either of us are speaking, we'll still understand each other."

"You created the translation charm?" Nero 51 felt chilled. Whatever this entity was, it either had more power than Nero 51 anticipated, or it was lying.

"Yes. Does that surprise you? I'm not as young as I look."

"Apparently."

"I need to get off this realm."

Nero 51 closed his eyes. After several minutes, he opened them again. Odyon was still standing there.

"I can't help you. The overseers have frozen the library."

"We were just on Fantasia."

"I managed to escape through a pinhole but could not go anywhere because the overseers have sealed all the libraries."

"Yet, I managed to hitch a ride with you. How amusing. That means there is a flaw in the enchantment used to seal the portals. I must discover that flaw. You must use your vehicle to take me back through your pinhole."

"It is no use."

Odyon grated his teeth. "I am the greatest sorcerer who ever lived. I can say that because all the others who even came close have died. Except one—but that is my problem.

"Take me through the pinhole," Odyon continued, "so I can determine the enchantment used to create it. I will sense its energy, read its pattern, and find a way to merge with it and duplicate it, thereby giving us control of the portals."

Nero 51 stared at the Mysterian. If what he said

was true, there was a lot to be gained by humoring him. The curator inhaled before rising. "I will take you through the pinhole, but before I do, I want to know what I will gain from agreeing to do this for you."

"I just told you what you would gain. You would once again be able to travel through the portals, unchecked, and launch your attack for Garpa. Isn't that enough?"

"You said we would be in control of the portals. I want you to show me how I can have power over them."

"We have to gain control first, and we can't do that as long as you stand there trying my patience."

"You said you would teach me how to disappear and reappear like you do."

"Fine. I will teach you how to be a shapeshifter. Actually becoming one will be up to you. It requires finesse and practice. But I will give you the tools you'll need. Can we go now?"

"I am to be the only ruler of the Libraries of Illumination."

"First, you have to win your war, and it will never get started unless you take me back through the pinhole."

JACKSON HEADED HOME that afternoon armed with Emily's cell phone number, address, and equal measures of guilt and anxiety. He'd done what he said he was going to do, and he had warned Johanna he was planning to do it. *So why do I feel so bad?* Emily was hot. Not that Johanna wasn't, but Emily looked more like a delicate princess, compared to Johanna's sultry vixen. Too bad Johanna didn't *act* like a sultry vixen. If she had, he would never have asked Emily out.

True, he wouldn't have made the date without Logan pushing him. *Maybe it will be wonderful.* He just had to make sure Chris and Ava would be at home to help Johanna while he was out with Emily.

He felt hot and sweaty even though the weather was mild. As he rounded the corner and saw the library, his stomach flipped. He would rather do anything than tell Johanna he had a date Wednesday night. *But maybe I don't have to....*

Before going upstairs to relieve Johanna, he waited for Ava to get home. As soon as he heard her come in the door, he walked out of his bedroom holding two shirts. "Which one of these shirts do you think looks nicer?"

Ava looked them over and pointed to the blue one. "Where are you going?"

"Emily Brent and I are double-dating with Logan and Cassie tomorrow night. I just want to set it aside to wear, so I don't forget."

His sister looked like he had physically punched her. She didn't say another word to him. She just dropped her books on a chair and left the suite. He knew she would go upstairs and tell Johanna. He was counting on it, because he was too chicken to tell her himself.

—LOI—

17

THE MILITAIRRES DID not stray far from their respective tables after lunch. No one wanted to miss the announcement.

The two younger Jolen sisters returned with several signs. "We made a lot," Milencia said, "because we thought it might be nice to invite members of the community as spectators. It will make the games more exciting, don't you think?"

Natalia pulled over one of the signs. "Not to mention it would be impossible to keep them away once they do hear about it."

✠*These will do quite nicely.*

"Nice," Arraba said, after reading one of the signs. She paused for a moment. "If we're inviting everyone to watch, I think we'll need to keep them to one side, rather than all around us. I wouldn't want anyone to be hit by a stray arrow."

Horatio Blastoe pointed to an open area next to the one they had cleared for their tables. ✠*The spectators could sit in the shade at the edge of the forest. The militairres would, of course, await their chance to compete at their respective tables. And I think a platform would be nice on the other side of the spectators.*

"Why do we need a platform?" Felicia asked.

✠*You don't. However, I think it would be nice for overseers who wish to attend and visiting dignitaries, like Furst, to have a special place to view the competition. Not to mention, your judges.*

Arraba turned on a dime. "Won't we, as commanders, be the judges?"

✠*Yes and no. I believe you all deserve a vote, as does Furst, who helped train you. But I also think the overseers and your former curator, Dame Erato, would contribute wonderful insight. Besides, selecting a winner won't always be easy. You may have to disregard a friend's performance in favor of someone not previously regarded as highly. To have the winner selected by committee removes the perception of favoritism and allows you to lead without shadows dimming the light of your command.*

MAL WALKED AROUND the Adventuran lab. "What about housing? Where do hu*bots live?"

Prophet IAN c. spoke without stopping his work. "We have built recharge units into some of the abandoned buildings around the city. We do not need to eat or sleep or provide for our families, so there is no need for individual residences. We only need a minimal column of space for each hu*bot, and we can rotate the recharge periods so that one column can serve several hu*bots over the course of a day. A large structure that may have housed four people in the time before, now can service five thousand hu*bots. It allows Adventurans to stay close to their work in the cities, rather than waste time commuting from the outer districts."

"How would a stranger, like myself, know which hu*bots have earned special prestige?"

"The most prestigious hu*bots quickly move up in rank and can be distinguished by the type of metal sheathing on their arms. You can also tell by their eyes. Most hu*bot eyes are clear glass lenses set into their artificially colored skin. However, some higher ranked hu*bots have earned glass human-like eyes. They may come with yellow, or violet, or red irises. The most prestigious color is violet, with the amount of status declining as colors run through the spectrum from violet to red."

"So, Adventurans don't have money, or personal vehicles, or large houses to symbolize their position in society," Mal said, "but a hu*bot with a gold arm and violet eyes is considered more influential than one with a copper arm and red eyes. And both are more distinguished than a hu*bot with polymer skin and clear glass eyes."

"Yes," Prophet IAN c. agreed. "And no hu*bot can buy those items. They have to earn them with their contributions to our society as a whole."

"I HATE MY brother," Ava complained to Johanna.

"What did he do?"

"He asked some other girl out on a date for tomorrow night."

Johanna felt like someone sucker punched her in the stomach. "You're not talking about Chris, are you?"

It was not a question.

"Jackson is such a jerk." Ava pulled the decimator out of Johanna's hand.

"Ava." Johanna's voice was sharper than she would have liked.

"What?"

"You're too riled up to be holding a dangerous weapon. Hand it back and go cool off."

"I'm all right. I swear. It's just that Jackson makes me so mad sometimes."

"Jackson has to do what he thinks is best for him. Besides, I don't want a boyfriend who is interested in seeing other people. I'm not into playing the dating game. It's better that it came out now, before our relationship progressed."

Ava sighed. "I know...."

"Will you be okay on your own?"

"Yes."

"Good. I didn't eat much for lunch and I need to make dinner."

"You don't have to make dinner. You can order room service."

"Under the circumstances, I think it would be better if I make my own." Johanna gave Ava a hug before leaving the cupola.

Back in her apartment, she looked around for ingredients. Before Jackson declared his freedom, she had ordered everything she would need to make him a lasagna dinner. She originally planned to cook it on the night she would finally confess her love for him. Just because he had a change of heart didn't mean she couldn't enjoy the pasta herself. Instead of thinking about Jackson, she turned on a radio and sang along to the songs being played. The love songs were tough to listen to, but the upbeat songs got her moving, and before she knew it, she was placing her dinner in the oven.

Johanna set the oven alarm on "loud" and left her front door open while she ran upstairs to the cupola to make sure Ava was okay. She found the younger girl pacing like a soldier. The fourteen-year-old took ten steps, turned on a dime, and took another ten steps in the opposite direction.

"You're going to wear a groove in the floor."

"I can either wear a groove in the floor, or make one in Jackson's head."

"You don't mean that."

"Oh, but I do," Ava said.

She was interrupted by Chris. "Good. You're here," he said. "I have to go out tonight for a...study group, and I wanted to make sure you and Jackson are here to help Johanna. See you later." Without waiting for a reply, he was out the door in a shot.

"I'll bet he's not going to any study group," Ava said. "He looks too happy and he smells too good. I bet he's going out with Brittany."

"On a school night?"

"On any night he thinks she might succumb to his charms."

OZZRO HEARD DUNGEN criticizing soldiers in the Dramatican barracks before he actually saw the man. It was soon evident Dungen was looking for Ozzro. Dungen stomped over to him and stood within inches of his face. "Looking for Lenc, you are?"

"Yes," Ozzro replied, trying to keep his voice calm, even though he knew his hands were shaking. He clasped them behind his back to keep them still.

"Why?" Dungen demanded.

"Share a meal, I wish to. Seen him, I have not."

"Nor will you," Dungen said roughly.

Ozzro felt his nerves jitter. *Is Dungen going to confess to Lenc's murder?* "Say that, why do you?" he asked as calmly as possible.

"Gone away, he has. Out of this region, he is."

"Oh?" Ozzro didn't know what else to say.

"Stop looking, you can. Stop asking about him, you can. Gone, he is."

Ozzro sighed. *Is it that easy to kill someone?* "Yes. He is, I suspect."

Dungen narrowed his eyes and stared at Ozzro. "Mean by that, what do you?"

"Nothing. Agreeing with you, I am."

Dungen lowered his voice. "All you're doing, that better be."

Ozzro was scared, but he could smell the other man's fear as well, and wondered if Dungen had already guessed that he knew what happened to Lenc.

THE TIME MACHINE still contained the coordinates Nero 51 had used to propel himself through the pinhole during his last attempt to escape the Terrorian library. Odyon took up a position beside Nero 51 and then disappeared.

"Now where did he go?" Nero 51 screamed as he jerked back a tentacle to fling the crystals used to operate the time machine against its transparent walls. He stopped himself when he thought better of it.

Odyon appeared, demanding, "Are we going, or not?"

"I would have left if you hadn't disappeared."

"I cannot merge with the energy in the pinhole while in human form." Odyon hissed. "I am going to disappear. As soon as I do, go."

Odyon evaporated from sight and Nero 51 thought of his destination. The time machine soon bounced in between the layers of time, looking for the appropriate exit.

Suddenly, Nero 51 felt like he was falling. He blacked out. When he came to, he found himself in a Library of Illumination that was definitely not his own.

HUE THE ELDER called Mal back to Mysteriose. "We have agitators in our midst who are opposed to the tax, or at the very least, currency that has a 'chip' in it. They are afraid of what the chip might do to them."

"I would say, 'that's ridiculous,' however, coming from Fantasia, I can understand their fears. Perhaps a little essential water will allow me to gather my thoughts before speaking to them."

Hue smiled. "Yes, my friend. I can see how that will provide the liquid courage you'll need for this crowd."

The essential water helped galvanize Mal's thoughts. He addressed the crowd, dispelled their fears, and finally got a majority of them to agree to the basic need for a collection of resources, if not taxes.

Hue replaced Mal at the center of the discussion ring and explained that the chip in the currency was developed to keep people from making their own notes and stealing unearned resources from all the others. "The chip you all seem to be so frightened of is there only for our protection. If you prefer not to have it, we can print our own notes, but don't come crying when you go to pick up your allotment of platinum, only to find there is none left because others with forged notes took it all."

The crowd buzzed. Mysterians were not exactly known for their honesty. In the end, the leaders agreed that the notes provided by the College of Overseers were in everyone's best interests, and Mal assured them while he personally took responsibility for the legitimacy of the notes, Hue the Elder would make sure he did it in a way that would not reduce Mysterian resources.

JACKSON SLOWLY CLIMBED the stairs to the cupola. He dreaded seeing Johanna, but he'd promised to take over for Ava. By the time he reached the top of the stairs, all he could think about was the aroma of food coming from Johanna's apartment.

"Hey," he said when he found Johanna with Ava.

"Hi. Are you here to relieve your sister?"

"Yeah."

"Good." She turned to Ava. "Want some lasagna?"

"You made lasagna?" Ava's eyes opened wide. "That's my favorite, but Mom doesn't know how to make it."

"Well, I do, and I'd say it's just about ready for the two of us."

"Hey. What about me?" Jackson asked.

Ava narrowed her eyes. "What about you?"

"Nothing." He picked up the decimator. "See you later."

* * *

MARBOL GATHERED HIS Bullaroot players around him. "I know you all want a chance to score in the final tri-match, but it looks like Duddu is onto us, so I need a second disrupter for his field. Harlo, I think you're the one for the job. And, Waxmo, I need you to replace Fibber, because they expect him and you'll be a big surprise." He meant it literally. Waxmo was bigger than Fibber in both height and weight.

On the opposite side of the field, Duddu discussed a similar strategy with his team and told Elmie and Boxer to continue the good work. Neither of the other two teams assigned disrupters, because none of the players wanted to be prevented from a chance to score.

The shrill vibration of a whistle curtailed the antic chatter of Juveniles. They returned to their spots in the stands to watch the third tri-match.

"Play on!"

Once again, the crowd roared as the players took their respective fields. The captains stood ready to pitch, and when the second whistle sounded, they sent out their best shots.

Both red and blue teams scored target shots on the first pitch. Red scored slightly higher than blue because the ball made contact closer to the center. It seemed like a team scored every single minute, which kept up the excitement and the sound level.

The red team scored another double rebound, which created a frenzy in the stands.

Duddu signaled Boxer, and when their eyes locked, Duddu nodded once. Boxer nodded once in return and positioned himself near Marbol for the next play.

The balls were fired toward the targets and the captains crouched down, ready to run. As Marbol scored a shot once again, he took off toward the left, only to hit the ground hard. He hadn't seen what tripped him and was knocked unconscious when Boxer's foot made contact with his head.

"Captain down! Captain down!" the players called out, and a whistle signaled time out. Red team players carried Marbol off the field to the deafening thunder of stomping feet.

A delay ensued while the three remaining captains discussed discontinuing the game. Duddu assured them that Marbol would have wanted the game to go on.

The game continued with less enthusiasm, but Pye was determined to win—not only for Marbol's sake—but because he, too, had been in the tunnels when the Terrorians had fried, and he didn't want to return. Pye managed to keep the red team two points ahead of the blue team, and the game ended with his own powerful kick sending a ball into the net just before the final whistle.

The red team butted heads, chests, fists, and butts with each other in a show of victory. Duddu and his blue team were strangely quiet, considering they came in second and wouldn't have to clean out the storm drain.

Pollo's teammates whooped with joy when they looked at the scoreboard and realized they had edged out Guffle's green team by one point. They could celebrate with the others while Guffle, Flugle, and their team members excavated the Terrorians' remains.

"Do it now," Pollo advised Guffle, "and you'll

get back in time for some of the celebration."

The yellow team shuffled off, picking up shovels and wheelbarrows along the way. When they got to the storm drain, they divided into groups. One dug a hole to bury the Terrorians in. Another agreed to act like a conveyor, passing buckets of *whatever* from one to the next until it could be emptied in a wheelbarrow. A third would cart the remains to the graves. But the group no one wanted to be part of was the team that had to travel to ground zero inside the storm drain and fill the buckets. Guffle and Flugle accepted that responsibility and grabbed a pile of buckets.

"Wait." Cici walked over and tied a flashlight to the top of Guffle's head. "This way you can see what you're doing." She did the same for Flugle.

The two boys trudged inside the storm drain with their human conveyer belt following behind.

"Yuck," one of the conveyors yelled. "It stinks in here."

Marbol had told them to take the left tunnel, but even if he hadn't, all they would have had to do was follow the overly ripe aroma. They tried not to breathe too deeply. Their progression was halted by a mass of black sludge. Guffle picked at it with his shovel and a chunk fell off. He shoveled it into a bucket, and when it was full, he told them to pass it on. He and Flugle continued on, scraping at the giant mound and shoveling up what fell off. As they continued, it got harder and harder to break apart the remains. But they kept at it, knowing the sooner they finished, the sooner they could join the party of celebrants.

"At this rate, we're never going to finish." He

rammed his shovel into the black mass as hard as he could and screamed—starting a panic—when the mound shifted and moaned.

—LOI—

18

JOHANNA FELT SORRY for Jackson, even if he did have a date with another girl. She had to work with him and depend on him and didn't want to make an enemy of him, so after Ava left, she reheated some lasagna and brought it up to him.

His eyes lit up when she appeared with a plate of food. "Is that for me?"

"Yes."

"I didn't think you'd give me any." He took hold of the plate and dug a fork into the noodles.

"You're my best friend and my co-worker," she said. "Regardless of anything else going on between us, I've still got your back. And considering it's attached to your stomach, I thought I'd bring you some lasagna since there's plenty of it."

Jackson closed his eyes while he swallowed. "This is so good."

"Just bring down the dirty dish when you're done."

"Will do...but it will be late."

"What do you mean?"

"Chris won't be here. He has a hot date tonight, so I'm covering for him."

The smile that Johanna had plastered on her face faded. *I wonder if that's because Chris will be covering for Jackson tomorrow night?* "Right," she said quietly before walking away.

NERO 51 EXITED the time machine and looked around a devastated library. Most of the books and shelves were gone, making it hard for him to tell which realm he and Odyon had managed to penetrate.

Odyon took shape. "From what I can tell, this library is on Romantica. I originally thought it was abandoned until I found several of your species half-unconscious on the ground floor. The outer doors and windows of this facility are locked. I may be able to penetrate them to the outside, but you won't. Is there a particular reason for your species to be on Romantica?"

"I sent them here to destroy the books. Without knowledge, Romantica will crumble. All the realms will crumble when we successfully destroy their libraries. Terroria alone will have all the knowledge in the universe—all the power in the universe. We will rule the realms and everyone on them."

Odyon tilted his head. "You will not rule the realms without my help, and I don't wish to live on Terroria, so you will have to make an exception. I prefer either Mysteriose or Fantasia, having lived on both worlds. Or, perhaps Lumina. What, exactly, *are* your plans for Lumina?"

"Lumina is not one of the twelve realms."

"Of course not, but you cannot conquer the twelve realms without overthrowing Lumina. The deans of the College of Overseers will do everything in their power to quash your rebellion as long as they remain in a position of power. The deans must be taken prisoner, and Lumina must be under your control for any plan to work."

"I did not plan on squandering resources on a world where the overseers have the power to reverse everything I put in place. Without the other realms at their beck and call, Lumina will be an empty power."

"Are you blind or just plain stupid? As soon as you destroy books on any realm, the overseers will replace them. You will not be able to make any meaningful progress until you take Lumina." Odyon ripped off the edge of a broken shelf and threw it to the ground.

"You want me to decimate the overseers?"

Odyon paused. His mind raced. "No. I'll handle the overseers. Lumina will be my new home. Continue what you're doing. You've given me an idea."

"You told me you would teach me how to appear and disappear like you do. You told me we would have power over the portals. Both of us. I will do nothing until you have made good on your promise."

Odyon disappeared.

Nero 51 waited for the shapeshifter to reappear. He waited hours. When Odyon didn't reappear, he went in search of his troopers. Perhaps he already had power over the portals now that he had successfully landed on Romantica. If so, he could start transporting his soldiers home.

He found a few Terrorians lying listlessly on the main floor. He tried to rouse them, but they had too little energy to respond. He sighed. *I'm going to have to drag each of them up the cupola stairs.* He approached the closest soldier and dragged him a short way. The strap to the soldier's decimator caught onto a piece of furniture. He dropped the soldier's shoulders and pulled the decimator free. He looked at the others littering the floor. *They are no longer any use to me.* He grabbed a decimator and put them out of their misery, turning them all to dust.

JACKSON WATCHED JOHANNA retreat down the stairs, momentarily forgetting about the plate of food in his hand. *What am I doing? What have I done?* Guilt flowed into every cell of his being. He thought about his date with Emily. He felt more anxious than excited and very confused.

His phone vibrated in his pocket. He answered it awkwardly. "Hello?"

"Hi Jackson, it's Emily."

He nearly dropped his plate. "How did you get this number?"

"Cassie Turner just called and gave it to me. We're double-dating tomorrow and she called to tell me you just got this new number. Is it okay that I called?"

"Sure," Jackson said, keeping his voice down.

"Why are you whispering?"

"Uh…because I'm in a library."

"Oh, that makes sense."

And I don't want Johanna to hear me.

* * *

"EVERYBODY OUT NOW!"

Juveniles scrambled out of the storm drain after Guffle screamed. One or more could have been trampled, but instead, they ran out one after the other, linking hands like a long chain.

Bungie abandoned the grave he was digging and ran to the mouth of the storm drain. "What's wrong? What happened?"

"One of the monsters is still alive," Flugle said. "We heard him moan."

"Someone's got to kill it, then," Bungie said. "Who will it be?"

Flugle gasped. "It's not going to be me."

They all looked at Guffle.

"What?"

Bungie grabbed both his shoulders. "You've got to go back in there and kill that thing."

Guffle's head rotated from side to side. "I already removed the other one. It's someone else's turn."

"It should be one of the older kids," a younger boy shouted. "You have 'sperience."

Bungie and Guffle were the two oldest ones. They tried to outstare each other until Flugle said, "Rock, paper, scissors. It's the only fair way to do it."

Everyone nodded, recognizing the wisdom of Flugle's words. They started to chant, "Rock, paper, scissors... rock, paper, scissors...rock, paper, scissors...."

Finally, the two eldest boys nodded and took position.

"Best three out of five," Flugle said.

"No," someone else cried. "Do four out of seven."

"Do I hear five out of nine?" Bungie's words dripped with sarcasm.

"Yeah," Guffle said, staring at him. "Five out of nine."

Bungie accepted the challenge. "You're on."

The two of them pumped their hands as they said in unison, "Rock, paper, scissors, shoot."

Guffle took the lead to cheers from the team when his rock crushed scissors. But Bungie quickly rebounded when his paper covered Guffle's rock. Bungie won a second round in a row, but Guffle tied the score with his next move. They each scored another point in the fifth and sixth rounds.

The seventh round went to Bungie, followed by two tie rounds. Then, Guffle evened the score again. The ninth and last round would be the deciding game. "Rock, paper, scissors, shoot!"

Bungie put in paper.

Guffle put in scissors.

Mope 98 put in a tentacle.

DEAN PROTEUS BLIGH walked through the Mysterian caves and observed all the natural resources the realm had to offer. Off to the side, tables were set up where community leaders packaged equal measures of minerals or herbs, numbered the package, assigned it to a note of currency, and inserted the information on identical master lists to be held by Hue the Elder at the Library of Illumination and Malcolm Trees, the Chancellor of the Exchequer.

Ψ*You have your work cut out for you.*

"Yes," Mal agreed. "It's a bit more structured than Mysterians are used to, but necessary to ensure all are treated fairly."

"It will certainly keep me busy," Hue the Elder added. "It's much more documentation than I previously had to worry about. We've gone from a single notation, like 'a cart of silver ore,' to dozens of entries for smaller packages of the same ore. But once it is set up, our reserves will be easier to track."

"Can anyone enter and exit the caves at will?" Malcolm asked.

"We've never had a problem before," Hue answered, "a least, not a big problem."

Ψ*You're saying there has been some theft in the past.*

Hue nodded slowly. "Yes."

Ψ*I will ask Ryden Simmdry if the College of Overseers might agree to install gates in the caves.*

Hue squared his shoulders. "That move might upset local leaders, not because you're protecting resources, but because it looks like you don't trust the people of Mysteriose."

Ψ*They will have to learn to accept it. Malcolm, you'll handle that, won't you?*

"Of course," Mal agreed. "They already dislike me. They might as well have a valid reason to hate me."

Proteus Bligh and Hue both looked concerned until Mal said he was joking and assured them he would be happy to help.

MAL LOOKED AT the deans gathered around the conference table at the College of Overseers. "So, as you can see, Adventura has absolutely no use for my services as Chancellor of the Exchequer, which means I have no excuse for visiting that realm."

⌘*A problem, indeed.*

π*Do you think they could be dangerous?*

⌘*Only in consideration of their role in history. They were part of the first triumvirate that instigated the Two Millennia War.*

"However," Mal said, "I've spoken with them, and in my opinion, there is no reason to believe they will repeat history."

Σ*When I first met with him to discuss the Terrorian invasion, Prophet IAN c. went so far as to ask, "If they," meaning the Terrorians, "choose to make the same mistakes over again, must we," meaning the Adventurans, "also be punished?"*

⌘*Unfortunately, this eliminates the opportunity for Malcolm to be our eyes and ears on Adventura, unless we can think of another plausible reason for him to be there.*

Mal looked around the table. "They seem overly impressed by earning prestige. Perhaps we could propose the Adventurans help us in a way that builds prestige?"

⌘*Continue....*

"I don't have any ideas right now, so any suggestions would be appreciated."

THE AIR ON Romantica was crisp and clean, perfect for the militairres' competition. The men who lived on Romantica had been employed overnight to help the women build a platform for visiting dignitaries, as well as several bleachers to accommodate a large crowd. Pairs of oversized platoon flags were created and nailed to poles, and flag bearers were selected to lead the militairres in a parade past the spectators and judges. Dame Erato had assembled a contingent of Romantican cooks to prepare refreshments. And, a group of musicians had agreed to play between contests. In all, the day of competition had taken on the spirit of a holiday.

In the hour following first light, Master Ryden Simmdry arrived to officiate, along with Deans Horatio Blastoe, Pru Tellerence, Zenith Fullova, and Chancellor of the Exchequer, Malcolm Trees. Furst and Dame Erato would be joining them on the platform. If Natalia Dalura hadn't been needed to command a platoon, she would have had a place of honor on the platform as well. However, as an active militairre, her place was on the field, even if her talents and those of the other commanders were not being judged that day.

Before long, the stands filled up and a flourish of horns signaled the beginning of the event.

The militairres had gathered under the tent with the flaps down, however, when the horns sounded, two civilians opened the flaps and each platoon marched forward two-by-two. The militairres split right and left, circling the entire field and passing each other at the midpoint, which elicited positive comments from the crowd, who marveled at their ease of movement without sacrificing Romantican style.

Once they all reassembled at the starting point, curator Natalia Dalura addressed the crowd.

"Friends, neighbors, and distinguished guests. Today is a proud day in Romantican history. While we wish the circumstances that call for a fighting militia did not exist, we are more than ready to rise to the challenge. Today, we will demonstrate all that we have accomplished in a very short time.

"Our reason is twofold. Not only do we want to give you a chance to share in the joy of our accomplishments but also to bear witness as the top two contenders in each specialty are elevated to the rank of captain for that platoon.

"We are honored today to be joined by Master Ryden Simmdry." Natalia went on to introduce the other deans from the College of Overseers and Furst.

"Now, I must take my place as commander of the hand combat unit so we can initiate our roll call."

She walked over and stood between her platoon's standard bearers. The crowd quieted. She nodded at Arraba.

"Archers. Roll call. Commander Arraba Jolen." Each archer down the line called out militairre and added her full name after it. Weaponry went next, followed by stick fighting, and hand combat.

Immediately afterward, everyone except the archers marched off the field.

NERO 51 REFUSED to wait any longer for Odyon. He'd had enough of the Romantican library. He entered the time machine and took hold of the crystals.

"It's about time." Odyon took shape right next to him.

The curator's voice held fire and ice. "Have you been here the whole time?"

"No. I traveled as a beam of light through a window pane and looked around the city of Roma. They have created a militia. A female fighting troop. They are busy competing against each other to prepare for your soldiers. If your troopers had been able to exit the library, they may have been able to take control of this city. I don't believe you will come up against much resistance here that your soldiers cannot handle.

"I suggest we return to your library. Once again, I will turn into energy so I can merge with the pinpoint you previously took us through. I believe it will take more than one trip to turn that tiny opening into a fully-working portal. In the meantime, I will teach you the skills you'll need to become a shapeshifter."

Happy with Odyon's explanation, Nero 51 thought about home as soon as the shapeshifter disappeared.

IN THE JUVENILIA Town Square, the children sang, danced, and boasted about their team's prowess on the Bullaroot field. In the center of the square, dozens of youngsters held the edge of a large trampoline-like net and bounced their friends into the air. Their squeals of delight were long and loud. But they were not unrivaled.

"Aaaeeeiiiyyy!" Not too far away, the youngsters who had been assigned cleanup duties panicked and bolted, not wanting to come face-to-face with a monster thought dead.

"Get the flamethrower," Guffle yelled.

But Bungie didn't budge. Instead, he appeared to be glued to the spot as he stared into the hollowed-out eyes of Mope 98.

The Terrorian said something unintelligible. Bungie remained paralyzed, his hand still held out flat like a sheet of paper.

Mope 98 turned and slowly moved away. He slipped into the water, and with what little strength he had remaining, propelled himself slowly to the center of the pond.

Guffle came running back with the flamethrower and lit the end.

Mope 98 pressed on his biometric band, releasing poison into his system. As he felt himself fading, he exhaled all his breath and sunk to the bottom of the pond.

Guffle and Bungie waited all night for the Terrorian to resurface, but he never did.

—LOI—

19

JACKSON WOKE WHEN he heard his bedroom door close. It was after two a.m. "Well, little brother, where have you been?"

"Having dinner with Brittany."

"Where did you take her?"

"We stayed in."

"Stayed in?"

"We ate at home."

"You ate with her parents?"

"No. Nothing like that. They weren't there."

"So you stayed in, because no one was there in a supervisory capacity."

"Now you're getting the picture."

"I hope it was worth it."

"It was worth every minute of it, big bro. Every minute."

Jackson rolled over. *I'm supposed to be the older, more sophisticated and worldly Roth. He's supposed to be the younger, eager, but not quite as sophisticated*

Roth. Where did I go wrong?

SEVERAL TARGETS WERE set up on the far end of what Romanticans now called Militairre Meadow. Five young women, each with three arrows, took a position on the field. Every time Arraba gave them the signal, they shot one arrow, until all three were fired. Everyone hit the target at least once, but no one hit the bullseye. The two best shooters for each round were told to wait at the edge of the field. The others were allowed to go back to their table under the tent. During the next phase of the competition, the remaining girls were asked to destroy flying clay and feather pigeons that they had all worked so diligently to make. Four of the women succeeded. Those four were instructed to do so again. Only one of them succeeded the second time.

Arraba approached the bench. "We have our first winners!"

⌘*The results seem far from conclusive.*

There was a moment of silence as the overseers telepathically communicated among themselves.

✠*We would like to see all four of the archers who advanced to shooting clay birds do so again. We are assuming you have enough devices for another round.*

"Yes, I'll see to it immediately."

✠*Not yet. We'll bring them back after the other disciplines have had a chance to compete. You can tell your sister she can begin the weaponry competition.*

Arraba told the girls to take a seat until later and nodded at her sister.

Milencia's troops lined up in much the same way as their predecessors while small wooden stands were each topped with a rock. On her signal, the militairres each fired three times. The best of them were then instructed to fire at rocks catapulted into the air. Once again, no final determination was made, and the militairres were told to wait with their platoon.

The sticks competition was a little more heated, because the women fought against each other. Some were graceful, others positively intimidating, but they all fought aggressively, trying not to be bested in front of their friends and neighbors.

Natalia's grapplers were the last group to go. These women not only relied on the strength of their arms but also on the agility of their legs and bodies. While the grapplers battled each other on the field, the spectators learned to fully appreciate the efficiency of the militairres' uniforms, for it was the grapplers who most needed the freedom of movement provided by pants.

Horatio Blastoe stood up after the last grappling session ended. ✠*We hope you will all enjoy the refreshments provided while the young women who are advancing to the final round are given their instructions. The competition will continue in a half-measure.*

During the intermission, several young women inquired about joining the militairres. The youngest adolescents were discouraged by Dame Erato, but a decision was made to allow older teens to try out for each of the four disciplines the following week. It would, however, be a private induction process, and not a public spectacle. Some would-be militairres turned away, disappointed, and withdrew their requests to join. They only wanted to perform in front of their friends and families. However, the majority of those showing interest agreed to return in five days' time.

Finally, the musicians stopped playing, and Dame Erato instructed everyone to find a seat.

JACKSON CLIMBED THE steps to the Fantasian cupola right after breakfast. He expected to see Ava guarding the portals, but instead he found Johanna.

"How long have you been here?"

"A few hours. I wanted to let your sister get some sleep."

Jackson smiled, but only on one side of his face, causing a dimple.

Johanna handed him the weapon. "She really likes guarding the portals."

"She probably feels like she'll prove her worth if she can kill some Terrorians."

"She doesn't need to kill any Terrorians to do that. Your sister has already gained my respect."

"I think I'll tell her you said that."

"Go ahead. She deserves to hear it."

"Why don't you go get breakfast. I've got the day off, so I might as well put in some time."

"Oh. Right. You're not going to be here tonight."

Jackson felt his face go hot. "Chris will be here. He'll cover for me. You won't even miss me."

If Johanna saw him blush, she didn't give him any indication of it. Instead, she turned and walked away. Quickly.

GUFFLE SHUFFLED INTO the Juvenilia Town Hall.

Everyone who saw him asked the same question. "Did you kill the monster?"

He shrugged. "He jumped into the pond. I never saw him again."

"Does that mean he's dead?"

"I don't know. We thought he was dead before. He wasn't."

"So now what are we supposed to do?"

Guffle snorted. "Stay away from the pond."

"What if he comes looking for us?"

"I don't think he will. He looked terrible. Burnt. Weak. He smelled like death. I think he went into the pond to die."

"Now what?" Pollo asked.

"I have an idea," Marbol said. He went into a room he often used to create gadgets and test new inventions. He picked up a bag and stuffed it with odds and ends.

Duddu leaned against the doorjamb, folding his arms. "You're not staying?"

Marbol closed the bag. "I need to test something out at home. I want to play with sound waves. I think if I find the right pitch, we can bust through the windows of the library and get inside. Anyway, you've got Guffle here to help you."

Bungie shook his head forcefully. "Breaking into the library is a terrible idea."

"We have to find out if there are any more of their kind here, and we have to deal with whatever we find. Or would you rather wait until someone is choked to death while they sleep?" He looked into the eyes of each person surrounding him, and when Marbol felt satisfied his remark had hit home, he left.

* * *

MASTER RYDEN SIMMDRY transported to Mysteriose for a quick visit with Proteus Bligh and Hue the Elder about the merit of installing gates in the caves storing the realm's natural resources. At the conclusion of their discussion, they visited the entrance to every cave, and an alarmed, locked gate system magically appeared. Even the smallest of openings was gated to ensure the safety of Mysterian assets. The master then excused himself, saying his presence was required on Romantica. Proteus Bligh and Hue the Elder were left to deal with the repercussions.

The new gates didn't sit well with a number of influential Mysterians, who felt their autonomy had been usurped. It scored even lower on the popularity scale with lesser citizens.

Dissenters crowded the discussion tiers at Town Hall to decry the gates. When the loudest opponents couldn't come up with valid reasons why the gates were such a bad idea, other than it made them look like they couldn't be trusted, their arguments were disregarded.

"It is too late," Hue the Elder said. "The system is in place. And for better or worse, it is here to stay."

A few people, however, refused to be dissuaded. They spoke together in hushed tones about measures that could be taken to destroy the gates.

ODYON PRACTICALLY HISSED at Nero 51. "You are not trying." The shapeshifter had asked the Terrorian to concentrate his thoughts as a precursor to transmogrifying into a beam of sound or light. The way things were going, it looked like that would never happen. Not that he'd ever thought it would. But he had to make sure

Nero 51 knew that he, Odyon, had done his part to train the Terrorian, and Nero 51 was responsible for his own failure.

"Take a deep breath, and hum a single note while exhaling. Like this." Odyon closed his eyes, inhaled deeply, and hummed, "Oooooooooooo...." He opened his eyes. "Now you do it."

Nero 51 closed his eyes. "Rrrihhhhhhhhrrr...." It sounded more like a death rattle than a tone. The Terrorian opened his eyes and stared at Odyon.

"What were you thinking about while you exhaled?" Odyon asked.

"How positively useless this exercise is."

"That is why you'll never learn. Your mind should be a blank. Like white light. Or a whisper. You will never achieve your goal unless you release all your thoughts, relax completely, and unite with the atmosphere around you. Try again."

Nero 51 closed his eyes and released the same strangled gurgle.

"Now what are you thinking?"

"How I'd like to wrap my tentacles around your neck and squeeze the life out of you."

"We both know how impossible that would be for you. I suggest you clear your mind and start again."

And so it went for the next hour.

"I'm tired of doing this," the Terrorian complained. "Is there no other exercise you could teach me?"

"You're not tired enough. I want you to run up and down the cupola stairs five times each way."

"That's ridiculous."

"No. I think it will help immensely. But it won't work if you don't do it as fast as you possibly can. Starting now. Go."

Nero 51 hesitated and Odyon picked up a ruler from the circulation desk and hit him. Considering it was crystal, it made quite an impression, of the painful variety.

Nero 51 ran up the cupola steps. By the time he reached the top, he huffed and puffed but knew descending the steps would be easier.

"Again," Odyon called out when the curator returned to the bottom.

It took Nero 51 considerably longer to reach the cupola on the second climb. He also descended more slowly.

"Again," Odyon said.

"No." Nero 51 had reached his limit.

Odyon whacked him with the ruler. "Climb!"

Nero 51 trudged up the cupola stairs. When he returned, Odyon told him to inhale, close his eyes, and hum.

Nero 51 was too exhausted to think. "Hmmmmmmmmm." For the first time, he realized that humming had a certain vibrato that filled him, not just his mind, but even the blood in his veins. He opened his eyes when he had finished exhaling and looked at Odyon.

"There was a difference. What were you thinking?"

"I thought about how the sound vibrated."

"You shouldn't be thinking at all, but at least you are making progress. Go off to your private chamber and show Garpa what you have learned. I think I need a little time of my own."

Nero 51 was happy to get away. As soon as he was out of sight, Odyon turned into a breath of air and entered the time machine.

OZZRO ENTERED THE Dramatican Library of Illumination, one of only two libraries still open to inhabitants of a realm. A soldier was stationed at the circulation desk.

"Come back, has Furst?"

"No. Still away, he is."

"Ever returning, is he?"

"Not say, he did."

Ozzro sighed. He needed to speak to someone about what was going on but knew the only person who could help him, besides Furst, was the father of the man he knew to be a murderer.

Someone entered the library behind him. "Morning, good."

Ozzro turned as he saw the soldier look over his shoulder. "You, Pondor, how are?" asked the soldier.

"Fine. Seen Lenc, have either of you?"

Ozzro felt the blood drain from his face but refused to let the moment pass. "Since he fought, seen him, I haven't."

Pondor's brows shot up. "Fought? Terrorians, more?"

"Not Terrorians. A Dramatican, he fought with."

Pondor's bushy red eyebrow shot up. "See him fight with, who did you?"

"Was dark, the night. In the shadows, they were."

Pondor pressed on. "Hear the man's voice, did you?"

Ozzro could feel sweat beading on his forehead. "Not sure, I am."

"Who you suspect, tell me."

Ozzro's stomach turned to a cold lump of clay. "Cannot…" He crumpled to the ground.

Ozzro choked, afraid he would drown. He sat up suddenly to find someone had thrown a bucket of water in his face.

"Ozzro, okay, are you?"

Ozzro felt his heart rate quicken as he stared into Pondor's eyes. His voice quivered. "Fine, I am."

"My office, please, come to," Pondor whispered. "Alone there, we can talk. Scared, I can see you are."

"No." Ozzro pushed himself to his feet. "Nothing to tell, I have."

"Something to tell, you do have. Feel it in my heart, I can. Be honest with me, you must." Pondor turned to one of the soldiers manning the library. "To my chambers, help him, will you?"

"Sir, yes." The soldier took Ozzro's arm and led him away.

Every step toward Pondor's office was steeped in agony. If Ozzro lied, Pondor would know. If he told the truth, Pondor would never forgive him.

Ozzro felt like he was being escorted down the *last measure*. Very few Dramaticans had ever been executed, but the last measure had been established following the Two Millennia War to execute war criminals remaining on Dramatica, and still remained in existence.

—LOI—

20

Johanna wished the cupola stairs would allow her to exit onto another level without having to go all the way down to the first floor. She didn't want to run into any of the Roths. She didn't feel like talking about Jackson, or explaining why she had tears in her eyes, or why her voice trembled.

She lucked out. She made it all the way to her residence without seeing anyone. She splashed cold water on her face and brewed a cup of coffee. Once she felt sufficiently composed, she returned to the main floor to check on new orders.

Part of her still felt numb, but she forced herself to work through the day as if nothing was wrong. She even managed to stay cool when Ava came out to relieve Jackson as a portal guard. "Hey, Ava. You're going up a little early, aren't you?"

"Yeah. Jackson said he needs time to shower and shave before he leaves for Logan's house. They're going to hang out for a while before…you know."

"Thanks for covering for him. I couldn't do it alone. I'll make sure you get something special for dinner later."

Ava smiled. "Okay."

THE INSIDE OF Pondor's office was inviting but not lavish. It exemplified the workspace of a humble justice of the people. Ozzro crumpled into a chair after Pondor motioned for him to sit down. Ozzro's erratic breathing gave away his mounting unease.

The judge wasted no time. "Threatened you, has someone?"

Ozzro's eyes went wide. "No." He practically choked on the word.

Pondor leaned forward and kept his voice even. "Happened, something has."

Ozzro thought carefully about what he would say. His voice registered barely above a whisper. "Hear a fight, I did. Like Lenc, one person sounded. Gruff, the other man was. Angry. In the shadows, he stood. Challenge him, Lenc did. A cape, the other man wore. From under it, a decimator, he removed. My eyes, I closed. Only one man I could see, when again, I looked."

Both Dramaticans jumped when the door to Pondor's office flew open with such force it slammed against the wall.

Dungen stomped in, his face red and his ringlets tight. "A liar, you are!"

Pondor stared down his son. "Know of this, what do you?" he asked in a neutral voice.

"To discredit me, Ozzro is here." Dungen placed his hands on his hips and leaned forward. "Move, his friend did, from him, to get away."

Pondor nodded at his son. "See, I." He gracefully stood and walked behind his desk. When he turned, he took in his son's appearance. "Joined the militia, have you?"

"No. Of myself, I take care."

Pondor nodded, then looked past Dungen at a clerk standing in the doorway. "A member of the militia, I will need."

Ozzro's shoulders sagged.

A hint of a smile crossed Dungen's face. "Failed, your plan to ruin my name has. A lesson, let that be. The key, I hope they throw away."

Mudge, one of Dramatica's military strategists, entered the room. "Need for a soldier, you have?"

"For a police matter, it is," Pondor said.

Mudge walked around Dungen and approached Ozzro, looking at Pondor for confirmation.

Pondor shook his head ever so slightly.

Mudge stopped as he stared at the judge.

Pondor tilted his head toward his son. "Dungen."

Mudge swung around in time to stop Dungen from unholstering the weapon. "You fool, not me," Dungen shouted. "To arrest Ozzro, you are here."

"Dungen, No," Pondor said in a steely voice. "Military, you are not. Permitted a weapon, you are not."

"At him, look!" Dungen shouted, turning his head toward Ozzro. "Shaking, he is, because, guilty, he is."

"Shaking, he is, because, you are my son, he knows."

"A fool, he is," Dungen yelled, squirming away

from Mudge. He ran from the room, managing to unholster the decimator. He aimed it wildly at anyone who got in his way.

"Sir?" Mudge said.

"Some soldiers, gather," Pondor said. "My son, pursue. The disappearance of Lenc, charge him with. And, a military weapon, illegal possession of."

"Did not, I..." Ozzro stuttered.

"Honorable, you were. But, my suspicions, I had. Confirmed, now they are. Erratic, Dungen has become. Like his mother, he is. Unstable."

JACKSON EMERGED FROM the George V suite looking like a male model. He wore a fitted shirt and his leather tie with a pair of black jeans. The scent of his aftershave swirled around him like a heady cloud. He saw Johanna looking at him. "Hey. Going over to Logan's. Everything okay?"

She nodded. "You may overpower him with your aftershave. But it will probably fade in time for your date."

Jackson's jaw dropped a bit. "You think it's too much?"

"A little. For now. I'm sure Logan will let you know if it's too strong. Or at least Cassie will."

Jackson squirmed. He felt funny hearing Johanna talk about his date and his friends. *Our friends.* "I'd better go. You're right about Logan, though. He'll keep me from making a fool out of myself. I think."

She smiled. "Good night."

Conversation over.

* * *

MAL WALKED THROUGH the walled garden in the College of Overseers, collecting his thoughts.

⌘ *Greetings, Malcolm. Communing with nature?*

"No. Just trying to work out a plan that would allow us to interact with the Adventurans. I think the best way to handle it is to appeal to their pride. Tell them that we know they will not repeat history like the Terrorians, and it is because of their strength and commitment that we would like to establish a three hu*bot panel to advise us on how Terrorians might react to certain specific situations. However, I don't know if telling them they are the only realm to assist us in this way would make them suspicious or believe they are wrongly being interrogated."

⌘ *First of all, only two realms could possibly fit the bill: the Adventurans and the Mysterians. It is pretty universally known that some Mysterians can't be trusted. That would include the former curator named Magra, a high priestess who was removed from that prestigious position after Pru Tellerence discovered her selling the services of her library, rather than allowing residents to freely use its books for recreation. It was an ugly occurrence that resulted in the downfall of Magra, as well as Pru Tellerence's eventual re-assignment to Dramatica after she lost her effectiveness on Mysteriose.*

⌘ *So there is no reason to think the Adventurans would be suspicious of your motives. But, let's take it a step further. What do you think, besides prestige, Adventurans want, perhaps not individually, but rather as a civilization?*

"I don't really know. They don't seem to have a need for anything."

⌘*I believe there was mention of how their population is slowly diminishing in diversity as some bloodlines died out.*

"Yes. Prophet IAN c. mentioned that. But he said it wouldn't happen any time in the near future."

⌘*Suppose we offered them live cell cultures from some of our most accomplished individuals. Luminan scientists, engineers, even poets and musicians. Imagine if entities, who have already proven their abilities beyond the average being, could be used by Adventurans to replace originators who die out. That might be incentive for them to agree to consult with us on a regular basis. It would give them something they need, and would give those brokering such an arrangement a certain amount of prestige.*

"Yes. It would, wouldn't it." Mal placed his hand on Ryden Simmdry's shoulder. "I can see why you are Master of the College of Overseers. You certainly master all the problems laid before you. As if by magic."

⌘*Magic, Malcolm? I didn't think you believed in magic.*

"How could I not? I used to be curator of a Library of Illumination. If they're not magical, I don't know what is."

⌘*I like to think they have* special properties. *When most people hear the word "magic" they think of a lot of hocus-pocus. Special properties is a much better way to describe what takes place in our libraries.*

GUFFLE INSPECTED THE back wall of the Juvenilia library, looking for broken glass. He'd shattered one of the windows the first time he used his sonic scrambler. But he and his friends couldn't enter the library through the opening. An invisible force field prevented them from going inside. There were other glass windows, and he hoped if he found the right frequency, he'd be able to shatter one of them and get inside. But first, he needed samples of the glass to test his theory.

He didn't design the sonic scrambler to break glass. He made it to scramble people's brain waves and cause confusion. However, considering one of its frequencies had worked on glass, he would attempt to fine-tune it. He didn't want to break all the glass in the library. That would be irresponsible and would cut down on everyone's candy and ice cream allowance, because they'd all have to forfeit *something* to fix the windows. Only a couple of Juveniles knew how to make glass, and they only accepted candy and ice cream vouchers as payment. The good thing was, they didn't like cake and cookies, but still, those desserts didn't taste as good without chocolate, and you could only get that with a candy voucher.

Back at home, he grabbed the parts he needed to create a second sonic scrambler and sat at his workbench. He didn't want to mess up his first scrambler. It worked just fine on the bullies who bothered his sister. This second one might not work as well on people, but he had every intention of making it a vital enemy to glass.

SHORTLY AFTER THE Mysterian sun began its descent, a dozen agitated residents stormed the cave housing their iridium. They carried a large log, which they rammed against the gate with all their strength in an effort to take it down. A half-dozen tries later, they gave up. The gate not only held but also didn't show a scratch. They concluded the gates must be enchanted.

Pagaron, a young man training as a priest in one of Mysteriose's more arbitrary orders, studied the edges where the gates met the stone walls. "We need explosives."

A local trader looked unconvinced. "If we couldn't even make a dent with a battering ram, what makes you think explosives will work on this gate?"

Pagaron looked at her as if she were an ignorant child. "It's not what explosives will do to the gate. It's what they will do to the rock surrounding those gates. If we can't go through the gates, we'll just have to go around them."

"I have an even better idea," said the assistant of a Mecox priest. "Val Dvir has a weapon, of reportedly Terrorian design, that pulverizes its targets. I've seen it work. It's supposed to have come from the overseers themselves to help protect our realm against the creatures who designed it. All we have to do is borrow it."

Pagaron stared at the man called Nycose. "What makes you think he would lend it to us?"

"He is reproducing them in bulk, and he probably wouldn't notice if one went missing."

Pagaron eyed the assistant warily. "When do you plan to make that happen?"

Nycose stretched and stared for a moment at the setting sun. "I'll meet you back here at daybreak."

"WHAT WOULD YOU do, Garpa?" Nero 51 asked the portrait of his grandfather after reflecting on what had almost seemed like a wasted exercise. The Terrorian realized something had changed and decided to not stop training with Odyon. But confusion overwhelmed him. He'd felt like he lost control the last time he had chanted, and even though he presumed it necessary for shapeshifting, it made him feel uncomfortable. He cherished being in control of himself and the situation around him. Garpa had ingrained within Nero 51 that loss of control equals failure.

His last exercise with Odyon left the curator totally fatigued. He was even too tired to wonder what the shapeshifter was up to, while he stood talking to a picture on the wall.

ODYON FELT CONFIDENT he knew the inner workings of the time machine better than its creator. He wanted Nero 51 to return and project the machine back through the pinhole. He was sure, this time, he would be able to restructure the apparatus internally so that it could transcend the portals and deliver him wherever he wanted to be, at any point in time. However, he knew Nero 51 needed time to grasp what he had learned earlier in the day.

Odyon thought about their lesson. At first, he couldn't believe Nero 51 had trouble emptying his mind and concentrating on a single tone. *It's child's play*. Later, he was equally astounded when the curator actually changed his tone and admitted the vibrato had taken over his being.

Odyon wasn't sure he wanted Nero 51 to succeed as a shapeshifter, but he wouldn't bother worrying about that until it came to pass. Right now, he needed him to power the time machine.

* * *

THE ROMANTICAN ARCHERS and weaponry militairres who had advanced earlier were given an opportunity to shoot additional targets. Some militairres who had not performed well that morning hit their marks later in the day, while others who had scored in the earlier session, missed their afternoon targets. Two people consistently hit every target they focused on, making the choice easier.

⚕*Ryden Simmdry, as always, your wisdom has proven that decisions made in haste are often ill-fated.*

⌘*Indeed.*

The final sessions for the stick fighters and grapplers was not as precise. The judges had to consider whether ground was gained during the confrontation. And they needed to determine who was truly talented, compared to those who were merely lucky. While some finalists fought against each other, a few were paired with people from their platoon who did not make it to the finals, but who were equal to them in size and weight. One of the women disqualified during the morning actually ended up as one of the top two choices for her platoon. Her skills were formidable, but earlier in the day she had been paired with someone much smaller than herself whom she had been afraid of injuring.

The musicians were asked to play a flourish signaling the conclusion of the competition. Horatio Blastoe held up his hands to silence the crowd. Ryden Simmdry stood to announce the winners. But first, the master discussed the difficulties the judges faced weighing the performances of each young woman, and the adjustments they made to their initial assessments. The crowd listened patiently. Finally, he divulged the names of the top competitors. Each new co-captain walked to the platform to thank the judges when her name was announced. Pru Tellerence presented the women with silver and sapphire triquetras to affix to the left side of their uniforms and jackets. Afterward, she invited Natalia, Arraba, Felicia, and Milencia to come up to the platform and gave each commander a pair of gold and diamond triquetras to signify their leadership roles.

Dame Erato presented the commanders with bouquets of rosalies, fragrant long-stemmed Romantican flowers that combined the best features of roses and lilies, ending the formal presentation.

As everyone chatted amiably in the afterglow, a sudden explosion rocked them.

Beyond the trees, where the Romantican Library of Illumination stood, a massive column of smoke and flames soared up toward the heavens.

—LOI—

21

LOGAN AND CASSIE waited in the car while Jackson went to the door to get Emily. He felt a wave of relief when she answered the door herself, but the butterflies in his stomach went ballistic when she pulled him into the family room to meet her parents. Her father grilled Jackson about school and his plans for the future, as well as where Jackson would be taking his daughter for dinner, what movie they'd be seeing, and what time he would bring her home.

Jackson answered all the questions and used the time as an excuse to leave, because they wouldn't want to "miss" the movie.

As they walked to the car, he said, "Does your father interrogate all your dates like that?"

"Yes."

"Wow."

"He wants to make sure you have the best of intentions. I'm an only child. I guess that's what parents do when they've only got one child."

"Oh." Jackson didn't know what else to say. Most of his past "dates" had been group dates with girls he'd known forever, so he'd never had to "meet" anyone's parents. Johanna didn't have any parents, so he didn't have to go through that with her. *I hope I don't have to go on too many more first dates. Meeting a girl's family is a killer.*

Cassie turned when they got into the car. "Hey, Em. Welcome to Brad."

Logan thumped the steering wheel with his hands. "This car is *not* named Brad."

"Sure, it is. It's a Mini-*Cooper*."

"Hi, Cass. Logan. Did you notice how fast Jackson dragged me out of the house? I'll bet he thought my father was going to tie him to a chair so he could batter him with more questions."

Cassie laughed. "At least you got the whole meet-the-parents thing out of the way."

They talked about classes, graduation, and summer plans all the way to the theater and until the movie began.

Without thinking, Jackson put his arm around Emily like he always did with Johanna. He turned red, but no one noticed it in the darkened theater. And Emily didn't push him away or squirm, so he just left his arm there. Halfway through the film, two of the zombie characters fell in love. He felt Emily nestle her head against his shoulder. He turned to joke, "their love will never die," when he saw Logan and Cassie sucking out each other's tonsils. He stopped dead. Emily tilted her face toward his and kissed him. *Surprise.* All thoughts of Johanna evaporated. *Emily Brent wants to kiss. Who am*

I to deny her?

The problem with movie theaters is the utter lack of privacy. And space. And he knew Logan's car would be too small to do anything more than push them together. Snuggling was one thing. Maneuvering would be out of the question. *Why am I thinking about this? We haven't even had dinner yet.* He felt his stomach drop. The thought of eating at Piccolo Italia where he could run into anyone he knew, including Johanna, or his mother, didn't feel like a good idea, but he'd suck it up and accept the consequences.

In the end, he needn't have worried. Logan pulled up in front of a restaurant in a neighboring village. Jackson helped Emily out of the car. "Where are we?"

"Mama Marcella's Trattoria," Logan said as he locked the car. "I thought we'd try someplace new for a change."

Jackson looked through the leaded glass windows into the dimly-lit restaurant and saw couples sitting at candlelit tables.

Emily grabbed Jackson's hand. "It looks so romantic."

"Doesn't it?" Cassie agreed with enthusiasm. "I've always wanted to eat at a place like this."

Inside, the maître d' asked if they had a reservation.

"Elliott," Logan answered. "Party of four."

They were shown to a table near the window.

Logan pulled out the chair for Cassie, but she had other ideas. "Where's the ladies' room?" The maître d' pointed out the way, and she grabbed Emily's arm and dragged her off.

Logan smirked at his friend. "Are you going to thank me for coming here instead of going to Piccolo Italia?"

"That's exactly what I was thinking of doing, until the girls started talking about how romantic it is."

"Isn't that what you want? A little romance?"

"No. Yeah. I don't know."

"Whoa, pal. Make up your mind. You and Emily sure looked like you were enjoying yourselves in the movie theater."

"How would you know? Are you telling me you actually came up for air long enough to notice us?"

Logan sighed. "A man's gotta breathe."

"Right."

"So, what's going on with you?"

"I don't know. It's like every time I relax and *go for the gusto*, I think of Johanna and it brings me down a notch. A dozen notches, actually."

"They're coming."

As soon as the girls slipped into their chairs, the waiter arrived for their drink orders. The girls and Jackson ordered soda, but Logan asked for a beer and was served one. Jackson looked at Logan with raised eyebrows. Logan smiled and leaned over to whisper, "I've got *big boy* proof, and for fifty bucks, you could, too."

Jackson stared at the bottle. "You're driving."

"One beer isn't going to affect me."

"Famous last words."

"Don't say that!" Cassie said. "Besides, I'll make sure he only has one."

"Great," Logan replied, sounding defeated.

"So, what are you ordering?" Emily asked Jackson.

"I don't know." He picked up the menu and looked at the choices. "I guess I'll have lasagna."

"Chicken Parm for me," Logan said, putting down his menu.

Cassie and Emily chose lighter entrées. They talked until their dinners arrived. At that point, Cassie and Emily continued the conversation while Jackson and Logan stuffed their guts.

"That was so good," Logan said, pushing his empty plate away.

Jackson's dish was still half-full. "Johanna makes better lasagna."

Emily put down her fork. "Who's Johanna?"

NERO 51 FELT Odyon staring at him. The curator opened his eyes. "This place is off limits. You are not welcome here."

Odyon flicked his hand as if batting the curator's words away. "It is time to fulfill destiny. I believe I can successfully redirect the time machine and remove us from this form of hell." He walked around the curator's private meditation space. There was very little to it. A different picture of Garpa hung on the glowing orange wall. A small altar-like edifice stood beneath it. On top, glowing embers provided a little more light. The remainder of the room was unadorned, aside from the floor mat the curator sat upon.

The curator stretched his tentacles, snaking them around the space, but said nothing.

Odyon made his taunt sound like a question.

"Surely you're ready to give your grandfather everything you promised him?"

The Terrorian huffed. "Do not talk about my ancestor as if you're intimate with him. This is not your domain."

"Thank the creators!"

Nero 51 stood. "Come. Let's see if you are as competent as you say you are."

Odyon narrowed his eyes but kept silent and followed the curator to the time machine.

THE ROMANTICAN MILITAIRRES took off at lightning speed for the Library of Illumination, which was so completely engulfed in flames the evening sky was tinted orange. The townspeople followed their lead and morphed into an amateur fire brigade, running for buckets, hauling water from wells and fountains, and passing it to the women standing closest to the fire.

The overseers didn't have to run. They transported themselves there in an instant and took stock of the scene before them. They watched as the residents of Roma joined together to fight a common cause. The women tossed individual buckets of water at the blaze, but they did not do much to quell the intensity of the flames.

⌘*It appears our assistance may be required to save the library.*

⌘ *We are in agreement that help is necessary.*

The three overseers spread out, triangulating themselves around the library. Ryden Simmdry nodded toward the buckets of water being passed by the fire brigade, and the onlookers gasped as the water rose out of the buckets into midair. The overseers used their powers to swirl the water around the library, building it into a circular wall of water that curved in at the top like a dome. The three nodded at the same time, and water drenched the Library of Illumination, transforming the flames into columns of steam. The structure hissed as rivulets of water found the last of the burning embers.

Natalia stood at the front of the building, caked with soot, except where her tears had allowed channels of her now reddened complexion to show through it. She said only one word. "Why?"

Ryden Simmdry disappeared, causing a few more gasps. Inside the library, he used his mind to reconstruct what happened in reverse. In what looked like a glowing video blueprint, the master watched the now-collapsed cupola rise to its perch at the top of the building. He observed as the flames lessened and lowered until they were merely concentrated in the center of a sub-level room. He saw a pile of books and furniture grow higher as the flames diminished. And when the fire went out, he watched the books and furniture fly into the tentacles of two Terrorians, who scrambled backwards to the places where their kindling had come from. Then, Ryden Simmdry watched the troopers shiver, and realized the overseers had triggered the event by shutting down the nuclear power supply to each library when they sealed them off from the portals. In doing so, they had made the buildings inhospitable to the two trapped Terrorians Nero 51 had overlooked when he exterminated their fellow soldiers.

He reappeared outside the library's blackened shell.

⌘*The Terrorians brought it upon themselves.*

★*We are partially responsibility.*

✠*Not at all; if the Terrorians had not made the unwise decision to invade, this would not have happened.*

⌘*They are to blame for their own demise.*

★*Will we rebuild this library?*

⌘*Not until the threat of war has ended. To do anything else would be a waste of natural resources.*

★*I feel the Romanticans are being unfairly punished.*

✠*Natalia will feel the displacement most. The others, less. And it will give them a cause to rally around. The restoration of the library will be the final reward. But, Ryden Simmdry is correct. Any premature rebuilding could be a waste of resources, best laid aside for now, in case of war.*

JACKSON FELT HIS face grow warm. Logan told him earlier that the first rule of dating is to not talk about your ex with your new girl. Jackson especially didn't want to discuss Johanna with Emily.

"May I clear your plates?"

Jackson looked up at the waiter. He had never been so relieved to see someone in his life. "Yes," he answered, "and we'd like to see your dessert menu." He turned to Logan. "Right?"

"Wouldn't be a meal without dessert," his friend answered.

Jackson turned to Emily. "You'll have dessert, won't you?"

"I don't think I could eat one by myself. Would you share one with me?"

"Sure," he replied, taking a dessert menu from the waiter. "What looks good?"

Logan groaned. "Chocolate Hazelnut Truffle Cake."

Cassie slapped his arm. "That's too fattening. Let's share the Triple Sorbet."

"Triple Sorbet?" Logan shook his head. "You want to share frozen water? Sorbet isn't dessert. At least, not for me. But, I'll order one just for you."

Cassie looked appalled. "I can't eat an entire order by myself."

"You don't have to." Logan placed the menu on the table. "Leave what you don't want."

Jackson looked at Emily. "You don't want Triple Sorbet, do you?"

She blushed. "I was thinking the Triple Sorbet or the Crème Brûlée."

"What's Crème Brûlée?"

"It's delicious," Emily answered.

Logan wrinkled his nose. "It's egg custard."

Jackson made a face.

"I've got it." Logan raised both arms. "Jackson and I will each order manly desserts. And the two of you," he looked at Cassie and Emily, "can share an order of sorbet. Everybody wins."

Emily sighed and looked away. Cassie glared at Logan.

"What?" he asked. "It's the perfect solution."

"I need to go to the ladies' room. Emily?" Both girls got up and walked away.

Jackson played with a spoon. "Did something just happen here that I missed?"

"It's a female thing, I think. It's okay for them to share dessert with a guy but not with each other."

The waiter returned. "Have you decided what you'd like for dessert?"

"I'll have the Chocolate Hazelnut Truffle Cake," Logan said. He handed the waiter his menu.

"Me, too." Jackson turned to Logan. "Should we order them sorbet?"

"Yeah. Or else they're going to call us thoughtless and cheap."

"And one Triple Sorbet with two spoons," Jackson said as he handed the waiter the menu.

Logan waited until the waiter walked away. "You don't look like you're enjoying your date."

"It's bad enough trying to decipher what Johanna is thinking at any given moment. At least I know her and can guess half the time. Trying to do it with a whole new person is ridiculous."

By the time the girls returned, the sorbet was waiting for them. Logan and Jackson were both nearly half finished eating slabs of cake that each looked big enough to feed four people. The girls picked at the sorbet, and then at what was left of the guys' cake. Emily acted as if nothing had happened, but every so often, Cassie gave Logan a look that said, *you really screwed this up*.

ODYON INSTINCTIVELY SENSED the moment Nero 51 focused his thoughts on the two crystals he clutched in his tentacles. The shapeshifter disappeared as the time machine propelled itself out of the Terrorian library and merged with the power of the crystals. He could feel the buildup in energy as the vehicle approached the pinhole. Suddenly, he felt himself dispersed like threads through the fabric of time and space and used his power to reverse their polarity, ultimately hurling the vehicle outside its trapped destination and directly to one of his own choosing.

At first, he had considered returning to Fantasia but had second thoughts. By now, everyone in his circle of colleagues knew he was someone other than what he said he was and would not trust him or offer him sanctuary. Not that he needed their approval or help to live anywhere he wanted, but existence as a beam of energy left a lot to be desired.

He then considered returning to Mysteriose. He was Mysterian by birth, and considering they would know nothing of his adventures on Fantasia, he would blend in until he could establish an identity. However, he hadn't been there in many millennia and wanted to give it further thought.

The time machine came to rest without traveling very far at all. It materialized in the Terrorian town square, where dozens of troopers were training for battle.

"NERO 51, YOU'RE finally here." Terrorian military leaders gathered around the curator. "We haven't received any news about the invasion. What is happening in the other realms?"

Nero 51 stared at the soldiers surrounding him. *How is it possible they know nothing about the library being cut off?*

His chief military strategist gave him a two-tentacle salute. "Why is the library locked? We tried to gain access but can't get in. We've seen troopers inside, trying to batter the windows, but it appears they can't get out. What is going on?"

So they do know. "Kelsis 384, it is good to see you," Nero 51 replied. "There appears to be a force field surrounding the library. We had a devil of a time getting out."

The strategist looked confused. "We?"

Nero 51 looked around for Odyon. There was no sign of him. He could feel an uncomfortable tightening of his skin but refused to allow his wariness to show. He clasped a tentacle around the strategist's shoulders. "I was speaking metaphorically, of course."

JOHANNA'S ALARM WENT off just before midnight. She stretched, grabbed a bottle of water and an apple, and headed up to the cupola.

"Thank God," Chris muttered. "I'm bushed, and I've still got to do geometry homework before I can hit the sack."

"Don't you have tomorrow off?"

"Ava has tomorrow off. Jackson has tomorrow off. But I have a tutoring session because I suck at geometry. So, technically, I have a *class* I have to attend. And since I'm the only student, he'll know if I didn't do my homework. He'll call my mom. Things will get ugly."

"Why didn't you bring it with you and do it up here?"

"Because if I'm doing homework, I'm not guarding the portals. And I'm here to guard the portals."

"Admirable. I don't think your tutor would agree, but you can't tell him, so it doesn't matter."

"Right. Like Vegas. What happens in the library stays in the library." He yawned loudly as he made his way down the stairs.

Johanna wondered if Jackson was home. He might have come in while she was asleep. But, somehow, she didn't think so.

—LOI—

22

JACKSON WALKED EMILY to the door.

She smiled, her dimples showing. "I had a nice time."

"Me too."

She closed the space between them. "A really nice time." She tilted her face up toward his.

She wants me to kiss her again. Jackson felt a pang of guilt, followed by a jolt of testosterone. *Oh, what the hell.* He leaned in and kissed her.

She wrapped her arms around his neck and pressed into him.

He responded in kind.

The porch light went on and he could feel the vibration from Emily's groan.

"I've got to get inside. But I had a really, really nice time."

"Yeah." Jackson waited for her to disappear behind the closed door before walking back to the car. As soon as he was inside, Logan pulled a U-turn and headed up the street. Jackson narrowed his eyes but said nothing. Five minutes later, Cassie turned to Logan before getting out of the car and stated abruptly, "Don't even think about walking me to the door." Logan shrugged as Cassie stormed off toward the house.

"I'm coming up front." Jackson switched seats and studied his friend's profile. "Why did you take Cassie home first?"

"She was fuming about something, and I didn't want to hear it. I knew she wouldn't get into it with you in the car. So you are my savior; thank you very much."

"This happen often?"

"Once a month. That's what happens when two people have been going together for a while. They get touchy about certain things. I'm not sure what's bothering her this time, but I'm sure I'll hear all about it before too long." Logan stopped for a red light. "How were things between you and Emily?"

"It was okay. It's easier to be with Johanna. She always knows what I'm thinking. But Emily is nice."

"You asking her out again?"

"I don't know. Maybe. She's not as reserved as Johanna. I might as well take advantage of the plusses in our potential relationship."

"How many plusses are you talking about?"

"If tonight is any indication, we're talking higher mathematics."

Logan pulled to the curb in front of the library. "Maybe *I* should have dated her."

"Didn't you tell me she's Cassie's best friend?"

"Yeah. I guess dating her wouldn't be a smart move. Cassie can be vindictive."

"Besides, I might date her again."

"You already said that. But, I'm not convinced, higher mathematics or not."

MOST OF THE Mysterians who had gathered the previous night to try to batter the gates at the iridium cave did not believe Nycose could get his hands on the weapon he described, so they didn't bother showing up at the cave at sunrise. However, Pagaron and two of his brethren from the priesthood stood waiting at the gate when they saw Val Dvir's assistant approach, dragging a small dray behind him.

Pagaron looked from Nycose to the dray. "Is it a cannon?"

"No. Just this." The assistant uncovered a large metal tube wrapped in a bundle of rags. He settled one end on his shoulder.

One of the men with Pagaron snorted. "You needed a dray to carry that?"

"No," Nycose answered. "I needed a dray so people wouldn't be able to tell what I had taken. If they saw this, they would talk about it. But all they saw was a dray."

"Do you know how to make it work?"

"Like this," Nycose said, aiming at a boulder. He pulled the trigger. Not even dust remained.

The priests' eyes widened.

Pagaron grabbed Nycose by the arm. "Quickly then, before anyone comes. It's time to remove these walls."

They entered the cave and Nycose took aim at the gates.

"Not the gates, you narf," one of Pagaron's companions complained.

Pagaron held up a hand to silence his fellow priest. "Let him shoot the gate. Let's see what happens."

Nycose focused on the round piece of solid metal that appeared to hold the gates closed and fired.

MAL ASKED RYDEN Simmdry to explain his plan to offer Adventurans living cells of highly accomplished individuals. Dean Artemus Rexana agreed that it might work and accompanied Mal to Adventura. They found Prophet IAN c. at work in one of the labs and discussed their proposal.

The Adventuran's answer was simple. "No."

Mal couldn't help but show his surprise. "You're turning us down?"

"We are an accomplished race. Our history has inflicted many setbacks, but we have always surmounted them on our own. We have worked hard to overcome the hurdles that make other races susceptible to failure. It is a major source of pride for us. You are suggesting we water down our own civilization by introducing other races. It is an appalling suggestion. We would be taking a step backward. Doing so could invite discord due to unexpected personality disorders, external politics, and possibly new pathogens that might infect the future viability of our own hu*bots. It could be catastrophic. On behalf of my fellow hu*bots, I refuse. Any type of immigration at this juncture is abhorrent to us."

OZZRO REPORTED FOR military training the next morning and found the compound buzzing with news of Dungen's arrest. Many of the stories were highly embellished. One stated Dungen had attacked his father, Pondor, in a drunken rage. Another said Ozzro hunted Dungen down and, calling him a traitor, had delivered him to the military sentinels. Both stories referred to Dungen's illegal possession of a decimator, which was a fact, and Ozzro referred to it whenever anyone asked him what happened. Besides that, he only admitted to being in Pondor's office when the arrest happened. There were rumors of Dungen's claim to "get even with Ozzro" after the "misunderstanding" was handled. Ozzro hoped that someone would lose the key to Dungen's cell and never find it.

The library on Romantica smoldered well into the morning. The outer walls remained intact, and since the library was sealed off, no one could really look inside to see the extent of the damage. But the dome and cupola could no longer be seen from the ground, so the fire had clearly caused the roof to cave-in.

Around the corner, Natalia sat at Dame Erato's front window, staring forlornly at her former home. Everything she cherished most had been locked inside the library, and now it was all gone.

"Good morning, Natalia," Dame Erato said. "Did you manage to get any sleep at all?"

Natalia felt a tear slip down her cheek. She opened her mouth to answer, but there were no words that could describe how profoundly sad she felt. She closed her mouth and shook her head.

"What you need is some fresh brichi. Do you want to come out into the garden with me and select the flowers you would like, or should I surprise you?"

"Choose whatever flowers you think are best," Natalia whispered.

Dame Erato nodded and headed outside.

THE BRICHI NO sooner came out of the oven than there was a knock on the front door. Dame Erato greeted the Jolen sisters and invited them for breakfast. The sisters couldn't help but notice the feeling of complete desolation, which was triggered by the waves of despair that seemed to roll off Natalia.

Arraba plucked a bit of soft brichi from the center of her slice. "I think the rebuilding of the library will be a wonderful task to help unite Romanticans, while giving our militairres purpose."

Natalia closed her eyes for several seconds before focusing her gaze on the eldest sister. "Only the overseers can rebuild the library. It has special properties that only they can address."

Arraba took a sip of tea before answering. "Maybe they'll rebuild the structure, but it's up to us to replant the gardens surrounding the library, which were trampled while we extinguished the fire. And we must haul water from the river to refill the fountains that we emptied last night fighting the flames. Your overseers can handle the interior of the library, but it's up to us Romanticans to refurbish the exterior and return it to what it was before."

Natalia nodded but said nothing.

"Finish your breakfast and we'll meet you at the field. Now that we have co-captains for our platoons, we need to discuss their responsibilities and divide the ranks. There are some pairings we'll need to be leery of, so a little pre-discussion on our part will go a long, long way."

Felicia smirked. "You mean like pairing Della with Leisha? I can see how that might turn into a bigger battle than any Terrorian invasion."

Milencia shuddered. "Della would never take orders from Leisha. Or from Patra, for that matter."

"Which is why we cannot allow Natalia to moon over what's happened to the library. It was a devastating event, but life goes on and we have work to do."

"Dame Erato," the sisters said in unison as they stood to leave.

"Natalia will meet you at the field, even if I have to hypnotize her to get her there."

MARBOL AWAKENED TO the sound of someone pounding on his door. He had fallen asleep sitting at his workbench, putting together another sonic scrambler. It was nearly done. He just needed to attach the outer casing. The call of the weapon was stronger than the knock on the door. Whoever wanted him would inevitably return. Right now, he wanted to test his new gadget.

He took a piece of glass he'd collected the previous night and inserted it into a groove he'd cut into a block of wood. He stood it on the workbench and stepped back. Taking aim, he pulled the scrambler trigger. Five seconds passed, then a minute, then several minutes. All that time, he'd stood there with his finger pressed tightly against the trigger. The piece of glass still remained unscathed in the stand he had made. *Something is wrong*, he thought as he released his hold on the trigger. He grabbed the pad he'd used to note his research and started recalculating each step. When his numbers proved right, he went back to the source of his research and re-read it. Somewhere in the chain of information he relied on to create his new scrambler, there existed a weak link, a mistake, and he needed to find it and correct it.

Hours passed and he stopped only when his stomach grumbled with hunger. It didn't help that someone was again pounding on his door. He reluctantly pulled it open and found Selly standing there holding a steaming bowl of corn pudding.

"I brought you something to eat. Guffle said you were on a mission, and that usually means you stop eating and sleeping until you're done."

"I slept," he said, grabbing the bowl of pudding and heading toward the kitchen for a spoon. He left the door open. If Selly wanted to follow him inside, it was her choice.

She looked around the room. "What are you working on?"

"Another sonic scrambler."

She wrinkled her nose. "Another what?"

"A sonic scrambler to intensify sound waves at a high frequency pitch that will break glass."

"Why would you want to do that?"

"To get into the library. That's where the monsters came from. But every time we try to get inside, there's something stopping us. We can't even get in through the window we already broke."

"So what good would breaking more windows do?"

"I don't know. Maybe if we break it at a different

frequency, we'll be able to get inside. It's worth a try."

"If you can get in, won't that mean that monsters can get out?"

"Yeah," he answered, scraping the now-empty bowl clean with his spoon.

Selly took the bowl from him. "Stupidest idea ever."

His face fell. He really liked Selly and didn't want her to think he was stupid. But he had to try. *If she doesn't believe in me, that's her loss.*

NERO 51 IMPATIENTLY awaited the reappearance of Odyon. At first he'd assumed the shapeshifter was somewhere in Ter 0, the capital city. But when Odyon didn't reappear after a few hours, the curator began to wonder if the shapeshifter had deserted the time machine for some other location. The thought made Nero 51's bile rise. *How dare he promise to teach me to transmute and then shirk his responsibility.* But even without the shape-shifter, the curator practiced recreating the hum that had taken over his body, and after a few hours, managed to do it at will, without having to exert himself running up and down library stairs.

BOOM!

The sound made by the bombardment of energy from a Terrorian weapon on the gate in the Mysterian cave sounded like a sonic boom and literally shook the earth, releasing clouds of dirt and debris upon the small contingent of men trying to open it. When the dust settled and they could see again, they were surprised to find the gates unaltered.

"Well, that was a fine little experiment," one of Pagaron's companions complained. "I'm pretty sure everyone in the village heard it and will be flocking here to see what's going on."

Pagaron took the weapon from Nycose and examined it. "And they'll be overjoyed to see we have put the overseers in their place and have rightfully reclaimed what is ours." He placed the weapon on his shoulder, mimicking what Nycose had done, and aimed at the rock wall framing the gate. He drew in a deep breath and pulled the trigger. Once again, a sonic boom shook the ground and large chunks of debris fell. Pagaron was knocked to the ground. A boulder crushed one priest's skull. Another severed Nycose's legs. It took a while for the dust to settle.

"Pagaron, I'm hurt. I can't move my legs. Help me," Nycose begged.

Pagaron rose and approached Nycose but knew instinctively that he was beyond help. A large pool of dark blood puddled around the site of the injury. "Close your eyes." Nycose did as he was told. Pagaron aimed the weapon at Nycose and ended his pain forever.

He walked over to where he had blasted the wall. The rock was gone but was now replaced with a type of crystal he had never seen before. He banged against it with the edge of the weapon. It was solid.

He changed position and aimed at the opposite wall

BOOM!

More debris fell. A razor-sharp shard sliced Pagaron's ear off. He dropped the weapon and wrapped his arms around his head, trying to dull the pain and protect himself. Blood crawled across the sleeve of his garment and pooled on the floor under his head. He soon lost consciousness.

—LOI—

23

Morning sunshine flooded in through the "halo" windows of the Fantasian library. Ava climbed to the cupola with an almond croissant and a cup of coffee. "Hi. I thought I'd bring you some breakfast."

Johanna reached for the coffee. "I was hoping you came to relieve me. I have some business to take care of today."

"I can relieve you, but I have to run down and grab something to eat first."

Johanna offered to return the pastry. "Do you want this?"

"No. I know that's your favorite. Besides, I need a chocolate fix—hot cocoa and a chocolate donut. I'll be right back." True to her word, Ava returned less than fifteen minutes later, ready to guard the portals.

Marbol's eyes focused on the piece of glass he had tried to scramble. *Why didn't that work?* He walked over to it and tried to remove it from the frame he had built. He felt his fingers touch. It was as if the glass wasn't there, but he could plainly see it. Yet when he reached for it again, his hand passed through it, as if it was merely a hologram and not something solid. *As if the molecules were scrambled.*

He backed away from the workbench until he hit the wall and slid to the ground, his mind racing. For all intents and purposes, his scrambler worked, but the glass appeared to be untouched. That didn't matter to him. What mattered was that he might have found a way into the Library of Illumination. He didn't know if that would be a good thing or a bad thing, or if hallucinations from lack of sleep were causing him to think the glass was no longer solid. There was only one way to find out.

He packed up his new sonic scrambler and headed to the library. *This is a one-man job*, he told himself, even though he could feel his palms sweating. He didn't need the others laughing at him if his plan failed. And, he didn't need them blaming him if more monsters got out and hurt someone.

At the library, he stood a short distance from the windows on a side wall. He took aim with his scrambler and held down the trigger for a full five measures. He didn't know how long it would take for the glass to disassemble, and he couldn't tell by merely looking at it.

Finally, he tucked the scrambler into his waistband and went around back to grab some of the boxes he had stood on the last time he fired his scrambler into the library. He piled them up and climbed to the top to look inside the library. Some of the interior walls were missing. He could tell where they had been because of the pattern they'd left on the floor. His eyes came to rest on a withered tentacle sticking out from behind one of the few remaining bookcases. He stared at it for several minutes but saw no movement.

He took a deep breath. He hadn't touched the windowpane, afraid it might still be there. His thoughts were interrupted by barking. Several dogs, running in a pack, shot out from around the corner of the library and crashed into the box tower he stood on. He lost his balance and swung his arms in wide circles, trying to regain it, but it was too late. He fell forward, right into what had once been the executive boardroom of the Library of Illumination.

NATALIA PREPARED TO dress for field duty with the militairres. Unfortunately, when she reached for her uniform, she found it singed and stained. A tear rolled down her cheek, and she ran to splash cold water on her face to prevent herself from slipping into despair. She put on her dress whites instead and told Dame Erato she needn't accompany her to the field. *I can do this on my own.*

Groups of militairres were already practicing their specialties by the time Natalia arrived. She met with the Jolen sisters and the co-captains under the tent. She was the only person wearing a dress uniform. The others' uniforms smelled of smoke but were not burned. Natalia looked down at her own. "I had no choice."

"It's no wonder. You were in the front of the line," Felicia said. "I'm surprised your hair and eyebrows didn't burn off."

Natalia involuntarily reached for her forehead and felt her brow. "I guess I should be thankful for that."

"And for the support of the community. And good friends. And Dame Erato's brichi." Milencia ticked off the list on her fingers.

Natalia sighed. "Of course you're right. I'll get over it soon enough."

"I hope so," Arraba said, "because we have a lot of planning to do." They spent the next few hours going over their training plans and breaking up each platoon into two groups.

Felicia's stomach growled noticeably. "Can we take a break soon?"

"Of course," Natalia answered. "I didn't realize how long we've been at it."

"I think we should tell the militairres to take a meal break and meet us back here afterwards to learn their platoon assignments. Once that's done, we should leave this afternoon's training in the capable hands of our co-captains while the four of us go to the library and start planning the restoration of the gardens and the fountains. It has to be done, and it will give you back a feeling of control."

Natalia smiled at her friend. "I agree." She turned to the co-captains. "Ladies, please inform the militairres."

MAL'S TRIP BACK to Lumina was a quick one. He couldn't believe the Adventurans rejected the offer to add to their gene pool. "That didn't go well."

∑ Yet it should have, logically speaking. It is in their best interest.

"I sense they are a proud species."

∑ That is a reasonable conclusion, considering they managed to survive near extinction totally on their

own.

"I can't help but think they may be making a mistake."

∑*It is their mistake to make. Do you have an alternative plan?*

"Not at the moment, but I will continue to think about it."

∑*As will I.*

HUE THE ELDER and Proteus Bligh were awakened by the blast caused by Pagaron and his friends at the Mysterian cave. The overseer hurried toward the cave.

Hue kept pace one step behind him. "I hope no one was hurt."

Ψ*It was a powerful blast. It would be naive to think there were no casualties.*

"I should have known something like this could happen. Mysterians are fiercely independent and do not like outside interference. They probably tried to bomb the gates."

Ψ*That would be regrettable. The gates are designed to return force. If someone tried to damage them, they would repair themselves while retaliating with equal force.*

Hue stopped suddenly and grabbed the overseer's arm. "I was not told that."

Ψ*It had not occurred to me that someone would try to bomb the gates so soon. I'd planned to discuss that feature today at Town Hall so everyone would be aware of the precautions that had been set into place.*

They encountered a crowd already gathering around the mouth of the cave. Some men busied themselves, removing the pile of rubble that blocked their entrance. There was too much.

They had to wait for the assistance of a mammoth beast to move the largest boulder. When it finally arrived, they tied ropes around the biggest stone blocking the entrance and attached them to the harness of the animal. Even with its help, the boulder only moved an inch.

Proteus Bligh closed his eyes and communed with the other overseers. The rock started to move more freely. In a short time, the entrance to the cave was cleared.

Inside, they found the bodies of Pagaron's two associates, who had been killed by the wreckage. Paragon was unconscious but not dead. Nycose was nowhere to be found, but the weapon he had taken remained. The gate stood intact, although the walls surrounding it had changed.

A Mysterian high priest managed to rouse Pagaron. He moaned as he tried to move, but otherwise, remained dazed. "What happened here?" the priest asked.

"Nycose..." Pagaron whispered.

"Nycose isn't here. We found only you, Geera, and Zologg."

"He is gone." Pagaron coughed.

The priest looked at the crowd. "Quickly. I need water." Someone handed him a flask, and the priest held it to Pagaron's lips. "What do you mean, 'he is gone'?"

Pagaron took a breath. "He used...Terrorian weapon...on walls surrounding gate... ceiling collapsed... he lay dying... weapon removed Nycose." The effort to speak was too much for him. He passed out.

"There's a dray outside," one of the men in the

crowd said. "We should use it to take Pagaron home. His mother is a powerful priestess. She will help him."

Hue the Elder picked up the Terrorian weapon. "Nycose should not have had this."

"Don't blame Nycose," one of the men shouted. "This," he moved his arm in a wide arc, "should never have happened."

Ψ*He brought it upon himself. If he wanted to withdraw some iridium, he should have handed in the currency he was given for his share. Trying to blast his way into the cave proves he was up to no good.*

"No. It is you who is no good," a man shouted. He picked up a rock and hurled it at Proteus Bligh. The overseer disappeared.

"Where is he?" someone else asked. "Where did he go?"

"I don't know," Hue replied. "Maybe the force that took Nycose took the overseer as well." The curator didn't believe his own words, but he knew how the crowd would react. They began backing up. If Nycose went missing, followed by the overseer, maybe the cave wasn't the safest place to be. It didn't take long after that for the group to disperse.

AVA TURNED WHEN she heard the curator stairs squeak and groan. She smiled when she saw Jackson. She'd started guard duty right after breakfast, and lunch was way past due. "Thank God."

Her older brother reached for the decimator. "Have you been here all night?"

"No. Just since breakfast. But I'm kind of hungry and Johanna isn't here." She paused for a moment. "How was your date?" She emphasized the last word of her question.

"We ate at Mama Marcella's Trattoria in Lowell. It was good. Where did Johanna go?"

"Are you seeing her again?"

"Johanna? Yes. I see her every day."

"Stop. You know what I mean. Are you going to date Emily Brent again?"

"I don't know. I might."

Ava sighed. "I think you're making a mistake."

"It's my mistake to make. I thought you were hungry?"

"Yeah," she mumbled. She had prayed Jackson's date would be awful. Apparently it wasn't.

Ava trudged down the stairs, making more noise than Jackson had climbing them. *This is not going right. He belongs with Johanna.* But as far as she could tell, neither he nor Johanna were open to listening to reason.

JOHANNA WAITED IN the reception area of the administrative offices of Cranford University. An approved Library of Illumination borrower had recommended his former protégé and successor as someone who could be trusted to use the library's resources and not reveal the properties of the books. Johanna wanted to meet the man in person before lending him any materials.

She heard door hinges squeal as a handsome young man walked out to greet her. She didn't mean to give him the once-over and blushed when she realized he was staring at her.

"Johanna Charette?" he asked.

"Yes." She stood. "Are you here to take me to

Professor Thorne?"

The Adonis standing before stuck out his hand. "I'm Cameron Thorne."

She became momentarily lost in the warmth of his smile and the sparkle in his eyes. "You're Doctor Murchison's successor?"

"I am. Were you expecting someone older?"

"Yes."

"People usually are. I've worked under Doctor Murchison's tutelage for the past seven years. I assure you, I'm fully tenured. And, I know something about the library you represent, thanks to Doctor Murchison." A group of students laughed right outside the office. "It might be better if we talk in my office. It's more private there."

Johanna followed him down a long corridor, around a corner, and up a flight of stairs. He led her through an outer office with a sign that said *Department of English* and past a door with *Dean Cameron Thorne* painted on a frosted glass windowpane.

Her eyes widened. "You're the dean?"

He laughed. "Please take a seat, and let me explain." He sat across from her. "I guess you could say I was a gifted child. I graduated college when I was thirteen years old and received my doctorate by the time I turned seventeen. I worked a year at Standwell College, then applied here when an opening became available. I originally graduated from this school, and I'm very proud to be teaching here now."

She shook her head. "I just applied here as an English major to take courses in the fall. I thought Doctor Murchison would be my dean."

His brows dropped. "I'm sorry you're disappointed."

"I'm not disappointed. Just surprised."

"Good. I assume you're here because of my request for materials?"

"I don't have them with me. I wanted to meet you first." She hesitated. "There doesn't seem to be anyone here to confirm you're really Dean Thorne. Do you have any I.D.?"

A look of uncertainty crossed his face as he reached into his pocket for his driver's license. "Will this do?"

She looked over his picture, his license info, and noted his date of birth. *Aquarius.* She handed it back to him. "I'm sorry, but I had to be sure you are who you say you are."

"That's okay. I can understand why you'd want to be careful. Is there some kind of contract or agreement I need to sign?"

"Yes. We require blood oaths from all our borrowers."

His eyebrows shot up. "You do?"

"Just kidding," she answered, laughing.

He laughed with her.

She stood to leave. "I'll deliver the books you requested tomorrow."

He stood as well. "Would it be easier if I come to pick them up?"

"No. At least, not for you. The library is tricky to find."

"How tricky can it be?"

"Trust me. It will be better if I deliver them."

"Maybe we could meet in the middle somewhere. Let me take you to lunch. That way I can ask you more about what I can and can't do as a client of the Library of Illumination."

"Oh." Once again, he had surprised her. "Okay. Maybe we could meet at the Willow Inn in Gainesford. It's not very expensive and the food is great."

"It's a date," he said, extending his hand.

She took it and blushed when he held it for a second too long. She rushed out of his office before he could notice her reaction.

—LOI—

24

MARBOL OPENED HIS eyes. He lay splayed against the bare stone floor in the Juvenilia library. He spotted a bit of chipped tooth about three inches away. He felt inside his mouth with his tongue and confirmed it was his. He looked around without moving. Satisfied that he had not disturbed any monsters, he pushed himself up until he knelt on all fours. *Okay. I'm probably not hurt if I can get up like this.* Slowly, he rose to his feet.

His eyes came to rest on a Terrorian tentacle. It had not moved since he spotted it through the window. He took a couple of deep breaths. He had to go see what lay behind the bookcase that hid the creature.

He walked as quietly as he could and peeked around the bookcase and then gagged. He hadn't noticed from the other side of the library, but up this close, the smell of decomposing Terrorian was quite strong. And there was more than one. There were four of them, all huddled together. He stared at their ugly faces, praying he wouldn't see an eye open or a tentacle stretch out in his direction.

His brain felt like mush. *Think*. He suddenly smiled. *The scrambler works. I'm inside the library.* But now that he was there, he wasn't quite sure what to do about it.

I need Peer Meap. He's the curator. He'll know what we should do.

Marbol climbed out the window and ran to the City Center. He found Duddu and asked him about Peer Meap.

"I'm going to have to find him. The easiest way is with my diary. But it might take time." Duddu ticked off an imaginary list on his fingers. "I have to run home and find my diary, then ask him to meet us here, then wait for his answer."

"Okay. Do that. I'm going back to the library to poke around inside."

"I thought we couldn't get inside?"

"Yeah. Well, I modified my scrambler, and let's just say, it worked. One of the side windows shattered and I was able to get in. But there are a lot of rot-gross monsters inside, and I don't know what to do. The curator will. That's why I need him."

Duddu turned and screamed, "Pollo, you're in charge." He turned back to Marbol. "I'll be there as soon as I can."

"Flayed for this, I will have you," Dungen screamed from his cell. "Or worse. Put to death, you will be."

Most Dramaticans would agree, Dungen was not a model prisoner. He ranted and raved all the way to the provisional jail and continued to scream from behind the barred door of his cell.

The guards feared for their lives, knowing Dungen's father was the chief judge of the Commonwealth Court. Most did not know, or refused to believe, that Pondor ordered the incarceration of his only son. The guards feared retribution. And if Dungen's words were to be believed, their lives, and that of their family members, were no longer safe.

Because of the guards' uncertainty, Dungen received special privileges—an extra serving of food at mealtime, a pillow on which to lay his head. Pondor did not order these treats and comforts, nor would he approve them if he were asked. But the guards did not know that. And so, Dungen was treated better than other prisoners, if there were other prisoners.

Dramatica prided itself on being a very honorable world. Most men took each other at their word, and there were few petty jealousies. Most disagreements embodied the spirit of competition but disregarded malice.

Dungen's wrath was a phenomenon, and because it was such a rarity, hearing his vile threats made his jailers unhappy.

PAGARON MOANED AS the cart that was carrying him hit a rut. His head exploded with pain at every jostle. When he tried to open his eyes, he felt like they were glued shut. He listened to the sounds around him, but everything seemed muffled.

As his pain continued to shock him into unwanted consciousness, he thought about the weapon he had used to blast the walls of the supply cave. *How could I have been so stupid?* Yet, it didn't make sense. The weapon had been strong enough to change stone into crystal. Why did the stone ceiling cave in? Why didn't it turn into crystal as well?

He felt his face engulfed in warmth. It was almost comforting. The sounds around him softened. He took a shuddering breath. He would never learn the answer to his question. His pain faded away with his heartbeat.

JACKSON'S NEW CELL phone rang. He placed the decimator on the floor next to him so he could answer it.

"Hello?"

"Hi, Jackson. It's Emily."

"What's up?"

"I had a really nice time last night."

"Me too."

"I was wondering…umm…I realized the senior prom is Saturday. I had been planning to go with my ex, but now that he's history, I'm wondering if you're available? I mean, I know you may already have plans and everything, but I thought I'd ask anyway. Are you going?"

"I hadn't actually thought about it."

"So you're not going?"

"No."

"Do you want to go? With me? I mean, I would love it if you would be my date for the prom. What do you think?"

He hesitated for a second before saying, "Sure. Why not?"

"You will?"

"Do I need to buy tickets or something?"

"I already have them. All I need is you."

"Okay."

"I've got a million things to do. I'll talk to you later."

"Sure."

"Bye, Jackson."

A shadow passed over his face. He looked up. It was Johanna.

She looked around. "Were you just talking to someone?"

"My phone." He pointed to it in case she didn't believe him.

"You should give me your number."

"I should?" He wondered if she wanted to get back together with him.

"In case I need to reach you."

"Oh. Sure." He gave her his number and watched her punch it into her own cell phone. His phone rang and he quickly looked to see who was calling.

"That's me. Just in case you need my number. Now you have it in your 'recents.' Are you okay up here, or do you need me to take over for you?"

"I just got here a little while ago. Take your time."

THAT AFTERNOON, NATALIA and the Jolen sisters walked the perimeter of the library. Arraba carried a pad and noted plants that needed to be replaced, burnt grass that required replanting, and soot that needed to be washed off stone benches and fountains. She pushed the renovation even farther, suggesting new flower beds and planting new trees where none previously existed. Natalia was so engrossed in their planning, she didn't have time to be depressed.

"Good afternoon, ladies," Dame Erato said. "Horatio Blastoe and I saw you roaming around the garden and wanted to see what you're up to?"

The overseer looked contrite. ✠*I'm sorry to say, as long as the libraries are on lockdown, nothing can be done to replace the interior.*

Arraba clutched her pad. "These gardens are communal. There's no reason why they should remain an eyesore."

✠*You're quite right. It's commendable that you wish to restore them to what they were.*

"Oh. Not 'what they were,'" Felicia said. "We plan to make them so much more, with meandering paths between additional beds of flowers and a new meditation circle. It will be different and even more beautiful than it was before."

"We plan to get the community involved," Arraba added. "Donations of plants and labor should help keep costs to a minimum."

✠*As I said, commendable.*

JOHANNA DRESSED CAREFULLY for her lunch date. She didn't want to appear too childish. She would scarcely admit it to herself, but she wanted to impress Cameron Thorne.

The Roth siblings were back in school and Mrs. Roth had gone to work, so no one was available to guard the portals. *Not a problem.* Johanna searched for the 1862 edition of *Les Misérables*. She opened the book and was struck by the stench of nineteenth century France. It didn't compare favorably at all to the lovely city beyond the Roth's balcony in the George V suite.

She ran her finger over Inspector Javert's name

and the man sprang to life. *No wonder the city smells so bad. These people have horrible body odor. And, apparently, no deodorant.*

The inspector looked around warily. "Où suis-je?" *Where am I?*

Johanna closed her eyes and channeled the incantation Plato Indelicat had used when he enacted a translation charm on Terroria. She inhaled, wished she hadn't, and opened her eyes and answered. "You're in the Library of Illumination, and I need you to stand guard for me."

"The Commissioners of Police have approved this?"

"Yes," Johanna answered. "Come with me." She led Javert to the cupola and handed him the decimator.

"What manner of weapon is this?"

"It is designed to stop anyone from entering through this window." She pointed to the portal opening.

"What enemy would be so small as to enter through that opening, yet be so lethal as to concern you? Rats?"

She didn't have time for this. "Hopefully, none." She closed her eyes again and enacted one of the spells she had seen in *Myrddin's Memoir*. She showed him how to use the decimator. "It is only meant for enemies entering through this portal. Do not aim it at anyone else."

Javert nodded.

Johanna descended the stairs, hoping she had just made the right decision. When she reached the circulation desk, she took the open copy of *Les Misérables* and hid it in a drawer. She picked up the books Cameron

Thorne had requested and headed out the door to meet him for lunch.

ODYON WAITED UNTIL the next morning to seek out Nero 51. During his time on Terroria, he determined the troopers were clumsy but well prepared for battle. He saw hundreds of them, but wondered if there were thousands waiting in the wings. *Perhaps it's time to make another deal with the Terrorians*. If they were hell-bent on going to war, he might be able to use them for his own purposes.

SOLAR FLARES FROM the Adventuran sun erupted so violently, scientists studying the cyclical electromagnetic disruptions could see them from the planet surface without the aid of a telescope. The enormous bursts of energy were brief but alarming. The flares were powerful enough to cause power grids on the planet surface to blow out, disrupting the delicate process of hu*bot cloning.

Curator Prophet IAN c. called for an emergency meeting of violet-eyed "Gold Arms"—the most prestigious strata of ruler*bots.

"The magnetic bursts are interfering with the cloning process and are expected to get worse. The disturbances are responsible for the death of originator tissue, and we are on the verge of a crisis. I have called you all together for your ideas concerning possible solutions."

Prophet CARL a. stepped forward. "Solar flares are cyclical. We have survived them before. Why are they a problem now?"

Prophet IAN c. pointed to a live image of the sunbursts. "In the past, they have rarely coincided with

hu*bot tissue failure. Many of our most notable originators are dying off, and the power disruptions are
preventing us from successfully cloning their brains and
hearts. We are currently rendered helpless."

Prophet DAVID 1. stepped forward. "Refrigeration
is the key. We have to freeze the failing tissue until a time
when we can viably clone it."

"The power grid disruptions can affect refrigeration as easily as our cloning operation," the curator
argued.

"Yes," DAVID 1. replied, "but if we place
cryogenic refrigeration units in several different areas,
our statistical chance of tissue survival will increase. The
Fantasian cliché, 'divide and conquer,' comes to mind."

The Gold Arms thrashed out the details and
assigned groups of Adventurans to install the necessary
units. As soon as freezers were in place, viable tissue
samples from dying originators were dispatched to those
locations.

In the Exeter High School cafeteria, Jackson found
Emily and Cassie having a lively discussion about prom
logistics while his best friend, obviously bored, ate
lunch. Logan looked up as Jackson slid into the chair
next to him. "Thank God."

Jackson raised an eyebrow. "What's going on?"

"Apparently my car isn't good enough anymore
for the prom." He nodded at the girls. "They want to hire
a limo."

Cassie looked up momentarily. "Everybody does
it. It's expected."

Jackson shrugged.

Logan nudged his elbow. "You know what else is expected?"

Jackson shook his head.

"Tuxedos. I imagine you'll be accompanying me when I go to the House of Luxe after school to rent one."

Cassie's head jerked up. "You don't have your tux yet? I can't believe you haven't done that already. You knew about the prom months ago."

Jackson took a bite of his sandwich.

"You have to wear tuxes." Cassie turned her attention to Jackson. "You'll look like complete jerks if you don't. And you'd better hurry. The prom is tomorrow."

Jackson finished chewing his food before answering. "I guess that says it all. What else do I need to know about this extravaganza?"

"Flowers," Cassie said. She leveled her gaze at Logan. "I'm wearing pale pink." She turned to Jackson. "And Emily is wearing the most delicious shade of teal."

Jackson swallowed. "Delicious?"

Logan snickered. "But not as delicious as your sandwich."

Cassie took a deep breath. "It's tradition to give your date a corsage that complements her dress. No carnations. Lilies are acceptable. Roses are preferred. Just ask for a corsage of roses and tell them her dress is teal. Perky Petals will know what to do."

Logan pushed his food tray aside. "What about the after-party?"

Emily smiled. "Bring your bathing suit. We're renting a cabin at The Dunes. We can use it as our base of operations and a place to change. Plus, we can lock up our stuff while we're on the beach. We can build a huge bonfire after the prom and bring in some food and stuff so we can party until dawn. Then we'll sit on the sand and watch the sunrise. It's perfect."

Logan nodded. "I'll get a keg. There's nothing like beer on tap to make a party soar."

"No," Cassie said. "We should get champagne. It's way more sophisticated."

"Sophisticated, schmafisticated," Logan replied. "I'm ordering a keg. If you want champagne, you can bring it."

Cassie rolled her eyes at Emily.

"Where's the food coming from?" Jackson asked.

"Carnie's Deli. We're collecting fifty dollars from each couple." Cassie took out a large manila envelope and wrote Jackson's and Emily's names on one line. She looked at Jackson. "Can you pay me now?"

"Uh, sure." He pulled out his wallet and handed Cassie the money.

She put a big checkmark next to his name before turning to Logan and rubbing her fingers together.

"What?" Logan asked. "You want the money right this minute?"

"Yes. We have to put a deposit on the food as well as the cabin."

Jackson leaned back in his chair. "Does that cover the limo too?"

"Nope. That's separate."

"Don't worry about it," Emily said sweetly. "I already convinced my father it's the safest way to travel. I'm sure he'll pay for it."

"Finally," Logan said. "Some good news."

25

Marbol carried a thick tree branch with him when he returned to the Juvenilia library. He climbed through the window he had shattered earlier and slowly walked around the library with his scrambler in his waistband and the branch poised above his head, ready to strike.

Aside from the group of Terrorians lying in a lump on the main floor, he didn't spot any other wayward visitors. He took a deep breath before climbing to the residence level, where he looked around. There wasn't much to see. The shelves and books had all been decimated, even the ones at the entrance to Peer Meap's apartment. However, unlike the rest of the library, nothing inside the residence appeared damaged. Marbol had only been there once before and really wanted to check it out. *Why not?*

Once he had satisfied his curiosity about where the curator lived, he inspected the other levels. That went pretty quickly, considering there was nothing remaining on them to look at. The only level he couldn't reach was the cupola. He'd heard Peer Meap complain enough to know he'd have to go back to the main level and climb the cupola staircase. But, at this point, he held the wood more like a walking stick than a weapon. He relaxed once he confirmed for himself that no monsters remained hidden on the other levels.

The very first step of the cupola staircase squeaked. He smiled when he realized that he had scared himself. But as he took his next step, he heard glass crunching. Marbol froze in his tracks.

JOHANNA ROUNDED THE corner to the Willow Inn and saw Cameron Thorne waiting for her by the front entrance. She broke into a wide smile, and he returned her smile when he caught sight of her.

"I hope I'm not late," Johanna said, looking at her watch.

"Not at all. You're right on time. I've been studying the menu that's posted, and I've worked up an appetite just reading it." He held open the door to the restaurant for her, and they went inside. The host nodded at them and led them to a table in the corner.

"This is perfect," Johanna said. "I hate to talk about the library when there are a lot of people around, but this is kind of secluded. I like that."

"Are those my books?" He nodded toward the bag.

"Yes. But I don't want to hand them to you before I explain more about them and what to expect."

He laughed. "I feel like you're the dean and I'm the new student."

"Sorry, Dean Thorne, but—"

"Please call me Cameron. Everyone else does. You'll find college etiquette fairly relaxed at Cranford."

"Okay. Sorry if I sound like I'm going to lecture you, but what I have to tell you is really important."

He picked up the menu. "Let's order first, and we can talk books after lunch."

During the meal, they got into a minor discussion about the food on the menu, followed by a major discussion of Johanna's college goals and how she planned to get a degree while working full-time at the library.

"I hope you're not planning to carry a full course load."

Johanna shook her head. "I thought I'd start small with two classes. *English Studies in a Digital World* and *Shakespeare 101*."

"That sounds doable." He raised his eyebrows before continuing. "I'm what you might call a Shakespearian scholar, so if you have any problems, feel free to come to me for help."

"Thank you for the offer, but I actually thought, considering I'm curator of the Library of Illumination, if I have any problems I'll just ask Shakespeare for help."

Cameron's jaw dropped just a little. "You can do that?"

She smiled. "Yes, I can."

"God, I envy you. What I wouldn't give to be able to talk with The Bard."

"You can. As long as you're a patron in good standing with the Library of Illumination."

He inhaled sharply. "Wow."

"Welcome to my world."

"Can I visit you there?"

"Of course. As long as the library knows you're coming, getting there shouldn't be too bad."

"What does that even mean? It sounds so cryptic."

She lowered her voice to barely above a whisper. "The library protects itself with a shielding charm. Finding it is never easy for people who don't have business there. But as long as I have you entered onto the calendar as a guest and give you explicit directions, you should be fine.

"When were you thinking of visiting?" she asked.

"Tomorrow?"

"Okay. Let me write out the directions."

THE DISCUSSION PITS in the Mysterian Town Hall were crowded beyond capacity. Several citizens removed tapestries used to separate seating areas so they could enter into the discussion about the death in the storage cave. "Why did it happen?" some asked. "Outside inter-ference," others answered. The noise level grew as more and more people pushed their way into the pits, all wanting the best placement possible. Tempers flared, and the massive gathering was on the edge of erupting into an all-out brawl.

Hue the Elder held up both arms to gather everyone's attention. The gesture did little to reduce the cacophony. Overseer Proteus Bligh closed his eyes and hummed. The sound reverberated perfectly and soon everyone quieted down. Hue turned to the overseer and said under his breath, "You must teach me how to do that."

The overseer smiled and merely held out his arms

as if to say, you have their attention.

Hue looked over the crowd. "Honored brethren, we are here because of a tragic incident at one of the caves in which a number of people were killed."

Everyone around him spoke at once, each trying to be heard over his neighbor. After several wasted minutes of shouting, Proteus Bligh hummed once more, which resulted in the desired effect—silence.

Ψ*Be it known that the deaths would not have taken place if the victims were not trying to illegally enter the caves with a weapon that should not have been in their possession.*

The crowd wanted no part of the explanation. This was their realm, their goods and resources, and their caves. They didn't need anyone telling them what was legal or not.

Proteus Bligh knew another hum would probably fail. Instead, he made a half-circle with one hand while reciting a short chant and was met with complete silence. Mouths still moved; fists were raised in the air. However, no one's voice could be heard. As the citizens of Mysteriose realized what had happened, they stopped flapping their jaws.

Ψ*That's better. As I said, the victims discharged a weapon they had taken possession of illegally, and they brought about their own demise. The gates had been in place less than a day before someone tried to breach them. I can see you're angry, as you should be, but your anger is misplaced. I would like to know why you aren't focusing your irritation on those who tried to steal from you? Those men, the victims, were trying to get past the gates so they could remove resources that did not belong* *to them. You each would have suffered a loss of goods to someone else's unearned benefit. Is that what you want?*

Hue the Elder nodded in agreement. "If we had not been so busy yesterday responding to the cave fiasco, we would have been meeting here to inform you that the gates are enchanted. The meeting had already been scheduled; the spell was put into place to protect our assets."

Ψ*The lives of the victims were forfeited because of their own greed. It is not something we wish had happened. It is merely what has occurred.*

"We all know Pagaron's history," Hue continued. "This was not his first transgression. It is tragic that he paid for an act of theft with his life, but he had several opportunities to reform and chose not to. He preferred to get out of trouble with a glib tongue and an empty promise. Unfortunately, he did not get that opportunity yesterday."

Ψ*Operations at the caves are now re-opened. If you choose, you may remove all your personal assets and keep them at your homes. I believe that would be ill-advised. They are better protected in the cave. However, they can be removed during daylight hours as long as you have the proper notes for the resources you wish to withdraw. That is your choice.*

"We are finished here," Hue concluded. "Pagaron's death and those of the others are appalling, however, the blame rests with him and his followers and no one else."

The overseer and the curator walked out of Town Hall together. The noise level suddenly returned. The crowd, relieved to have their voices back, spoke among themselves, but the fevered pitch of their earlier conversations did not return.

A SINGLE BEAM of light widened in front of Nero 51 and settled into the form of Odyon.

Nero 51 merely nodded. "Shapeshifter."

Odyon raised a single eyebrow. This was not the reception he expected. He shrugged it off. "Are you ready for your next lesson?"

The curator finished signing the dispatches in front of him before answering. "What new feat will you teach me today?"

"First," the shapeshifter said, "you must perfect the hum."

Nero 51 hummed perfectly as he stood. He towered over Odyon.

The shapeshifter felt the intimidation in the curator's stance.

Nero 51 glowered at Odyon. "I believed I used the word, 'new.'"

"Of course. Yesterday, while you worked on using tonal vibration to clear your mind, I studied the time machine and the adjustments I made to it to escape the confines of the library. We did not have to travel through the portals to do that, but we might have to use the portals to go elsewhere. I thought, at first, we'd be able to travel through time at will, but then I realized the distances between the realms might create problems. So, today, I would like to try a different experiment. Like before, I want you to think of a time and a place that I will give you. Before the trip is completed, I will ask you to change both those elements. If I'm right in my calculations, we can bypass the portals entirely. If not, we'll have to adapt on the fly, so to speak."

"Why can't you give me the correct time and location to start?"

"Because the time machine will automatically want to start the journey by passing through the portals. That is how it's designed. However, if we gain acceleration before changing gears, the machine may be traveling too quickly through time to readjust for location and should bypass the portals entirely. That is what we want to happen. It is an untested theory, so we will have to make adjustments as we go along."

"I had the time machine moved in case of an impromptu visit from the Luminans. It is in a warehouse not too far from here. If you're ready, we can depart."

Odyon gave Nero 51 a mock bow. "Lead the way, your lordship."

JACKSON WATCHED THE overgrowth on the side of the road whiz by. "Where were you this morning?" he asked Logan. "I tried calling you."

Logan changed lanes before answering. "I would like to point out that you sound just like my mother."

"I just wanted to find out what time you were picking me up."

"Now you know."

"What's eating you?"

"I can't believe how much this prom is costing us."

"C'mon," Jackson replied. "It sounds like fun. And, what do you care? Your family's loaded."

"My father has informed me that since he will

be paying for college in the fall, he's putting me on a budget. And why aren't you complaining? You never have any money."

"I got a raise at the library, so I'm good. What I want to know is, how are you going to survive on a budget?"

"I may have to actually go out and get a job."

"You mean like slinging burgers at Big Buns?"

"I will never sling burgers, even though I could probably eat all the burgers I want for free. I was thinking more along the lines of selling men's clothing at the Gainesford mall."

"Like suits and stuff?"

"More like jeans and motorcycle boots."

"Yeah. I guess you could do that."

"Unless you guys need help at the library?"

Jackson's eyes widened. "I'm not saying we do, but that's a possibility worth exploring. I'll have to ask Johanna. And, you'd really have to be serious about it. She'll tolerate nothing less."

"It's not like I need full-time or anything. I already signed up for a summer internship, so I'll be doing that a few days a week."

"Doesn't that cost extra money you say you don't have?"

"If it's 'educational,' the family sperm donor will pay for it. If I work full-time, the pater will just make me save it for the fall. If I lie and say my internship is full-time and work on the other days, I'll be able to have my cake and eat it too."

"That didn't work out so well for Marie Antoinette."

"I'm not some spoiled French queen; I am an Elliott."

"A spoiled American brat."

"I prefer playboy."

"So, what kind of internship is it?"

Logan's face lit up. "It's pure white light. I'm interning as a reporter at the university's nightly news program. It's carried on the local cable channel, so you'll be able to watch my reports."

"Watch you make a fool out of yourself, you mean."

"They won't let that happen. The reputation of Graydon Ransom University News Tonight is on the line."

"That's a mouthful."

"They call it GRUNT for short."

Jackson snorted. "I knew you'd just be doing grunt work."

"Not true, my little naysayer. They teach interns what to do and how to do it. They'll help us write our stories and put them on the air and online. I'm slated for stardom."

"You're slated for something. I'm just not sure what. And, don't expect Johanna to go easy on you at the library."

"No wonder you dumped her."

Jackson's face reddened. "I didn't dump her. I was trying to motivate her, and she took it the wrong way."

"So, what are you saying? You're stringing Emily along? Because, according to Cassie, Em's 'in deep' for you. If you hurt her, I'll never hear the end of it."

"When did this conversation nosedive from you wanting a job at the library to my choice in women?"

"Sixty seconds ago. You have to keep me in the loop as far as Emily is concerned so I can lay the groundwork in case you decide to go back to Johanna. If Cassie thinks she got blindsided, she'll go into DEFCON 1. That won't be pretty."

"If Johanna would even take me back...."

"Of course she'll take you back. It was your idea to expand your horizons. And, from what you've said, she's not exactly throwing herself at any other men. Does she even see other men?"

Jackson shrugged. "She sees Chris."

Logan shook his head. "That would be a real kick in the butt, wouldn't it? If the former love of your life took up with your little brother."

Jackson's face turned red, but his voice remained eerily calm. "For the sake of everyone around, that better never happen."

UNIFORMED MILITAIRRES FANNED out across the Romantican capital seeking donations of plants, labor, and money to offset the cost of restoring the library gardens. There were so many enlisted women reaching out to family, friends, and neighbors, it seemed like the entire populace of Roma elected to take part in the reconstruction. The militairres remained persistent, and by late afternoon, many of the them were able to stop soliciting donations and start digging up flower beds for the plants that had been readily donated. The co-captains placed monetary donations in a large urn on top of a previously soot-covered bench that had been cleaned by several volunteers earlier in the day. As the day progressed, carts of evenly cut stones to line the pathways began arriving, and the badly charred lawn was soon hidden under piles of masonry supplies.

PRU TELLERENCE ACCOMPANIED Furst back to Dramatica, now that his assistance in training militairres was no longer needed. He was glad to be back on his own realm. The Terrorians had done massive damage to the Dramatican library, but it remained in far better shape than its Romantican counterpart.

Pru Tellerence thanked him for his assistance on Romantica and departed for Lumina. Furst eagerly wandered about his library, just to make sure what little was left remained intact. Afterward, he crossed over to the town square to catch up with his friends and kin. "Has changed since I left, not much, I see."

"Change, there has been. The murder, you weren't here for. Lenc."

Furst felt his jaw drop. "Dead, Lenc is? Him, who killed?"

Instead of answering Furst, everyone turned and stared at Ozzro.

Furst's curls tightened as he turned toward Ozzro. His voice thundered. "Lenc, you murdered?"

Ozzro's eyes opened as wide as his mouth. "No. It, Dungen did!"

Furst couldn't believe his ears. "Dungen?"

Ozzro nodded. "His arrest, Pondor ordered."

Furst's curls loosened. "A sad day, it is. At once, I must see Pondor. Offer solace, I will. Happened, has anything else?"

There was a moment of silence until Berra filled the void. "Enough, isn't murder?"

—LOI—

26

UNAWARE OF THE solar flare crisis, Mal and Artemus Rexana arrived on Adventura to speak with the curator about refusing their offer of living cell tissue from Luminan luminaries. They found him in a lab, babbling oddly to the people working with him. "Specimen 42 goes to the Uven unit. No. It goes to the Vern unit."

"We just sent specimen 76 to the Vern unit and were told the unit is full."

"The Cada unit, then," he said shrilly. "Or the Lodi unit."

Mal whispered to Artemus Rexana, "I've never heard an Adventuran express any level of emotion. What is going on?"

Before the overseer could answer, another worker shook his head. "The Cada and Lodi units are not available. Those units were designated for specimens 18 to 22, and specimens 66, 68, and 90 through 111. That would fill them to capacity."

$\sum$ *Prophet IAN c. Is there a problem?*

The curator turned abruptly, unaware Artemus Rexana and Mal had entered the lab.

The curator stared at the overseer. "What can you do to remediate solar flares?"

Σ *They occur naturally and are way beyond any power an overseer might possess.*

"New organs for our oldest and most revered bloodline are dying off. Prophet EZECHIA q.'s will soon fail, and there are no freezers left to store his tissue. We are about to lose another cherished line of citizens. How am I going to tell Adventurans that our bloodlines are dangerously imperiled?"

Artemis Rexana closed his eyes, and a moment later the College of Overseers agreed unanimously to provide refrigeration. He chanted as he widened his arms. The far wall of the lab was suddenly lined with a dozen freezer units.

"Quickly, Prophet DANIEL p. Place Prophet EZECHIA q.'s tissue in one of the new units. And gather a company of men to move half of those freezers to other locations. Once they're in place, we will divide EZECHIA q.'s tissue."

Mal rubbed the side of his head, disturbing his chaperon. He tugged it back into place. "Why move those units, at all, when you clearly need them here?"

The lights blinked but stayed on.

"That is why," IAN c. explained. "Our power system is in a state of flux because of solar flares, and we've had an extraordinary number of power outages. We cannot take the chance of storing all the freezer units in one place. Nor all the tissue from an originator at a single location. We will surely suffer losses but are trying to lessen the severity."

∑I fully understand why you rejected our earlier offer to offset the loss of dying originators with some of Lumina's most renowned citizens. But the offer remains if you should suffer a remarkable amount of loss.

IAN c. shook his head. "It is too much to consider at this time. Our first priority is to preserve our heritage."

MARBOL CROUCHED INTO a tight ball when he heard glass breaking and stayed in that position for so long, he could no longer feel his legs beneath him.

He'd heard no other sounds since the initial disruption and decided it was safe to continue inspecting the library. Besides, from his vantage point halfway up the cupola stairs, he hadn't seen any movement, although he did have his eyelids squeezed shut most of the time. He looked around, took a deep breath, and continued on his way.

The cupola was barren. It resembled a wheel hub with empty aisles extending from it. No shelves. No books. Just a layer of powdery dust covering the floors. *Peer Meap isn't going to like this.* He wondered where the curator had disappeared to, now that the library was defiled.

Tick...tick...tick. He froze again. More noise coming from below. The teenager shook his head. *I'm getting too old for this.*

THE TERRORIAN WAREHOUSE, where Nero 51 took Odyon, looked like an abandoned structure. The walls were cracked, the windows blackened, and wild growth crowded the walkways. Nero 51 picked up a stick and pressed it against a rock on the far side of weeds surrounding the building. A whirring sound accompanied the movement of undergrowth, which seemed to fold back onto itself, and the ground opened up, revealing a steep staircase leading way down below the building. Odyon followed Nero 51 inside.

The curator relied on his tentacles to keep him from toppling down the stairs. Odyon shifted into a beam of light and descended without trouble. At the bottom, Nero 51 pulled a lever on the wall, and daylight disappeared as the opening rumbled to a close. Overhead lights clicked on automatically, and the time machine stood in the middle of a mist-covered dirt floor.

Odyon looked up. "This is an unusually deep subterranean chamber."

"It is a very safe place, designed to misdirect outsiders."

"I can see how it might do that. But we're not here to discuss the space. Let us start working on a way to bypass the portals for time travel."

THE OVERSEERS AND Mal sat around the conference table at the Library of Origination.

⌘*I'm surprised the Adventurans refused our donation of tissue samples.*

Σ*I believe they are currently preoccupied with lessening the impact of solar eruptions on their electrical system.*

"I don't think we need any more than that," Mal said. "Surely, if I appear regularly as your emissary to assist with their cloning crisis and get updates, they would not regard it as an intrusion. By now, I've been

there enough times that those closest to IAN c. recognize
me."

*You have a point. Our original offer was predi-
cated by our desire for you to be able to freely visit that
realm in a capacity other than as an overseer.*

*∑Unless they feel too inundated by the current
crisis to acknowledge your presence.*

"Do you think that might happen?"

*⌘Adventurans are not emotional by nature and
could dismiss your visits during this critical juncture as
unnecessary.*

*∑Actually, IAN c. was as emotional as I've ever
seen a modern-day Adventuran. He appeared...frazzled.*

"I was just thinking the same thing. Their brains,
after all, are human. Why wouldn't they have emotions?"

*⌘For centuries, they depended on logic and
scientific study to survive, burying their emotions. But
now that neither of those have prevented a perceived
catastrophe, Adventuran emotions may be resurfacing.*

*⌘Mal, go as our emissary with an offer of
additional refrigeration units. If the Adventurans accept,
your telepathic request for the units will be acted upon
immediately. We could arrange for you alone to provide
them, but we think it might be better to keep your role
separate from that of an overseer. The Adventurans may
feel they can speak more freely in front of you than they
could around an overseer.*

THAT AFTERNOON IN the library, Johanna actually whistled
while she worked.

Both Ava and Chris noticed how lighthearted she
seemed and compared notes in the cupola. "Do you think

she and Jackson made up?" Chris asked.

"Not that I know of."

Four stories below on the main level, Johanna hummed as she laid out Shakespeare's First Folio in the display case.

The front door swooshed open and Jackson rushed in.

She looked up. "Wow. Somebody's in a hurry." She looked at the clock. "Oh. Is it that late, already? I didn't realize you weren't here."

"I...uh...had to do something."

Chris's sneakers pounded as he raced down the cupola stairs. "Where have you been, bro? We've been waiting for you."

"Uh..."

"C'mon. Out with it."

"I had to rent a tux."

Johanna's face lit up. "Really? Where are you going?"

"Prom," Jackson mumbled.

"That's so nice for you," she said, before turning and walking away. She continued humming as she replaced the key to the display case in a drawer.

Jackson's eyes narrowed. He looked at Chris. Chris shrugged. Something had rocked Johanna's world, and neither of them knew what it was.

TICK...TICK...TICK.

"Marbol, are you in there?"

Marbol's shoulders relaxed. *Duddu.*

"I'm here," he shouted, and he practically flew down the cupola stairs. He ran to the broken window and saw Duddu outside.

"You got in," Duddu said in amazement.

"I told you I would."

"What's in there?"

"Come in and see for yourself."

"Is it safe?"

"I'm standing here talking to you, ain't I?"

"I tried to enter through the back, but I can't."

"No. You can only come in through this window."

"But there's glass here." Duddu lifted his hand to knock on the glass and gasped when his fist went through it without a sound.

"Told you…."

Duddu hesitantly hoisted himself through the window. "What's that smell?"

"Dead monsters."

"Ugh." He paused momentarily. "Are you sure they're dead?"

"Come take a look." Marbol led the way to the heap of decaying Terrorians.

Duddu made a face. "Peer Meap is going to have a fit when he sees this."

"Where is Peer Meap? Did you bring him with you?"

"Nope. Can't find him."

"Where did you look?"

"Everywhere. You know. All the usual places. I got everyone I could find together and sent them out in different directions. They're all knocking on doors, looking for him."

"I thought you already looked everywhere?"

"I looked in all the usual places. I sent the others

to look in the unusual places."

"We'd better look, too. We need him."

NERO 51 WATCHED as Odyon paced, displacing the mist that hugged the dirt floor of the hidden Terrorian warehouse. It had been the shapeshifter's habit during the entire night. They would try something. It wouldn't work. Odyon would pace. They would try something else. It wouldn't work. Odyon would pace. And so it went. Nero 51 had expressed his displeasure at first, but Odyon's bitter rebukes had now resigned the curator to silence.

Odyon spun around and walked back to the time machine with purpose. "You said you took possession of the time machine following the overseer's challenge. Head toward Lumina with that date in mind."

"Lumina is the last place I want to travel."

"Which is why it just might work. Come."

Nero 51 activated the time machine, and it whooshed into dark space, nearly leaving his stomach behind.

"Mysteriose, now!" Odyon demanded, and the curator switched his thoughts. He and Odyon were thrown against the side of the vehicle before either of them could prepare for the rapid change in direction, and they both lost consciousness.

THE NEXT MORNING, Jackson left the library before either of his siblings woke up. He had a lot of stuff to do, and if he didn't do it right, there would be hell to pay. Logan already had the Mini Cooper warming up. Jackson dropped his bike in Logan's driveway and hopped in the passenger seat. "What's the plan?"

Logan pulled onto the main roadway. "First thing, we're going to The Dunes to pay for the cabin. Cassie called last night to make sure there was one available."

"And it's just for the four of us?"

"No. Kaden and Madi, and Darrius and Shayna, are also in on it. But we are the team leaders. They're just footing half the bill."

"Once we have the key," Logan continued, "we're going to pick up a kegerator, and then we'll hit the florist."

"Do you think they were annoyed at having only one day to fill the flower order?"

"Nah. Florists always get last minute orders. You can't very well call 'em and tell 'em Uncle Ned is going to die in an accident next week, so you want to pre-order flowers for the casket."

"Good point. And House of Luxe promised the tuxes would be ready by noon."

"That's because we're dashing, debonair, and perfect specimens of manhood, and our tuxes didn't need any alterations."

"And that's it?"

"Except for the food, but that won't be ready until one. We're supposed to run it back out to the cabin with the kegerator and set everything up."

Jackson twisted in his seat to stare at Logan "We're setting it up? Why aren't the girls doing that?"

"Because they're at some hair salon getting done up."

"Figures."

Logan pulled up in front of The Dunes office. "If

you're feeling left out, I could fluff up your hair for you."

Jackson made a face. "And file my nails, too?"

"That would cost you extra."

THE ROMANTICAN SUN hovered just above the horizon when teams of militairres, their friends, and families arrived at the Library of Illumination to continue their work on refurbishing the library gardens. Many picked up spades and shovels and got to work building flower beds and laying new pathways. A second large group used soapy water, brushes, and brooms on the exterior stone surfaces, scrubbing away the soot that clung to seams and crevices. The generosity and devotion of the workers transformed the once-charred garden into a beautiful landscape, and they swore an oath to protect Roma against any invader who might try to infiltrate their realm and harm their fellow citizens.

It was a powerful sentiment, foreshadowing a future time when their adversaries would seek dominance over the citizens who now worked shoulder-to-shoulder. And it wasn't lost on the platoon leaders, who knew better than their fellow citizens that a serious threat remained.

Around midday, Natalia suggested the rest of the restoration be left to the citizens under the leadership of Dame Erato while the militairres returned to the compound to practice their skills. "We need our women to be better prepared, and planting flower beds isn't the way to do it."

"That is a perceptive observation," Dame Erato said. "Do you also have a solution?"

"Yes. We must train to be self-sufficient. And we should do it sooner rather than later. I believe a three-day mission in the forest, in which the girls have to do every-thing on their own without being able to retreat to the comfort of their homes, might prove useful."

Felicia's eyes widened with excitement. "We would be forced to perfect our survival skills if we suddenly had to take shelter in the woods and live off the land."

Milencia jumped into the conversation as well. "The militairres are adept in starting fires from flint and cooking on the fly, but not many of us are good at hunting and fishing for food. There are shops for that, and the people who trap game for the trades are experts at it. Most militairres barter or pay for game but have no idea how to catch it on their own. We must learn to do that."

Arraba joined in. "I agree, and we should do it without warning. Each team of girls and her co-captain should be responsible for either capturing game for consumption or fishing for it. It's not as easy as it looks, but the only way to learn is to try."

"Should we have a professional trapper come in and teach us how to catch game?" Milencia asked.

"No," Natalia replied. "Let's see what we can accomplish on our own. Then, if we utterly fail, we'll ask for advice. The lesson will be better learned by militairres who have actually tried and failed than by women with no frame of reference."

"Let's do it right now," Felicia said.

"Tonight?" Arraba asked. "We'll make a lot of enemies with those women who have already planned their evenings."

"If we are attacked by invaders," Natalia reasoned, "any previous plans anyone has made would be scattered to the winds. I agree with Felicia. We do it now."

"But only for three days," Arraba confirm.

Natalia grinned. "This time."

—LOI—

27

MAL RETURNED TO Mysteriose for the reopening of the caves. There were long lines the first day, but they dwindled by the second morning. In all, one out of three Mysterians chose to withdraw all their assets from the caves. "It's a sizable number," Mal confided to Hue the Elder, "but it is still a minority of the population. I believe my occasional presence here is still warranted."

The two men slowly walked toward Hue's home for a midday meal. "I agree," Hue answered, "and while I hate to admit it, Mysterians are not the most honest of races; there will be thefts from the homes of people who have withdrawn their resources. You will be needed here to help judge the wild claims that will come in."

"Wild?" Mal asked.

"Oh, yes. Some complaints will be valid, but others will come from people who will lie about being robbed. There will be those who have not made any withdrawals at all, but will say they did, and they'll swear they've been robbed."

The afternoon was warm and humid, and Mal removed his robe and chaperon so he could eat more comfortably. "It's hard to believe anyone would think they could get away with that."

"Maybe on Fantasia. Definitely on Lumina. But here on Mysteriose, prevarication is to be expected."

PRU TELLERENCE SOUGHT solace in the garden behind the Library of Origination and found Horatio Blastoe contemplating its beauty under a brilliant violet sky. She sat beside him on a bench made of solid diamond. ★*Am I disturbing you?*

⊞*Not at all. I was thinking about the fire on Romantica and its devastating effect on the library.*

★*How are the women dealing with the aftermath?*

⊞*Natalia is, of course, heartbroken. And there's not much I can do at this point to help them rebuild.*

★*Do you really think the Terrorians will attack them again?*

⊞*None of us dares predict the future. That would be, as Malcolm Trees might say, "a slippery slope." But there is also the escaped shapeshifter to take into consideration. We do not know what he has planned for his future, and if it should, perchance, intertwine with what Nero 51 has in mind, no library will be safe.*

★*Would you mind if I traveled to Romantica to see how the women are doing?*

⊞*Not at all. I will accompany you.*

JUVENILES SEARCHED EVERYWHERE but couldn't find Peer Meap anywhere. They met back at the wreck-wroom.

"What should we do now?" Marbol asked.

Duddu took a step back. "How should I know?"

"You're supposed to be our leader. Think of something."

"I would ask Peer Meap what to do at a time like this, but there is no Peer Meap to ask."

"What about those old men in the long robes?"

Duddu shook his head. "They're Peer Meap's friends. I don't think they live around here. The only time I've ever seen them is with Peer Meap."

"Maybe they live in the library."

"I thought you checked the library. You told me there was nobody there."

"Nobody but dead monsters."

Duddu scratched his head with both hands. "I wonder if his secret book is there?"

"He has a secret book? What's in it?"

"I don't know. I saw it laying around on the desk, and when I opened the cover, he snatched it away from me and told me not to touch it."

"Did he say why?"

"Something about it being connected to one of those old guys."

Marbol picked up a dart and hurled it at a target drawn on the wall. "Maybe we should look for it. Who knows. Peer Meap may show up to yell at us if we open it."

"That's a plan!"

NERO 51 OPENED his eyes slowly. Shelves filled with manuscripts filled his field of vision. He pushed himself into an upright position. A noise sounded behind him. He shifted, as if attacked.

"It's about time. We've been in this god-forsaken library for more than an hour and there's no way to exit it. It's just like the one on your world. This has 'overseer' written all over it."

"Where are we?" the curator asked.

"Mysteriose. My home. Humph. I lived here for a short while a very long time ago. I'd tell you how it's changed, but I haven't been able to exit the library, so I don't know if it's changed at all. Anyway, this is what I need you to do." He outlined the same steps they took to exit the Terrorian library and told Nero 51 to concentrate on a glade far west of the library. "I wouldn't want to run into anyone unexpectedly."

Nero 51 reached for the crystals that controlled the time machine. He usually carried them in his pocket, but they weren't there. "The stones are gone."

"So, look around. You probably dropped them when you were thrown off-balance."

The inside of the time machine was empty, however Odyon spotted one stone right outside the vehicle. He handed it to the curator. "I've done my part. It's up to you to find the other stone."

"It's not here," Nero 51 grumbled.

"Then I suggest you look harder."

THE GRANDFATHER CLOCK at the Fantasian Library of Illumination chimed the one o'clock hour. Johanna rushed down to the circulation desk to await Cameron Thorne's arrival. The library looked perfect, thanks in no small part to Cinderella's fairy godmother, whom Johanna had summoned by opening *Cendrillon*, Charles Perrault's French version of the fairy tale.

The heavenly smell coming from the upstairs apartment was a simple roasted chicken with a crispy brown skin, compliments of chef Caesar Cardini, who also whipped up his signature Caesar salad under duress, because Johanna wanted it ready ahead of time. Cardini insisted it had to be prepared at the table moments before it was to be served. However, Johanna did not want Cardini waiting on them and threatened to used bottled Caesar salad dressing, causing the chef to throw an apoplectic fit before fulfilling her request.

When he completed the salad, Johanna closed the book in which the history of the Caesar Salad had been recorded. She didn't need him popping back in to check on the meal.

Cameron arrived right on time. Johanna had propped the front door open so he wouldn't have any trouble entering the library. He took two steps inside and stopped. He eyes swept the room, taking in the tall shelves, the gleaming displays, and the rich artifacts acquired by the Library of Illumination over the centuries. "This is phenomenal."

Johanna released the front door, which *whooshed* shut, and linked her arm in his. "Would you like a tour?"

"Yes!"

She showed him around the main floor, and they ascended to the residence level.

Cameron sniffed the air. "It smells really good up here."

Johanna laughed. "Roasted chicken and Caesar salad. It's ready if you're hungry."

"Will you continue the tour after lunch?"

"Of course."

"Then I'm all for a bite to eat."

THE MILITAIRRES INITIALLY reacted to the announcement of a three-day survival mission with excitement. But their smiles turned to looks of distress when they learned it would commence immediately.

"I have plans," one of them whined.

"My family won't know where I am," another lamented.

"Who is going to teach us to hunt?" a third asked.

Arraba stepped forward. "You are all learning the four disciplines. As archers, you can naturally use bows and arrows. As stick fighters, you can use a blade to sharpen a point on the edge of your stick and spear fish. Grapplers may stalk larger game, like pallid. Those of you who specialize in weaponry will be called upon to sharpen other skills. We will not be required to use decimators during this mission."

Natalia placed a hand on Arraba's shoulder and addressed the group. "You won't all be tasked with catching our dinner. Some of you will be expected to build lean-to shelters and fire pits for everyone. Others must look for fruit and vegetation that is safe to eat. And we need everyone to collect any plants they find that have medicinal properties, so we can create a medical supply of natural remedies."

And so, the afternoon began, with one girl from each platoon designated to return to Roma and inform the citizens that the militairres were on special assignment and would not be returning home for several days.

The hunters, fishers, and foragers set out in search of food while the remaining militairres cleared brush, lashed together narrow stalks to use for lean-tos, and gathered kindling and stones for the fire pits. Some militairres grumbled about their assignments, but most took their work in stride.

The day resulted in minor injuries and rashes from crawling after game in patches of poisonous plants, plus the inevitable insect bites, but many of the militairres brought back medicinal herbs, and a couple of women—who were already trained herbalists—made poultices and salves and attended to everyone's medical needs.

Skinning small animals made some of the girls squeamish, and they were reluctant to eat what they captured, even after being told it was the only food available to them.

Several militairres complained about petty thievery after someone broke into their backpacks and removed sweets and brichi. They were later chastised by the platoon leaders who had removed their snacks. They would be forced to survive on their own without the benefit of secret stashes.

Natalia and the Jolen sisters agreed that three nights was not sufficient time to hone the militairres' survival skills, but they had to start somewhere. Even as the girls recovered from their first afternoon in the woods, their commanders were already making plans for a second, longer, more comprehensive mission farther away from home.

One young militairre approached Natalia and the Jolens and asked, "Are we expected to sleep on the ground? Without blankets?"

Felicia, not knowing how to answer, looked at

the others and shrugged. "We'll get back to you," Arraba said.

"We may have jumped into this mission a little too hastily," Natalia said. "However, we could never foresee this problem without actually encountering it. We need some type of bedrolls for the girls that they can easily carry across their backs."

"It will have to be light and serve as both mattress and blanket."

"Gracyn's mother is a wool shearer and weaver," Felicia said. "Perhaps she can make us something?"

Arraba shook her head. "Not by tonight."

★*What do you need by tonight?*

Startled, all four platoon leaders turned to face Pru Tellerence and Horatio Blastoe.

"We are on our first outdoor, overnight mission to hone our survival skills," Natalia answered. "However, we didn't plan on needing blankets or mattresses."

Pru Tellerence nodded as she telepathically broadcast their request to the other overseers.

Natalia sighed. "Should we call it off?"

★*No. If necessary, the militairres will have to collect some hay or leaves to sleep on.*

Felicia closed her eyes tightly and made a face. "Insects."

✠*You must learn to rely on nature when everything else is taken away from you. Even if it means dealing with things that make your skin crawl.*

Milencia turned away from the group. "I will have some militairres collect leaves to place under the lean-tos."

✠*Very good.*

★*Now you're thinking like a survivor. If I may, I'd like to return later to see how you're doing.*

Natalia smiled. "We look forward to seeing you—" She was interrupted by a high-pitched scream that came from the woods.

—LOI—

28

FURST KNOCKED ON Pondor's door. A woman who cooked for the judge told Furst that Pondor had gone out for the evening. Furst sighed. He would be forced to wait until the next morning to offer his support.

He spent a restless night. He didn't particularly like Dungen and was glad he had been jailed. But he wanted Pondor to know he felt badly about what happened.

When he went back to see the judge the following morning, he was surprised by his attitude.

"I lost my son, it is not like. Breathing a sigh of relief, many people are. Like his mother, Dungen is. To think clearly, he is unable. A sickness, it is."

"Sorry, I am," Furst said. He wanted to say something nice about Dungen, but there was nothing nice to say.

Pondor sensed Furst's dilemma. "As an infant, he was a joy."

Furst nodded.

Pondor's eyes twinkled. "Past that, not much."

Furst's mouth opened, but nothing came out.

"All right, it is, Furst. What was happening, I knew. Remember him as he was, I will. As he is now, I will not."

Furst still felt uncomfortable. "Return to the library, I must."

Pondor walked him to the door. "For coming, thank you."

"Yes," Furst nodded, as he scurried away.

JACKSON DID A quick inspection of the cabin at The Dunes before laying out the food, napkins, and plastic utensils. "I'm done here. Is that going to take you long?"

Logan pushed the tap on the kegerator and watched beer spill into the plastic cup he held under the spigot. "Nope. I'm done, too." He chugged the beer and made a face. "Warm...."

"I thought the whole purpose of that thing is to keep the beer cold?"

"It is. I guess it needs time to cool it down."

"Fine. So we're done here. Can you drop me off at the library? I haven't done any work today, and considering I won't be there tonight or tomorrow, I need to log in a few hours."

"You don't have much time. The limo is picking me up at 6:30, and will probably get to the library by 6:45 so we can pick up the girls by 7:00."

"What about the others?"

"They've got their own limo. We're only sharing the cabin and the food."

Jackson looked at his watch. "That's cutting

things close. How about you pick up the girls and then come get me at the library?"

"Emily is going to want pictures of the two of you at her house, all dressed up."

"You're killing me."

"Okay. I'll tell her you had to work this afternoon. Your mom can take pictures of the four of us at the library and share them with her parents."

Jackson groaned. "I don't want Johanna and Emily to...uh ...."

"So what do you want to do?"

"Call me on your way over, and I'll wait for you out front. Then you can snap a few pictures on your phone in front of the library and we'll leave. And you can share them with Emily's parents."

"Now you're killing me."

THE FIRST MYSTERIAN robbery report was made that afternoon. A priestess, who said she had just withdrawn all her assets, claimed she had been robbed of everything—herbs, minerals and gold. Drace the Elder convened an immediate hearing to gather evidence and determine if an emergency payment should be made to the young priestess so she could barter for the resources she would need to administer to her followers.

Hue the Elder and Mal were interrupted in the middle of their meal and hurried to the Town Hall. The hearing would be held in one of the smaller, more private discussion pits toward the rear of the building.

After they arrived, Mal realized he left his robe and chaperon behind.

"I would not worry about it, Malcolm. I doubt

anyone will notice." Hue paused. "I will be right back. I need to speak with Val Dvir."

Mal watched as the priestess answered a series of questions about the different resources she had been carrying and why she'd needed to withdraw them all at once.

"What does it matter why I withdrew them?" she asked impatiently.

Drace sighed. "Can you describe the thief?"

She tapped her right cheek with her forefinger as she slowly gazed around the room. "He's here," she shouted.

Drace's head jerked up. "Where?"

"Right over there," she said, pointing directly at Mal.

MARBOL AND DUDDU began their search for Peer Meap's "secret book" in the curator's residence. They opened drawers and looked inside appliances, but found nothing. They searched under seat cushions and on top of shelves but still came up empty. In the bedroom, they poked through clothing in the closet and looked through all the curator's pockets.

"It's not here," Marbol said, flinging himself on the bed. "Hey. This is pretty comfortable."

"You'd better get up from there before Peer Meap finds you."

"I want him to find me." Marbol stood on the bed and started jumping up and down. "Peer Meap. Peer Meap. Peer Meap. Come out, come out, wherever you are." As he jumped, a pillow slipped off the bed, revealing a book that had been tucked under it.

"Stop," Duddu shouted.

Marbol looked around, expecting to see the curator. He turned to Duddu. "Why?"

Duddu pointed out the book. "That's why."

THE ADVENTURANS WORKED together to distribute the freezers and disburse equal amounts of brain and heart tissue to their various locations. Artemus Rexana provided a dozen more freezer units to help with the crisis.

∑ *Is there anything else we can do?*

"You have saved us from extinction. Thank you for your help. It is now up to us to make sure we have sufficiently protected our assets."

The overseer returned to Lumi to commune with his brethren. ∑ *They seem adamant about not accepting help, at least, not as far as living tissue is concerned.*

⌘ *It is hard to believe that a civilization that is three-quarters robotic would still be victim to their own pride.*

∑ *I can understand why they might be afraid of foreign integration. And we only suggested it to ease our own way into their confidences.*

⌘ *We'll have to find another way to have Mal infiltrate their society.*

NERO 51 BECAME frustrated as his search for the missing time machine crystal remained unsuccessful. He huffed and puffed and threw his tentacles around like a truculent child.

Odyon folded his arms across his chest. "Grumbling won't help you find the stone."

"What if the stone flew out of the time machine when we were thrown to one side? What if it's out there," he waved a tentacle, pointing to no place in particular, "somewhere, lost forever?"

Odyon's features hardened. "Well, I know I can survive on this realm, considering I was born here." He narrowed his eyes. "I'm not so sure about you."

In a burst of anger, Nero 51 attempted to pick up the time machine in his tentacles and fling it at the shape-shifter. The vehicle proved too heavy to hurl.

Odyon rushed over. "Again."

"What?"

"Do what you just did, again."

Nero 51 tugged at the giant orb, tilting it up, and Odyon—moving with the speed of light—snatched the second crystal out from under it.

"Here," he handed the crystal to Nero 51. "I've done all your work for you."

Nero 51 stared at the crystal. "It's fractured."

The shapeshifter had little patience. "What are you talking about?"

"It is not solid. It has cracks running through it."

"So what?"

"I don't know if it will work."

Odyon sighed. "Well, we'll certainly never know if it works until we try."

Nero 51 stepped inside the time machine, saying nothing.

Odyon followed. "Think about the open field far behind the library."

The curator closed his tentacle around the two stones and thought about the field as Odyon dissolved into a beam of light. Something about the light from the beam reminded Nero 51 of something, but he wasn't sure what.

PRU TELLERENCE PULLED Horatio Blastoe aside to share her latest idea for the militairres.

He appeared confused. ✠*Sleeping bags?*

★*If we are all in agreement, I can have one made up and the others replicated. The militairres will adapt more quickly if they can get a good night's sleep, and that may not happen if they're sleeping on leaves or hay when they're not used to it. Let them get acclimated to sleeping outdoors in something they may find more acceptable.*

✠*War seldom allows for such luxuries.*

★*These may have to have special properties in order to work. They must be thin and light enough to carry on their backs, yet warm and comfortable.*

✠*You are giving them an advantage by means of magic.*

★*Yes. But it is a small point, and if it would make you happier, we can offer them to all the realms.*

✠*How very democratic of you.*

IT WAS LATE afternoon by the time Johanna and Cameron finished their tour of the lower levels. Cameron pointed up toward the cupola. "You didn't take me up there."

Johanna hesitated. Ava was in the cupola. That wasn't the problem. Explaining the decimator, however, could be a problem. Cameron knew about the potential for the library's books to come alive, but he didn't know about its other peculiarities. She wasn't sure if it might be too much, too soon.

"Could you wait here, one minute?"

"Sure. Whatever you need."

Johanna raced up the cupola stairs and watched as Ava quickly trained the decimator on her and just as quickly lowered it to the floor.

The juxtaposition of Ava aiming a deadly weapon at her while Ophelia contentedly purred in Ava's lap made Johanna smile. "Ava. I have a guest. I'm giving him a tour and would like to show him the cupola, but I don't think I want to get into a discussion about the portals or," she nodded at the weapon, "that. Could you hide it nearby and pretend you're reading a book?"

"You like this guy?"

"He's a dean at the college your brother and I are attending in the fall, and he's an approved client of the library. He's familiar with what the books can do, but I think we should keep the Terrorians and the portals our little secret."

"Okay," Ava answered.

"Good," Johanna replied as she rushed back down the stairs to get Cameron.

While she did, Ava rested the decimator on a lower shelf of books and pushed it out of sight. She grabbed the closest book off the shelf and settled back. Grabbing the cover and first several pages between her thumb and index finger, she flipped the book open.

Johanna smiled when she saw Cameron. "It's okay. There's just one person up there, and she won't mind if I show you around. Ready to climb?"

Cameron looked up at the giant helix that formed the cupola steps. "As ready as ever."

As they climbed, Johanna recounted the different levels she had previously taken him to and told him what they were called.

"It all looks so different from here," Cameron observed.

"There's a wonderful symmetry to the library," Johanna said, "although this staircase is not dead center. There's a forced perspective from here that makes all the levels look uni-distant."

Cameron didn't reply. He was too busy studying his surroundings, looking for indications of symmetrical incongruity.

When they arrived in the cupola, Johanna began to explain how the founders of the library had named it the "first level," but she stopped when she saw Cameron staring at a series of two-dimensional, geometric shapes floating in the air and Ophelia playfully batting them with her paw.

"What are you reading, Ava?" Johanna asked.

The younger girl looked at the cover and read the title, "Edwin Abbott's *Flatland: A Romance of Many Dimensions*." The geometric shapes disappeared when she closed the book.

"I'm sorry we interrupted you," Cameron said. "Please. Read on."

Ava opened the book, and the circles, triangles, straight lines, and rectangles all reappeared.

Cameron shook his head as he looked at Johanna. "It's so extraordinary."

She tilted her head. "I thought you were familiar with the properties of our books."

"Only by word of mouth. I've never actually seen

one in action before. It's breathtaking."

She smiled. "And, sometimes, it's even more than that."

SEVERAL MILITAIRRES GRABBED weapons and ran into the forest in the direction of the scream. They fanned out but kept in sight of one another. The sounds of grunting and moaning became louder, and the co-captains motioned to the others to move as quietly as possible. "No," a voice screamed, and one of the militairres pulled back some foliage to get a better look at what was happening. Her laughter broke the tension.

"What's going on?" another militairre asked, pushing aside a mess of leaves and vines. On the other side she found one militairre hanging onto a wild pallid with her arms wrapped around its belly as it thrashed and darted, trying to keep out of the way of another militairre who was trying to wrap a vine around its neck like a leash. They were on the edge of a stream, and both girls were caked in mud.

The other militairres didn't let their laughter stop them from trying to lasso the pallid, and soon they proudly hoisted the live animal that would later become their dinner.

—LOI—

29

AS THE DAY progressed on Dramatica, Furst found it hard to concentrate. His discussion with Pondor left him feeling bewildered. The older man was correct in his assessment about his son, but Furst felt bad for Dungen because he apparently had alienated everyone, even those close to him. He thought about his past encounters with Dungen and wondered what he could have done differently to prevent Dungen from becoming so bitter he would murder Lenc. His jumbled thoughts prevented Furst from concentrating on his work. The only thing that brought him out of it was shouting outside the library.

HORATIO BLASTOE AND Pru Tellerence stopped by the Romantican library to see how the work was progressing. New flower beds were in place and planted, and stone walkways had been laid out running through them. A large section had been marked off with chalk powder in the shape of a meditation circle.

"It is taking shape beautifully," Dame Erato told

them with pride.

★*Yes. I'm surprised to see how far you've progressed without the help of all the militairres.*

✠*And with so few citizens helping.*

Dame Erato laughed. "We had quite a large crowd of people working here. But it is the dinner hour, and many of them have gone home to be with their friends and families."

✠*This is certainly impressive.*

★*We have a surprise for the militairres and should be on our way. But I really wanted to see how the library grounds are coming out.*

"May I walk with you to the encampment?"

★*Of course. They will be excited to hear of your progress.* Pru Tellerence took Dame Erato's arm and they made their way toward the militairres' camp.

THE TIME MACHINE came to rest on a verdant field with a dense forest bordering one side and a large platform with four tented tables on another.

Odyon swung his head from side-to-side as he stared at the landscape. "What have you done? This isn't Mysteriose. What were you thinking about when you started our journey?"

Nero 51 remained quiet for a moment. "This isn't my fault."

"Of course it is. I wasn't holding the crystals. I was busy transmogrifying."

"It was you. You gave off a glimmer when you changed. It reminded me of one of the recent curators."

"Which one."

"The Romantican."

Odyon held up a hand to silence Nero 51. The sound of voices seemed to be getting closer.

"Quickly," Odyon ordered. "Take us back to your realm immediately. We don't want to be discovered here."

The vehicle disappeared just before two overseers and Dame Erato came into sight.

JACKSON HAD PROMISED to pay Ava big bucks to relieve him from guarding the portals after only a few hours. He needed time to shower and shave, and wanted to make sure he would be dressed and out the door as soon as Logan called.

The guy in the tuxedo store had talked Logan into renting black patent leather shoes, and Logan made Jackson rent them as well. He hated the idea of slipping his feet into shoes someone else had worn but had to admit they looked really good with the tux. He took a deep breath and walked out of the bedroom, surprised to find his mother standing there.

"Mom. What are you doing here?"

She looked at him quizzically. "I've been living here ever since you and Johanna asked me to." She looked him up and down. "You look very handsome. Where are you going?"

"Senior prom."

"With Johanna?"

"No. With Emily Brent."

His mother sighed but suddenly looked up and smiled. "I have to take some pictures of you."

"Logan is going to take pictures. I'll have him send them to you."

"Nonsense."

Jackson's phone rang. "Yeah?...I'll be right out."

"Not until I take a picture."

"I can't leave him hanging. He has the girls with him."

"Good. I can get pictures of all of you."

Everyone piled out of the limo when Jackson said he couldn't leave until his mother took some photographs. Logan helped Cassie out while the limo driver opened the back door for Emily. Emily looked like a supermodel. She wore a beaded midriff top and what looked like a tight miniskirt under layers of sheer fabric that cascaded to the floor.

Jackson introduced her to his mother, and Mrs. Roth took no less than a dozen pictures of the teens.

Emily looked up at the library. "Is this where you live?"

"I work here. My family is just staying here while, uh, we get some work done on our house."

"Oh. Can we see inside?"

Jackson blanched. "I don't think that's a good idea. We'll be late for the prom."

She smiled. "The prom is only ten minutes away and doesn't start for an hour. Besides, we want to be fashionably late. Only the real nerdy kids arrive on time."

"I'll give you the short tour." He led them inside and raced through the main level of the library referring to "books, just like in any other library," and the gong on the circulation desk that no one was allowed to play with.

Emily stared up at the cupola staircase. "What's up there?"

Jackson looked up warily and then at her. "Nothing."

"You have this incredible spiral staircase going all the way up, to nothing?" She grabbed his hand and tugged him toward the helix. "Come on."

Mrs. Roth looked stricken. "I don't think that's a good idea. Your dress may get caught in your high heels and trip you or rip your skirt."

Emily gave Mrs. Roth a dazzling smile. "Okay. You all don't have to come. Just Jackson and me." She literally pulled him up the first several steps.

Cassie pulled Logan up as well. "I've never been up there. I want to see the view from the top."

THE TIME MACHINE appeared on the square across from the front of the Terrorian library, disrupting the drills of the troopers. Nero 51 found Barzic 922 and ordered him to have a platoon of all available troopers meet the curator in the square.

"What are you planning?" Odyon asked.

"The time to strike is now," Nero 51 replied.

"And where, exactly, do you plan to strike first?"

"Everywhere."

THE MILITAIRRES' ENCAMPMENT was nearly complete. Lean-tos formed a large circle with a small fire pit in front of each one for warmth. A large communal space sat in the center of all the lean-tos and contained a much larger fire pit with open flames on one side where several wild hares and hens roasted alongside a juicy pallid. The butcher's daughter—a militairre grappler—happily relinquished building chores to take on the job of preparing the wild game for dinner. She hated killing the pallid, but one of the archers did her a favor by ending its life with a single arrow.

The other end of the fire pit contained burning embers under a large flat stone, which the militairres used to roast vegetation. A couple of women had chopped down a tree and hollowed out slabs of wood to make rough-hewn serving trays, which now held nuts, berries, and apples. And they used the large curved leaves from the Romantican gylesso tree to hold roasted vegetables.

Natalia looked over the encampment and smiled. "Our militairres have really shown they can accomplish the impossible, even on short notice."

Arraba nodded. "They have such an array of talents, aside from their ability to fight, that they've all been able to come together and contribute to this impromptu mission."

The sky overhead was clear, with stars winking their approval. "It's so peaceful here," Felicia said. "I could live out here forever."

TROOPERS RECEIVED MAPS and orders to capture as many citizens in force fields as possible during one full solar rotation. A representative would be sent to meet with them at that time to determine the next course of action for whatever realm they were on.

The Terrorians waited until darkness to transport soldiers to the realms. Nero 51 personally delivered platoons of men to the fields behind each Library of Illumination. They were instructed to blend with the landscape until their bio-bands signaled them to begin. A small group was assigned to try to gain entry to the libraries and destroy the books, even though he thought that might be futile. It was far more important to capture as many prisoners as possible and transport them back to Terroria. That would open up negotiations, and while he made the other curators sweat it out, he would use the time machine to travel within the libraries and destroy them.

—LOI—

30

THE SOLAR FLARES on the Adventuran sun raged but did nothing to brighten the night sky. To the contrary—as their destructive power increased, massive explosions of energy proved too strong for Adventura's power grid. Section by section, the power on Adventura shut down until darkness bathed the entire realm, and all their shiny, new refrigeration units ceased working.

FURST GRABBED A decimator, but instead of running out the front door, he ran upstairs to the halo level and looked out the windows, trying to spot the source of the shouting.

It was past dusk, but the moon was full, and he could see what looked like a giant glass orb on the rear lawn. His hair curled tightly when he spotted Terrorians, and his blood raged when he saw them taking aim at his kinsmen, rendering them frozen in place. He felt impelled to run out and help the others but stopped when he saw senior officers from the militia running en masse with flaming arrows. Surely, they would quell the attack. But there were too many Terrorians, and they seemed to be more prepared to handle leaping Dramaticans, freezing them in mid-air and ignoring them as they fell to the ground. *Slaughtered, I will be, now, if I run out.*

THE MYSTERIANS CLOSED ranks around Mal as their voices rose in indignation. Who was this stranger in their midst? Drace the Elder called for order, but the crowd had ideas of its own. "Sacrifice him," one of the priests called out. "The gods need to be repaid for what he has stolen."

Hue pushed through the crowd until he stood by Mal's side. "This man has taken nothing. He has been by my side all day until just a moment ago. You probably don't recognize him without his robe and headpiece, but he is Malcolm Trees, the overseers' Chancellor of the Exchequer.

"The priestess is lying!"

Before the discussion could go any further, an elderly woman screamed. The crowd turned to see barbaric creatures aiming their weapons at everyone and rendering them inert.

"Terrorians," Hue said under his breath as he grabbed Mal's arm and ducked behind a wall hanging. "I must get you to safety."

ALL THE OVERSEERS felt a ripple of unease at the exact same moment.

ℋ*One of our curators is missing.*

MARBOL AND DUDDU sat across from each other on Peer Meap's bed and carefully lifted the cover to the "secret book." They began to read the entries and found they were boring passages about what had happened in the library or community on a given day, mixed with questions. Duddu threw the book down on the bed between them. "This is stupid. This book isn't going to help us find Peer Meap."

The pages started to shuffle to the back page and the words, *Where is Peer Meap* appeared.

Marbol snapped his head up. "Did you see that?"

"Yeah. But it's asking the same question. That's no help."

"But how did it know to do that?" Marbol thumbed through the pages. "Oh, secret book, if you can hear us now, please tell us how to find Peer Meap."

§*We have just become aware that Peer Meap is missing. What have you done to find him?*

At the sudden appearance of the overseer, the color in both boys' faces drained. Duddu passed out, slumping against Marbol.

Marbol grabbed his friend's arm but kept one eye on the overseer. "Duddu, wake up. Duddu—"

Zenith Fullova snapped his fingers, and Duddu's eyes sprang open.

"What happened?"

Marbol grabbed Duddu's head between both his hands and twisted it to face the overseer. "That happened."

§*I'm Zenith Fullova, the dean of Juvenilia. I work with Peer Meap to make sure the library is operating in the best possible way. You boys should not be in here. The libraries were sealed. But that is not as important as discovering the whereabouts of Peer Meap.*

"We don't know where he is," Duddu said. "We looked everywhere."

Marbol poked him in the arm. "Yeah, but maybe one of the other kids found him by now."

§*Where are the others?*

"Town Hall."

§*Then we should go there immediately.* Zenith Fullova placed a hand on each boy's shoulder, and before they could blink, they were inside the town hall game room. The boys, who had been sitting on Peer Meap's bed, tumbled to the ground.

"Wow," Waxmo and Pokkie said in unison. "How'd you do that?"

Duddu shook his head and Marbol just stared.

§*Has anyone here found Peer Meap?*

A dozen heads silently shook side to side.

THE MILITAIRRES WERE so excited to receive the overseers' gift of sleeping bags that their voices drowned out the shouts coming from the field abutting the woods where they were camping. Pru Tellerence and Horatio Blastoe sensed the intrusion and used a spell to silence everyone's voices.

The eerie silence followed by shouts in a foreign tongue caused several of the girls to jump. They dropped their food on the ground and began to run toward the screams.

The platoon leaders made sure they armed themselves before following the others. Milencia slipped the strap of the decimator over her shoulder as she ran, but she wasn't wearing her harness and it bounced around, slowing her down. She didn't notice until it was too late that none of the other girls were moving and slammed into Natalia, who crashed to the ground. *Why didn't she use her arms to brace her fall?* Milencia looked up. The militairres appeared to be frozen in place and several large creatures were pulling out arrows that had pierced their tentacles. Behind them, two overseers stood like statues, and Dame Erato was lying on the grass, bleeding out from an arrow in her chest.

THE NEW TERRORIAN invasion plan was not that different from Nero 51's original scheme, which didn't work. It was time to switch things up. He made sure he instructed the troopers on the strengths and weaknesses of the realms they had previously attacked and discussed ways to change their tactics so they could prevail.

He saved Fantasia for last and decided to personally lead that patrol. He hated that realm and its curator the most, and he wanted to savor wreaking havoc on Johanna Charette's world. Unfortunately, he was so intent on tormenting her, the time machine took him to her exact location, rather than the field behind the library.

AS SOON AS Ava heard an unfamiliar voice coming up the cupola stairs, she closed the book she was reading and just pretended to look at the cover. She glared at her brother when she saw him with Emily.

"Ah...Emily, this is my sister, Ava."

Ava looked Emily up and down. "Nice dress," she mumbled as she picked up the book she'd been reading and studied the cover again, shutting Emily out.

"Meow." Ophelia batted playfully at Emily's sheer, flowing skirt.

"Could you please keep that thing away from me?" Emily pulled her skirt out of Ophelia's reach. "I don't like cats."

"Figures," Ava mumbled.

"So this is the cupola," Jackson said, a little to loudly. "Just more of the same. C'mon. Let's go."

"No, Jackson. I think we should take some pictures up here." She leaned over the balustrade and shouted, "Cassie...Logan, up here!"

"Yeah, yeah, we're right behind you," Logan said without enthusiasm. *Jackson is going to kill me for this.*

Emily turned back to Jackson and quickly raised and lowered her eyebrows. "This is so exciting."

"What's all the fuss?" Johanna and Cameron walked out of one of the alcoves. She looked at Emily. "Hasn't anyone ever taught you that libraries are quiet places where you should keep your voice low?"

"It's okay. My boyfriend works here."

Jackson's face turned red. "I...uh...this wasn't my idea."

Johanna stared at him for a moment. "You look really nice." Suddenly, her eyes widened. "You're going to the prom, aren't you?"

Cameron had been silent until that point. "Maybe they're future Cranford University students."

Emily smiled at him. "Do you go there?"

Johanna smiled. "Doctor Thorne is the dean of the English Department."

"Really. I've been accepted at the Morgan School of Design, but I could be persuaded to switch colleges." She gave Cameron a sweet smile.

Johanna looked at Jackson and caught his

grimace.

The lights blinked and the air wavered. A second later, the grotesque figure of Nero 51 in triplicate appeared. Emily screamed, startling the Terrorian curator, and he snaked out a tentacle and grabbed her around the waist and pulled her toward him.

Ava darted for the decimator, but Johanna screamed out, "Ava, no."

Nero 51 suddenly realized he did not have the curator and froze for a second.

That was all it took for Johanna to chant a translation charm and say, "Release her. I'm the one you want."

Jackson threw himself in front of Johanna to shield her from the Terrorian, but she stepped around him. "She has nothing to do with the library. I'm the curator."

"Take me," Jackson blurted out. "I'm a curator, too."

"Johanna Charette," Nero 51 said as he snaked another tentacle out and grabbed her.

"Okay, Ava."

Ava lifted the decimator and aimed it at Nero 51.

"Release the girl," Johanna repeated.

"As you wish," the Terrorian said. He dangled Emily over the balustrade.

Johanna mumbled a chant that made the Terrorian involuntarily retract his tentacles. Another Terrorian aimed his decimator at Ava.

Logan and Cassie grabbed Emily and yanked her free, but Jackson wasn't quick enough to shield Johanna. Cameron had tried to pull Ava out of harm's way and was caught in a force field.

Nero 51 grabbed Johanna, and a split-second later they disappeared, along with Cameron Thorne.

—To Be Continued—

If you enjoyed reading Third Chronicles of Illumination, please share your experience with others. Take a moment to write a review on Amazon, or Goodreads—even if it's only one sentence long—and tell other readers why you liked 3COI. Indie authors, like myself, need reviews to survive.

And please, share the fun by recommending 3COI to your friends.

Email me after you review one of my books, so I can thank you. You can reach me at C.A.Pack@ LibraryofIllumination.com. I look forward to hearing from you.

Now turn the page for a "sneak preview" of the

Fourth Chronicles of Illumination

⊙

CAMERON THORNE, THE dean of English at Cranford University, grimaced and twisted his face to one side with his eyes tightly closed. "What is that smell?"

"Terrorians."

He squinted just enough to see Johanna Charette, curator of the Library of Illumination. "Am I dreaming?" he asked. "I just had a hell of a nightmare."

"It's a nightmare all right, but it's very, very real."

"How can this be real?" He quickly got to his feet to try to put some distance between himself and the Terrorian vapor that swirled across the floor. "Wait. Don't tell me. We're inside one of your books."

"I wish it were that simple." She sighed. "We're not even on Fantasia anymore."

"Fantasia?"

"That's what the College of Overseers, who run the Libraries of Illumination, call Earth. 'Fantasia.' We're part of the Illumini System."

"I have absolutely no idea what you're talking about, but I can say for certain, you're starting to scare me."

"You've got nothing to fear from me. But I can't say as much for our tentacled abductors. They absolutely hate me and would love to see me die a slow, painful death."

"That doesn't sound promising."

"I just hope Jackson managed to secure the library after we were taken."

"Is that hard to do?"

"It is with the Terrorians. They have our time machine, but I thought they were stuck between the layers of time and space. I guess they figured out how to break free."

"Meow."

"No," Johanna said as she searched the vapor in the area of the mewling. She lifted a bundle of fur, and Ophelia purred at her. "Now, I have to worry about you too."

Cameron scratched the top of Ophelia's head. "You know," he said to Johanna, "everything you're saying sounds totally off the wall—like you're just grabbing bits and pieces of your favorite sci-fi stories and mashing them together. Yet, my insides are tied up in knots because I believe every word of it."

Johanna managed a small smile. "I'm sorry I got you mixed up in this. It really was just supposed to be a pleasant lunch and a library tour for my future college professor and new library client."

"What do you think our chances are of getting out of here?" Cameron walked around the enclosed space that imprisoned them, looking for a way out.

"Normally, I'd say slim to none. But I've got a few tricks up my sleeve, thanks to the Eahta Frean fram

Drycræft."

"Welsh?"

"Yes. It's a secret society formed to protect the works of Myrddin Emrys, more popularly known as Merlin the Magician."

"Merlin the Magician is fictional."

"Nope. He's as real as you or I."

"I'm the dean of the English Department. I did my doctoral dissertation on medieval Arthurian literature. Myrddin Emrys may have been real, but Merlin is a complete fabrication."

"When we get back to the library, I'll prove it to you."

"Well, at least you're optimistic about us getting back to the library."

Johanna sighed. "I'm so sorry, Cameron. I really wish the Terrorians would have left you and Ophelia behind."

"But then you'd be all alone. At least you have me to protect you."

His comment took her breath away, if only for a moment. "Thank you," she whispered.

FURST USED HIS diary to contact overseer Pru Tellerence. He wanted to tell her about the Terrorians' sneak attack and how troopers were now capturing his kinsmen outside the Dramatican library. He walked back to the "halo" window and looked out into the field behind the library. He could see a half-dozen soldiers and a dozen immobilized Dramaticans. The fighting appeared to have stopped, although four of the troopers faced out from the field with their decimators ready.

Pick them off, I could, Furst thought. But the

sealed library window would pose a problem. *The cupola?* The curator looked at the railings above him before staring at the base of the cupola staircase below. *Too much time, that would take.* He slid the decimator behind his back and flexed his knees before jumping from the halo level to the cupola.

Furst took a deep breath after his feet connected with the floor. Dramaticans were known for their jumping abilities, but he took a leap that would be considered well beyond normal. He rushed into one of the alcoves and found an octagonal window that opened for roof maintenance. He opened his diary to ask Pru Tellerence if the window was sealed. He did not expect to see the words, *Furst, we are under attack.*

THE TERRORIANS WHO invaded Romantica were so intent on removing the arrows that had pierced their tentacles, they didn't notice Milencia's late arrival on the field.

She fell to the ground after crashing into Natalia and found herself staring into the curator's eyes. "Are you all right?" Milencia whispered.

"I can't move," Natalia answered. "We've all apparently been incarcerated in our own personal force fields."

"But you can speak."

"Yes. But I can't turn my head or use my limbs."

Milencia tried to touch Natalia, but the force field repelled her hand. "Did I hurt you when I crashed into you?"

"No. Apparently, it's also protecting me."

"What do you think I should do?"

"Unless you think you can pick off six large invaders before they see you, I'd say not much. It would be better for you to sneak away and warn everyone to lock themselves inside their homes."

"Dame Erato doesn't look good. Is she dead?"

Natalia couldn't move, but that didn't stop a tear from pooling on the bridge of her nose. "I don't know. It wasn't supposed to happen. One of the militairres shot an arrow at the Terrorians, but the arrow went wild. If Dame Erato dies, it's our fault."

"U zego a inca-gi." Milencia froze when she heard the Terrorians speak. She looked around for a means of escape. A massive willow tree was just a few arm-lengths away. She turned her head and saw the Terrorians cluster together to discuss something. Milencia crawled behind the tree and held her breath. Even though she didn't exert a lot of energy, her heart thumped heavily, and she tried as hard as she could to quiet her heartbeat and control her breathing. What felt like several minutes passed without incident. Milencia slowly crept around the trunk of the tree to see what the Terrorians were doing. Her jaw dropped when a large glass bubble appeared and two militairres were loaded into it. She gasped when they disappeared, ducking back behind the tree.

The invaders lined up the other frozen militairres two-by-two in a long line. At this rate, it could be hours before they went away. Or maybe not. The bubble suddenly reappeared, empty, and two more militairres were carried onboard.

A MELANCHOLY SPIRIT pervaded in the overseers' meeting room on Lumina.

⌘*The Terrorians have invaded Romantica and managed to capture Pru Tellerence and Horatio Blastoe, as well as the militairres. Fortunately, they ensnared their captives in force fields rather than killing them.*

∑ We must go free our brethren.

⌘ We do not need to go free them. The deans are still wearing their miters and can remove themselves at will. Right now, they are acting as our eyes and ears.

∎ How interesting. They say the prisoners are apparently being removed in the stolen time machine.

✳ This calls for an entrapment snare.

⌘ Pru Tellerence and Horatio Blastoe do not have that capability. Only you, Galio Abbingdon, and I can engage an entrapment snare.

∎ Will you be traveling there, then?

⌘ It is wiser to allow them to be transported to Terroria. They can give us information on what is transpiring on that realm.

Ω If I'm not mistaken, although I have no memory of the actual event, I did not fare well there even though I'm an overseer.

⌘ Ah, Plato Indelicat, that is only because you became separated from your miter. Pru Tellerence and Horatio Blastoe will take themselves away if they fear that is about to happen to them. You have provided them with that important lesson.

∑ Can we discuss Adventura, which is under attack by its own sun?

⌘ By all means.

∑ The power grids have failed across the entire realm. Previously, only their tissue cloning was threatened. Now, their very existence is threatened. They have no way to refrigerate the plasma they use to keep their brains and hearts functioning, nor any way to recharge their non-organic sensors. In less than seventy-two hours, their civilization will cease to function.

* * *

SCORCHING WINDS BLEW debris across the deserted landscape of Adventura's main cities. The massive explosions caused by their raging sun had destroyed the realm's interconnected power systems, plunging everything into darkness.

In the capital city of Venit, gold arms gathered in cohorts to discuss strategies to sustain the majority of their citizens in stasis. Physicians discussed ways to maintain heart and brain health. Scientists studied the phenomena that caused the massive blackout. Mathematicians calculated how long the solar storm would last and how much further damage it might do. Engineers concerned themselves with developing new mechanisms for generating power. And violet-eyed gold arms—the most elite echelon of all—weighed all the various approaches and considered how they might mesh together.

Few would admit it, but never had Adventurans felt so helpless, at least, not since the nuclear aftermath of the Two Millennia War nearly annihilated their civilization. Each of them still carried the cloned remnants of those same ancestors, and their forbears' ancient emotions stirred back to life.

THE JUVENILES WERE amazed to see an overseer. Most of them had never seen anyone so old. They circled around Zenith Fullova, touching his robe and marveling over his beard and hat. The overseer had visited Juvenilia regularly but mostly confined his stays inside the library. He was as concerned as the children over the disappearance of their curator.

§*When was the last time you saw Peer Meap?*

One of the younger boys stared at the overseer,

his eyes wide. "Did you see that?" he asked, without taking his eyes off Zenith Fullova. "His lips don't move. He can talk with his mouth closed."

All the Juveniles took a step closer to the overseer, hemming him in. "Say something," one of them called out.

§*Allow me to restate the question. When was the last time any one of you saw your curator?*

"Wow. Would you teach us how to do that?"

Zenith Fullova smiled. §*First, you must tell me about Peer Meap.*

"He's been gone a good, long time," Duddu answered. "I haven't seen him since before the monsters came."

§*Are there monsters here, now?*

"They're mostly dead. One drowned in the pond. We fried one in the storm drain. The others are making a big stink in the library. We don't want them here."

§*They don't belong here. It is the reason why we sealed the libraries. However*, Zenith Fullova looked at Duddu and Marbol, §*you boys still managed to get inside.*

Marbol held up his handmade weapon. "I used my sonic scrambler. The first time, it broke the glass in the window and the monsters escaped. But then, something happened, and we couldn't get inside even though there was no glass left. Then, I modified my scrambler and tried it again. It doesn't look like I broke the glass, but now we can get inside like there's nothing there."

Zenith Fullova carefully studied the device. §*May I borrow this?*

Marbol hunched his shoulders and made a face. "It's the only one I have."

§*I can get it back to you, unchanged, within moments.*

Marbol repeatedly sucked air in and rapidly blew it out of his pursed lips, making them quiver.

Duddu place a hand on Marbol's shoulder. "It'll be okay. He's Peer Meap's friend. He'll give it back to you." But Marbol continued to clutch the sonic scrambler to his chest while breathing heavily.

§*I have an idea. Let's take a trip.*

"All of us?" someone asked.

§*No.* Zenith Fullova put his hands on Marbol's and Duddu's shoulders. §*Just these two lads and I.* In the blink of an eye, they disappeared.

MALCOLM TREES, THE Chancellor of the Exchequer, hid on the floor behind a stone bench at the far end of a Mysterian discussion circle. He and curator, Hue the Elder, hoped the bench would shield them from invading Terrorians. Mal's biggest concern was his inability to commune with the overseers. He had left his robe and chaperon, a special hat designed by the overseers, at Hue the Elder's home after lunch. Without the special properties built into the chaperon, he could not inform anyone of the attack.

"This is quite undignified," Hue whispered, "and uncomfortable. But we must remain here until we can get away without being detected."

Mal nodded but doubted the curator could see his sign of agreement. He wriggled his way to the edge of the bench to try to peek around it. He caught a glimpse of a Terrorian trooper walking out of the building with each of his tentacles wrapped around an immobilized Mysterian.

* * *

JACKSON FRANTICALLY SEARCHED the Library of Illumination circulation desk for Johanna's diary. "She used to keep it in here. I'm sure of it."

Emily, his prom date, wrapped her arms around her body. "I don't want to stay here. This place gives me the creeps. Those ugly…beasts tried to kill me!"

"They're called Terrorians. You're okay now, which is more than I can say for Johanna."

"Are you calling the cops?"

"No. I need to get in touch with the overseers."

"If you're not calling the cops, I'm not hanging around here for a repeat performance." She turned to Cassie. "Do I look okay? Have I been slimed?"

"No," Cassie answered. "You look beautiful."

"Good. I want to go to the prom."

"The prom?" Jackson couldn't believe his ears. "I can't go to the prom. I have to save Johanna."

Logan shook his head. "Leave it to this place to turn prom night into a weirdo missing persons case."

Cassie gripped Logan's arm like she'd never let go. "What about that other guy?"

That got Emily's attention. "The cute college guy?"

Jackson allowed himself to be distracted. "Who did she say he was?"

"The dean of English at Cranford University," Logan answered.

"I've got to get them back." Jackson continued his panic-stricken search.

Cassie tugged on Logan's arm. "Do something."

Logan kissed the side of her head before saying to Jackson, "Dude. How about I take the girls to the prom while you take care of business here? There's not much reason for us to hang around. You know where to find us when you're done."

"Yeah. Sure. You go ahead," Jackson said, without stopping his hunting expedition.

Logan placed his free hand on Emily's back and led her and Cassie out the door.

"Wait," Jackson called out. He grabbed the corsage he got for Emily and ran over to her. "This is for you."

She took the corsage without looking at him. "Thanks."

After Jackson went back inside, Emily focused all her attention on Logan. "What was that all about? What is this place?"

"It's the Library of Illumination, and if you don't want to be considered a nut job, don't repeat anything that happened tonight to anyone. Jackson didn't want us coming here to begin with, and now I can see why."

Cassie pulled away from him. "Somebody needs to know about this place. It's...unnatural."

Logan helped the girls slide into the back of the limousine they'd hired to take them to their senior prom. "You're right. But if you say something without any proof to back it up, no one is going to believe you. And they'll start calling you a whack job. Just leave it to me. This gives me an opportunity to put my summer internship to good use."

"Where are you interning?" Emily asked.

"Graydon Ransom University News Tonight.

I'm going to be one of their new reporters. And, boy, do I have a story for them. This is my springboard to stardom."

—Coming in 2018—

Primary Characters & Symbols

Johanna Charette—18-year-old prime curator of the Fantasian Library of Illumination. She's a triple-B: brains, beauty, and bravery.

Jackson Roth—17-year-old co-curator of the Library of Illumination. He's cute, funny, and innovative.

Malcolm Trees—the former curator of the Library of Illumination who brought in Johanna as his replacement.

(Mrs.) Niamh Fitzpatrick-Roth—Jackson's mother

Chris Roth—Jackson's 16-year-old brother

Ava Roth—Jackson's 14-year-old sister

Logan Elliott—Jackson's best friend

Cassie Turner—Logan's girlfriend

Brittany Chelvie—Chris Roth's girlfriend

Emily Brent—Cassie's best friend

Cameron Thorne—Dean of English, Cranford University

Nero 51—curator on Terroria

Furst—curator on Dramatica

Pondor—Dramatican Judge

Dungen—Pondor's son

Ozzro—Dramatican soldier

Lenc—young Dramatican soldier

Natalia Dalura—curator on Romantica

Dame Erato—former curator on Romantica

Arrabia, Felicia and Milencia Jolen—three sisters who
    help establish the militairres on Romantica

Ingur Aguri—a white witch

Selestra (a.k.a. Bel)—Pru Tellerence's child

Hue the Elder—curator on Mysteriose

Prophet IAN c.—curator on Aventura

Odyon—shapeshifter (a.k.a. Robert Birk of the Eahta
Frean fram Drycræft)

The residents of Juvenilia only live to age fifteen and are then reincarnated as three-year-olds. Their lives are not short, however, because each year on Juvenilia is equivalent to five Earth years. Peer Meap, the curator of their library, is a transplanted teacher from Educon and is the only adult who lives in the realm

Peer Meap—curator

Duddu—teen leader

Pollo—Duddu's right hand man

Marbol—the oldest teen and the inventor of the sonic scrambler

Jee-Joy—teen girl

Guffle and Flugle—teen twins

Waxmo & Pokkie—teen twins

Selly & Cici—teen twins

Pye—Juvenile teen

Dee-Dee—youngest Juvenile

Boxer, Elmie, Fibber, Harlo, Bungie—Bullaroot players

The esteemed members of the College that oversee he Libraries of Illumination are known either as overseers or deans. Each dean is assigned to one of the twelve realms, which he or she benevolently controls. Ryden Simmdry is the Master of all the deans, and he oversees the main Library of Origination on Lumina, the thirteenth world and the center of the Illumini system. Overseers go by both their first and last names—you would never say one without the other. They are each identified by a symbol and can speak telepathically.

⌘ Master: Ryden Simmdry   Lumina

✠ Dean: Horatio Blastoe   Romantica

∑ Dean: Artemus Rexana   Adventura

⇌ Dean: Grappho Pluck   Educon

❋ Dean: Galio Abbingdon   Scientico

§ Dean: Zenith Fullova   Juvenilia

★ Dean: Pru Tellerence   Dramatica

☿ Dean: Reichel Bean   Comedia

■ Dean: Marsh Kierand   Inspiracon

Ψ Dean: Proteus Bligh   Mysteriose

πDean: Rubicon Zenicon   Numericon

ⱮDean: Selium Sorium   Fantasia

Ω Dean: Plato Indelicat   Terroria

The Eahta Frean fram Drycræft—The Eight Masters of Wizardry—live in various countries on Fantasia and protect *Myrddin's Memoir,* a collection of Merlin the Magician's spells.

Cathasach Caird of Scotland

Zendali Zendaga of Zimbabwe

Mateus Ferrari of Brazil

Alianessa Anjou of France

Robert Birk of Switzerland

Brychan Rhydderch (Beck) of Wales

Edmund Beasom of England

Veronika Veselov of Russia

This is a basic index of characters. Not everyone who appears in this book is noted above. For a more inclusive list of characters, please consult the *Illumini Compendium* (due 2017) or go to:

www.libraryofillumination.com